# LET THEM FALL

FALL SERIES
BOOK 1

SIMONE HOLIDAY

S. BRIDDELL PUBLISHING

# A NOTE FROM THE AUTHOR

Let Them Fall is my debut novel, so I really appreciate you taking a chance on it! I have sent this to an editor and have read it a million times, but we are both human. So please, if you spot something that looks funky please tel ME (not Amazon and the like) either via a message on on IG or email (authorsimoneholi day@gmail.com).

Again, this is my debut novel and I do not have the might and all the resources (yet!) of trad publishing, so your help and support is appreciated.

Also, this work is fictitious and any resemblance to real life persons or places (if not specified) is purely coincidental. Additionally, not all views in this book are shared by me but I tried to stay as true to the characters as possible.

This book is also not meant to be a guide to relationships or kinks. Should you have an interest in the type of relationships or kinks expressed in this work please do your research with a professional.

**Content warnings: Please take care.**

- Mentions of divorce (off page)

- Mentions of a depressed parent
- Alcohol usage (though not habitually)
- One MC is an adoptee which is part of their identity
- Acknowledgment of homophobia (though non-on page)
- Feelings of being othered due to race (mentioned)
- Rejection by a parent (on-page)

# LET THEM FALL

SIMONE HOLIDAY

# PART I

THE FIRST FALL

# 1

## MAYA MCDONALD-JACKSON

Maya's stomach knotted with every mile north on I-93, the world outside a flurry of New England yellows and reds. Her mother hummed off-key to Shania, and Maya pressed her forehead to her passenger window. She missed Boston, even though Boston wouldn't miss her.

She had lived there with her mother and father; except now that the divorce was final, her mother, Maggie McDonald, was moving back to her small childhood town of Maplewood, Vermont. She'd picked her up at school for fall break—*I need my babygirl,* her mother had said—and they were off.

Maya had complicated feelings about Boston. She'd grown up there, born to her white, beautiful, blonde mother whose eyes looked like the sky in June, and her Black father, his skin, eyes, and hair all complementary shades of a sturdy, deep brown.

Being biracial in Boston wasn't anything too abnormal. No, the thing about Boston was that the history of staunch racial segregation had deep roots in the city. Even on college campuses. She'd wanted to escape, but one just doesn't say no to the chance to attend Harvard, where she was reminded all the time how different she was.

"*So you got the looks, but—*" her mother theatrically put her fist in front of Maya's face like a microphone, waiting for her to fill in the lyrics.

Maya smiled weakly. "Mom, I don't sing unless it's karaoke and the last stop of the night."

Her mother scoffed. "Fine, it's just that you're so quiet! I know this is a change. I know," she paused and seemed to swallow what she was going to say. After a moment she said, "I'm sorry, Maya, thank you for coming with me, especially during your break. I'm—"

"We don't have to talk about it, Mom. I'll be fine, I didn't even live with you and Dad anymore, it wasn't—"

"It was still your home. Where you grew up. I don't care what you say, it was your *home. Your home is where you are kept safe. Your home is where you are loved, truly.* It was a part of you and still is, like Maplewood is for me."

"Is that why you're going back? You want to go back to your home? With..." Maya didn't finish the sentence. Her mom was cagey about her relationship with Maya's grandparents.

Maggie pursed her lips in thought. "Maplewood is one of my homes. But it was also the last place I—" Her mom seemingly brought herself back to the present, and Maya turned to see her expression tighten. "It just feels like a good place to return to."

Maya hadn't spent much time in Maplewood. She got the sense from her parents' hushed conversations and side comments that her maternal grandparents hadn't been big fans of her father, and so they didn't visit. Neither of her parents seemed close to their own parents at all. They'd attended her grandfather's funeral, but that was it. What Maya could glean from her parents' hushed whispers was that Maggie's parents were racist. Maya wondered if her grandmother saw Maya and her father as some kind of stain on her mother.

Maya was tall and curvy, with tawny brown skin and thick curly black hair. She wasn't the type of biracial girly who appeared ethnically ambiguous. She also wasn't close enough to white to achieve the level of "biracial" the Kardashian-Jenner clan seemed to have strived for the majority of their careers. No, she was a brown girl. There was no way around it, especially in the summer when her light brown skin deepened with every day in the hot sun. Like now, by fall, she'd reached her peak shade of brown.

"Will you see Grandma more now that you're going to live in Maplewood?" Maya was careful to emphasize that her mother would be the one living in Maplewood. Maya absolutely would visit, but she was not interested in taking up residence in a small, sleepy town.

"Hmmm," her mother pursed her lips, looking deep in thought as another Shania song filled the midsize SUV. Maya didn't press, afraid the answer would confirm her fears and hurt. She knew what rejection felt like, and she hated the idea that perhaps her and her father's brown skin was the reason her grandmother had rejected her mother.

Her skin had set her apart from her peers in Bedford. There had been a few outspoken asshats, but the majority of Maya's experience had been one of general acceptance and warmth, with this undercurrent of—*difference*. She couldn't describe it, but it was something that was always there, clinging to all of her interactions and stolen moments. It was the thing in between, "Oh is it possible for you to wash and straighten your hair before we all get ours done?" and "We just LOVE Michelle Obama, you could grow up to be just like her!"

Whatever it was, people tried to pretend it didn't exist, not with the massive *Black Lives Matter* sign just outside of the city. It acted like a talisman whenever there was a whisper of an accusation of intolerance.

Maya was sure Maplewood didn't even have a *Black Lives Matter* sign. No talisman there. Not that it mattered, she reminded herself. Her mom was setting up roots again in Maplewood, not her.

Still she wondered, would she be seen in Maplewood? Would she connect with anyone there? Her gut clenched in anticipation of something she knew her mother would insist didn't exist in her hometown. Her *mother's* hometown. Maya had the feeling they were driving towards both a new beginning and a goodbye of sorts, but Maya surmised that was how all new chapters began. Still, she was there for a long weekend and would at least settle for a good time.

"*Ain't nothing better, we beat the odds together,*" her mother's off-key singing brought her back to the car. "So you're really going to make me sing this one alone, too?"

"Seems like you've got it handled," Maya replied.

"Oh come on, it's SHANIA," her mother said, like Maya didn't understand that she was one of the Queens, *the* Shania Twain. Maya understood. It was just at that moment, Maya didn't care. She was too wound up with the anxiety her past experiences were dredging up. Though she supposed anxiety might be a permanent state for her during her final year of undergrad. Her professors and advisors tried to comfort her by telling her that she had the rest of her life to figure it all out— but that just made things worse. She tried not to picture herself wandering aimlessly, forever.

"Suit yourself, it's going to be a long trip for you otherwise," her mom lamented. "At least we're getting back for fall. This time of year is going to make our new home worth it — I can feel it."

"*Your* new home, Mom," Maya reminded her.

"*Our* new home. I know you have your apartment, but what if you don't want to stay in Boston? You can't tell me you are going to miss that city after all the grief you've given me and your father about it over the years," her mom said, laughing.

"Who knows, it's the home I know," Maya replied, turning to look out the window.

"Oh please, home isn't only a place. It's people, and your father and I are your home. You'll also see him obviously. But *I will be* in Maplewood and *I am also your home.*"

"Where are we staying again, and how come not with Grandma?" Despite returning to Maplewood, Maggie hadn't yet found a *physical* home, but Maya knew she was keen to leave the Boston area and her old life behind as soon as possible.

"Well, your grandmother can hardly fit us in the assisted living space she lives in now. No, we are staying with my friend, Diana Miller—I mean, Blake. She has this huge working orchard property with plenty of space. She and I went to high school together." Her mom shook her head in time with the music's beat, seeming distracted. Maya noted that Maggie had said "your grandmother" rather than "my mother".

This was the first time Maya had heard of this Diana Miller, now Blake. "So you have been friends since high school? How come she never visited us in Boston?" Maya hoped it wasn't the same reason she suspected of her grandmother.

Her mother was quiet for a moment, humming to herself and looking as though she'd lapsed into a memory. She shook her head and said, "We sort of...fell out of touch. Life happened. I moved away for school and then got married, and immediately had you — she has a daughter about your age." Her mother chuckled. "We always dreamed about having kids at the same time. Too bad we weren't able to raise you girls together." After another long pause she said, "Anyway—her family makes a mean hard apple cider. Maybe you can meet and make some friends now so you know who's who when you come home from school. She always needs help in the orchard—and I do know how you love a cider."

"I already have friends," Maya said, which was sort of true. Her course load currently kept her from making deep personal relationships, and navigating Harvard's social scene outside of certain spaces as a proud Black girl left a lot to be desired. Still, she had acquaintances. She wasn't totally antisocial. She filled any cracks in said social life with online writing communities and the occasional man or woman for the night. Besides, Maplewood was a small town. Everyone already knew everyone. She turned in time to see the pleading look on her mother's face. *Shit*. She felt a twinge of guilt.

"Fine, I'll indulge you. Tell me more about this cider?"

MAYA AND MAGGIE had fallen into comfortable silence all the way up the highway and through an exit that put them close, but not quite, to Burlington, in the small town of Maplewood. Maya thought the name was a little on the nose, even for Vermont.

"Wow this place hasn't changed a bit," her mom said. They were at a four-way intersection that Maya suspected was the center of town. There was a statue of an old white man on a horse. Presumably he had done something important, likely at the expense of the Indigenous peoples.

"Down there is downtown, well, downtown for Maplewood, shops and whatnot. I wonder if Mr. Hodge's bookstore is still there?" They made a turn in the opposite direction of where her mom had gestured, so Maya guessed they'd find out later.

They moved through town until it morphed into old school colonial-style homes, all well maintained.The fall foliage that lined the streets made them all seem like they were out of a film.

"I used to live on the other side of town," her mother said. "This is the nice part. I grew up under way more modest circumstances. Your grandmother would never admit to it, never let anyone drop me off or pick me up at our house." She said it lightly, but Maya detected a hint of bitterness. It was the first time in a long time that Maya had heard her speak about how she grew up.

They turned down a long, seemingly deserted road that inclined slightly. The trees became more and more uniform until they came to a clearing and Maya gasped. She was looking at a beautiful sprawling property that her mom's description hadn't done justice. The trees they'd passed were clearly part of the property's operation, and Maya could see that more groups of trees lined the perimeter, surrounding several structures. At the top of the hill sat a large house, with large windows and a wraparound porch.

Maggie drove past the parking lot, down a narrow path— *Were they supposed to be driving on it?*—and up what Maya realized was a private driveway leading to the large house she had seen a few minutes before.

"This is where we're staying? You said family orchard but I guess I didn't realize."

"Just for a little while," her mother said. Maya guessed that her mother probably felt some shame, having to ask for help from someone she had previously lost touch with.

"What do you mean? This place is stunning." *At least if the people suck, the view is great.* It looked like Maya could make it a good time.

## 2

## LILY BLAKE MILLER

"Are you fucking kidding me?" Lily felt her face grow hot. Her mother kept the apple processing center cool, so she couldn't blame the heat. The rectangular space was all grey concrete and the smell of fresh apples. "You're acting like *I'm* prejudiced? You do realize I was the one who got a Black Lives Matter sign and a Pride flag on the town bulletin board, right?"

"Lily, yes, we *all* know," Hanna said, with an exaggerated eye roll that made Lily's stomach twist—she'd tracked those gorgeous dark almond eyes on more than one occasion back in high school, hoping that they'd notice her. It was crazy to Lily that here she was years later, in her senior year of college, and Hanna still had this effect on her.

They were seated on a bench that the processing staff had nailed down for people to take breaks on. They were taking a quick break from sorting apples, deciding if they were "pretty" and could remain apples. The ones they deemed "ugly" would be used *in* apple products—pies, cakes, apple butter, donuts. It was work usually reserved for high school kids, but Lily was home for fall break and had nothing better to do. Neither, apparently, did Hanna McAvoy, whom she hadn't even spoken to since high school. And yet...

"All I'm saying is the annual festival doesn't have to end with some heteronormative bullshit thing like the 'King and Queen' of fall."

"Who's to say that the King and Queen can't be two dudes or two ladies?" Lily countered, because fuck this.

"It's implied, and you know how the town will react."

Lily knew she was right. Connotations meant different things to different people. They could all pretend words weren't gendered, but that's not the way the town would see it, not the way the local church—a major contributor to the festival—would. Lily and her mother were not religious by any stretch of the imagination. Her mother was more likely to pray to the harvest goddess than to go to church, but the festival included the whole town and was a major boost for their family business. There hadn't been a year they hadn't supplied the apples, cakes, and cider for the event.

*Nothing like a church-sponsored event that involves drinking,* her mother, Diana Blake, liked to remark with a tad too much glee.

No, what was bothering Lily was that she was being called out by the fucking straight girl, the *super cute straight girl*, who was bringing up gender and sexual orientation points left and right when Lily was one of the few folks in Maplewood who'd been out and proud since her first bra.

"It's just that..." Lily trailed off. She had no idea what she was going to say. Hanna was making all of the good points, but asking her mom to use her clout to influence the logistics of a festival Diana Blake didn't really care about beyond watching the clergy let loose didn't feel like a necessary win. They wouldn't even be there for the festival. This whole conversation was only because Lily made an off-handed comment that she could no longer even remember, and she didn't get why Hanna was pushing for this so hard.

"Look, I know we have traditions, but one of my classes taught me that we have so much tied to the ways we think about relationships and sexuality." After a beat Hanna quietly added, "And besides, it's important for people to...see."

Lily sighed and closed her eyes. Because it was Hanna, one of the few girls Lily had been too scared to approach back then, Lily was entertaining this conversation. Otherwise, she didn't care about the silly festival. But it was Hanna, even after all these years. In high school, Lily would have given anything to have Hanna coming apart underneath her. Pulling down her long black hair from her signature ponytail so it fanned around her head as she threw it back. Her cool mask cracking to reveal a mess of pleasure. The image that flashed through her mind outweighed the need to be intentional about what she asked of her mother.

Diana Blake believed in Lily *finding her own path* so she could *be sure about the family business,* about following in the family footsteps. Therefore, she rarely intervened or acted on behalf of Lily. What was more likely was that Diana would tell Lily to go to the planning committee meeting herself. She could just hear her mother say, "You should come with me when I have to go review all our permits." She shuddered. Getting things on the town bulletin board was one thing— people were often more okay with symbols representing something than they were with actually implementing it.

"Hanna, you do know I'm gay, right?" Lily said.

"Lily, plenty of lesbians are also TERFs."

"One, fuck you, and fuck TERFs. Two, I like *all* women. Three, I have been in the queer space longer than whatever fucking lecture you've had at Tufts."

"Lily, look, I'm Asian, okay? We can be different and still have room to grow."

Okay so fuck, she wasn't wrong but holy shit, how did they get here? Lily closed her eyes again for a moment before they began parading around their experiences of oppression and lost the plot altogether. She opened her eyes and looked at Hanna, expecting to see a smug expression. Instead she found something else, something like pleading.

"Fine, I'll talk to my mom," Lily breathed.

"Something like, 'Fall Royal Court'," Hanna pushed further.

"Fine, yes, whatever."

Hanna beamed at her, and Lily decided the conversation was worth earning that smile.

In high school they'd run in different circles, but since they were from the same town she'd seen Hanna on and off throughout the years from afar. A quick glimpse on a day the orchard was open to the public or at Hodge's, the funky bookstore everyone loved to visit. So having Hanna here lecturing her now was a bit surreal—an unexpected addition to Lily's fall break. They'd run into each other at the grocery store, and Hanna had offered to help out on the property for some extra cash, but Lily thought she'd sounded lonely. Lily got that, for more than one reason. After her dad had left, her mom buried herself in her work, expanding the business, planting new kinds of trees, and growing the staff. When she did have a little down time, she spent it in her office/studio on the phone with her sister, Lily's Aunt Julia, or sketching. Sketching what, Lily didn't know. At school, she thought she'd be able to find that *thing* she'd been missing at home, but aside from her good friend Eve who was always traveling anytime she could, no one really stuck around for more than a good time.

"Lily?" Hanna's voice broke through her thoughts, and Lily realized Hanna must have been saying something.

"Sorry, what?"

"I said thank you—it, um, means a lot." Hanna gave a small smile and her eyes grew warm.

God, Lily thought, she was beautiful. She wondered what it would take to keep Hanna's heart-shaped lips smiling at her. Hanna was a few inches shorter than Lily's 5'7, with a stocky build, soft in all the places Lily wanted to...

A knock on the door pulled Lily back from her thoughts. She had just enough time to realize she was staring at Hanna when another knock came, a bit more forceful than the first.

"Wha—" Lily started to say, but the creaky door opened. It was her mother.

Diana Blake smiled brightly and her navy blue eyes—just like Lily's—seemed to glitter with excitement. Her blonde hair hung in loose waves, and she wore her signature t-shirt, jean shorts and tall Hunter boots caked with dried dirt. She was Lily's height, but leaner and more petite. Following closely behind her was a tall woman Lily had never seen before. She had long, light brown hair and blue eyes, and was followed by a tall younger woman with tawny brown skin and curly black hair Lily suspected looked more brown in the sun. Something about her hair made Lily want to reach out and run her fingers through it, convinced it would be warm.

"Hey, Mrs.—I mean, hey Ms. Blake," Hanna said from beside Lily.

"Hey Hanna, again, thank you so much for your help." A look of warmth and genuine pleasure at Hanna's presence danced across Diana's face. She looked at Lily and Hanna on the work bench. "Aren't you girls cozy here?"

Lily realized, to her horror, that she was leaning into Hanna's space. She righted herself.

"Just taking a break before we get back to sorting apples," Lily offered.

"Uh huh," Diana said, holding Lily's gaze for a moment before turning to the two newcomers. "This is Maggie McDonald and her daughter, Maya. You know, they'll be staying with us for a while." The memory of Diana telling her about the mother and daughter duo from Boston snapped into place and she immediately regretted not having thought to stalk Maya's socials. Maybe then she would have been prepared for how much of a stunning babe she was. She had an assured grace about her; her perfect posture made her appear demure instead of uptight. She was in a t-shirt and shorts, the same as Lily and Hanna, but she somehow made the combo look *chic*. She looked like a girl who laughed a great deal. Lily wasn't sure how she could tell.

Diana continued, "Why don't you show her around, maybe show her the treehouse? You could even camp out there like old times." Lily inwardly laughed. Her mother couldn't have known that she got up to *a lot* more than camping with the girls who spent the night with her in the treehouse. *Did Hanna know?* Lily knew she had gained a sort of experiential reputation in high school—plenty of girls tried to explore their attraction to her in hushed and rushed interactions.

"Hey, nice to meet you both," Maya said, and Lily nodded to mask the fact that she was continuing to take Maya in: shapely legs barely covered by a pair of denim shorts, topped off by a small pink T-shirt that did nothing to hide the swell of Maya's breasts in a very, very thin bralette. Her lips were full and a warm pink brown, and Lily had to look away before she got caught up again like she had in Hanna. What was wrong with her? She definitely had an appreciation for the feminine form, but today it was like she had an overzealous cupid assigned to her.

Perhaps it was because it *had* been a while since she'd hooked up with someone. The semester had just started, and

Lily had been busy trying to work out a schedule for her ceramic artwork. She decided to do a play on her two loves: women and apples, which brought up biblical vibes she wanted to explore. Not because she was religious, but because she was convinced Eve was the first woman to let a man take credit for her work. She would try to balance both depth and playfulness, as was her style. This was the one thing she asked of herself, since she loved her art process but didn't take the final product too seriously. She knew that while it was all valid, she was still a rich kid who got to follow her passions because she had an orchard to inherit and run one day, so she let that show in the playful side of her work. This had been keeping her busy, as it would be her final series at school. But, she decided, when she got out of Maplewood and back to school, she was going to have to blow off some major steam.

"Hey, I'm Hanna."

Hanna's voice grounded Lily. She bit her lower lip to center herself before saying, "I'm Lily, Diana's daughter."

"Well," Diana said, "Why don't you show Maya around? It's the best time of the year to be up here." Diana gestured between herself and Maggie. "We moms will catch up at the house, and you girls can get to know each other. I know you're all just here for the long weekend, but you never know when you'll be back home around the same time. Feel free to help yourselves to cider, plain or hard."

Diana put an arm around Maggie and ushered her out of the room. Maggie seemed too surprised by the gesture to say anything and when Lily looked at Maya, she just shrugged.

"Yeah, okay, let's head out to the treehouse." They left the grey processing center and walked into a world of color.

# 3

## HANNA MCAVOY

Hanna breathed in the crisp air tinged with the smell of soil and rotting leaves as the trio made their way from the processing building towards a patch of trees. It was a smell she wanted to soak up as much as possible. Fall was going to pass her by in Boston—nothing but grey days and rain. Here in Maplewood, it clung to her skin and made her feel settled. Diana Miller, now Blake, had made out well in the divorce from Mr. Miller, securing her family's property in an obviously ironclad prenup.

*Good for her.*

Hanna was acutely aware of Lily and Maya as she took in the red and gold trees that could make any sky romantic.

"This place is gorgeous, can't lie," Hanna heard the newcomer, Maya, say behind her. Hanna wasn't sure what to think of Maya, but she had watched the impression she'd made on Lily, which had made her feel—unfairly, she knew—jealous. She pushed the feeling aside.

"Yeah it has always been beautiful, especially this time of year," Hanna said over her shoulder. "Never been to the infamous treehouse before, though."

"Infamous?" Maya questioned.

"Not infamous," Hanna heard Lily say behind her. "And thanks Maya, well, this is your home too for…"

Hanna heard the question in Lily's tone. Hanna was curious too.

"Fuck if I know," Maya said, somewhat dismissively—but Hanna could tell it wasn't directed at her audience. She added, "Sorry, it has been a lot. My parents' divorce is final, my mom has packed up and is moving back here. Those are the knowns."

"Been there," Lily said, as Hanna said, "Sorry to hear."

Maya sighed and then chuckled, as if she were trying to get the vibes back on track. "It's okay. Well–it isn't okay, but I'm glad my mom and dad are getting the fresh start they need." After another pause she said, "Not that you two wanna hear this."

Lily replied, "No skin off our backs, right Hanna? No judgement here, and besides, even if there were, you don't know us and don't owe us anything." Lily shrugged, but it wasn't dismissive. Hanna saw Maya's shoulders relax a bit.

"Very true, kinda like telling a bartender all your problems?" Maya said.

"Exactly," Lily hummed in agreement.

"Great, then I guess I can let it all hang out tonight," Maya added, laughing.

Hanna slowed and looked at Maya. They all just *happened* to be together, home for the break, perhaps only together for that night. A little honesty wouldn't hurt.

"For what it's worth, my parents divorced too, and it wasn't great. Dad just left. Haven't seen him since," Lily said.

Hanna didn't know much about the divorce; no one in town did. Before she could ask more, Maya turned to her expectantly.

"My parents were high school sweethearts," Hanna shared. She felt inexplicably guilty for not being able to commiserate, so she added, "I'm adopted though, so not all perfect."

"Why would that make your family less perfect?" Maya asked. "It's adoption, not domestic violence."

Lily scoffed, "Her family is perfect, not a hair out of place."

"Whatever," Hanna replied, irked. She was miffed by the way Lily spoke as if everything she thought was fact. Lily didn't know everything and didn't even ask.

"Is that right?" Maya asked, as if reading her thoughts.

"I mean, sure, my parents are churchgoing, very even-keeled people. There isn't any drama in our family—but still." Hanna wanted to choose her words carefully. Her parents *were* somewhat picturesque, but they'd still had their struggles, namely when they wanted to start a family. Those challenges had led to them adopting Hanna, but she carried their weight like a shroud. Her Chinese heritage made that story visible, something the town often picked at in conversation, trying to understand. A story that was both a reminder of the toll her parents had to pay, and the way she didn't quite *fit*.

"But still," Lily said, urging Hanna on.

"But still, I was an unplanned addition, you know?" Hanna said. "Not planned *but the best addition in the end.*"

Maya smiled sweetly in a way that Hanna thought held some understanding of what it was like to be so visibly different in a homogenous area. The brief exchange warmed Hanna, and she leaned into that rare feeling of being seen without explanation. She was one of the few Asian people in town, let alone her household, but she hadn't grown up culturally so. There was a disconnect in the way people treated her outside of Maplewood. She'd had one friend in high school who was Latine and thought they'd forever be an outcast because of an obsession with 80s music and Star Wars. But in college, they had learned that wasn't the case, discovered how diverse and expansive their racial identity was, and told Hanna she just needed to find her tribe. It was hard for her because there were so many layers she hadn't yet explored. She rarely felt like there were circles she fit in at all.

"Gonna need some cider, Lily," Hanna said, as they continued to crunch through leaves.

"Almost there," Lily replied and a silence fell between them. It wasn't comfortable, but Hanna bet it was the type of silence that would be washed away by the liquid courage the Blake family hard cider could provide.

Hanna continued to survey the land around her, having never ventured this far onto the Blake's property. The land had been in the family for generations. Plenty of time to perfect an apple cider recipe the town, including Hanna, was obsessed with. Though Hanna wasn't sure if it was the cider, or this feeling she got when she thought about the inside of Lily's mouth tasting just as sweet. That had been a revelation in high school that she hadn't dared explore. One, at the time she didn't know how, and two, being into girls had been Lily's thing.

In a small town that liked to think of itself as liberal, differences were exchanged as social currency. You were allowed to have just one depending on what it was, how interesting it made you, how edgy. You possibly could have two if you came from money, but being the adopted Chinese girl was already enough for Hanna. Being into women would have turned her narrative from "survivor" to "outcast" quickly.

Still, there was something about the way Lily parted her lips when she was thinking. Her pouty, almost-red lips against her pale skin, opening slightly like an invitation to something Hanna would always want to attend. Light blonde hair sun-kissed by the summer, dark blue eyes lined with thick dark lashes, a disinterested stare that made her look effortlessly cool. Like she didn't care if Hanna took the invitation or not. It made Hanna's throat grow dry with nerves.

"Holy shit," Maya whispered as they came to a stop. They

were deep into a set of trees, not exactly the woods, as Hanna could still see the main house in the distance.

*The main house, god.*

The fall sun was beginning its descent for the night, and light poured through the trees, bathing Lily and Maya in golden light. The result was striking; both women looked almost ethereal, and Hanna's breath caught in her throat. She had always known Lily was attractive; she'd thought about Lily countless nights in high school, even while she hooked up with her high school boyfriend. But seeing Maya this way, she felt smacked in the face with just how breathtaking she was. Maya's eyes moved to Hanna's and she melted.

"Yeah," Hanna heard herself try to say back, hoping it had come out of her mouth clearly.

"It's like something off of Pinterest," Maya whispered to her, which made her giggle a little.

*She was giggling.*

Hanna was suddenly less jealous of the way Lily had been checking Maya out. Now she saw that she couldn't *blame* Lily. Maya was magnetic. Sure, she'd been hoping that with her and Lily only home for a short stint, they might be able to help on the orchard, chat, and then get a little drunk off hard cider and stumble into something steamy. Being tipsy wouldn't be a requirement; she simply wanted all parts of Lily, and that included the taste of her family's sweet cider.

But the pull, the curiosity around Maya in that moment felt just as strong. Hanna suddenly wished it were possible for them *all* to stumble into something steamy, maybe even a little romantic. There was something about fall in New England that forced the latter, each reddening and yellowing leaf ushering in cuffing season.

"So this is a..." Maya started to say.

"....a treehouse?" Hanna finished. The treehouse Hanna had

heard of but never seen. It was like a mini cabin? Cottage? Hanna didn't know the true difference. The structure sat about eight or ten feet above the ground, built in a—hexagon? Hanna sucked at geometry, but an angular circle—and held up by five trees. The whole thing had windows and a plain wooden door at the top of a wooden staircase.

"Welcome! Let's get inside, it's somewhat insulated, but I also have a ton of warm blankets," Lily said, making her way up the stairs.

Hanna exchanged a look with Maya that was equal parts excitement and wonder.

*Being a rich kid was something else.*

"Okay, I mean, this is pretty fucking cool," Maya said as they all entered the treehouse. It was the size of a luxury studio in Boston.

"Thanks, this was definitely my corner growing up," replied Lily.

"Some corner." Maya used her hands for air quotes.

"This is insane. I'd heard about this place but—wow, you've got everything you could need in here," Hanna said, taking in the space. The treehouse had a teal futon, a mustard bean bag, and an oval forest green all-weather rug pulled the space together. The whole thing was made of wood and smelled of the outdoors and spice. Throughout the room, Hanna noticed small but substantial ceramic sculptures that looked like unraveling waves. Like they had frozen in motion and someone was peeling them apart layer by layer, with increasing speed. Each piece was painted a jewel tone. The three she spotted in the room were fuchsia, navy, and forest green, presumably to match the rug. Hanna could also see that there were shapes painted on the pieces with text like "puberty" and "war paint" on them.

"You even have highbrow art in here, some treehouse," Hanna said, taking a closer look at the fuchsia "puberty" piece.

"You think so Hanna?" Lily asked, smiling sheepishly, and Hanna noticed her cheeks had gone slightly pink.

"I mean, look?" Hanna said, gesturing around the room. "God knows what this would go for as an apartment in Boston or New York."

Lily laughed and Maya nodded in agreement.

"Is that a cooler?" Hanna said. On the floor was a solid shape, like a 70s old school fridge on its side.

"Yeah, we're going to need refreshments. I keep it stocked and cool. Hard cider good with everyone?"

Hanna and Maya grunted appreciatively at the same time.

"Now if you have to pee, there's an outhouse outside, around the back. I keep flashlights by the door," Lily added. "Figured we should get that known now before we start drinking."

"This can hold us, right? I kinda, don't always do well with heights," Maya said, walking over to one of the cut-out windows.

"I used to have all my...study sessions in high school...well, let's just say this place is durable."

Maya raised an eyebrow.

"Not a lot of people wanted others to know they were with me, this place is private. Perfect for an escape, though I suppose people would have to actually want you for it to be called an 'escape'." Lily mumbled that last bit, Hanna noticed.

Hanna couldn't help but think–what if Lily had brought her out here? Would she finally have experienced what she had yet to?

Lily handed them a cider each and looked around. "I would say let's all get on the futon, but it is not meant for three. Shall we all just sit on the bed?"

"Buy me dinner first, geez." Maya plopped down on what appeared to be a queen (*a queen!*) mattress against the far corner of the room. It had several blankets folded on top, and Maya pushed them aside and settled in.

"I got you a drink, there's plenty by the way, but no pressure," Lily said, grinning and stooping down over what looked like two glass canning jars. She turned a switch on each of the jars, and Hanna realized that they were filled with fairy lights. Lily grabbed a cord attached to what Hanna could see were more lights and turned them on. The cabin was aglow with soft light, and just in time the sun was quickly setting, taking the whole concept of "mood lighting" to another level.

"Points for mood lighting though, got any music?" Maya said, taking a sip of her cider. "Oh shit, that's good."

"Thanks—and one second, I'm working on it," Lily said, procuring a small pill-shaped Bluetooth speaker from the side of the mattress. "Any requests?"

"Whatever, something chill," Maya said, and then patted the spot next to her on the bed while looking at Hanna. "Come sit, girl," Maya said, her tone friendly and warm. Hanna pushed past the flood of nerves and settled in next to Maya.

*She was in the treehouse. Lily's treehouse. On a bed. With two hot women.*

She tried to cling on to the idea that they all just happened to be together, under circumstances that may or may not happen again.

Hanna took a deep pull from her cider, the sweet and sour flavor bursting across her tongue, tasting like possibility.

It was time to lean into the chance to be honest and maybe, into something steamy.

# 4

## MAYA

Maya didn't know how she'd gotten here, but the atmosphere was surprisingly warm. Like the invisible mismatched parts of them clicked. There was an air of taking advantage of the fact that they didn't know each other well, and may never, so why not lay themselves bare?

They were all sitting on the bed drinking cider, forced into a playdate like a group of six-year-olds, while Lily's mom, Diana, and her mother caught up. Maya made a mental note to ask her mom more about their friendship, but for now she was enjoying the present company. It didn't hurt that she was sitting with two absolutely gorgeous women, and her body took notice. Maya's busy school schedule didn't leave much time for romantic run-ins and trysts. Most people needed her to be someone she wasn't, someone she either couldn't be or wasn't at the moment. School was her focus, and after watching her parents' marriage slowly implode, there had been no reason to make romantic relationships a priority. It meant that she had to make events like this one count.

"Maya you're from Boston, and Hanna goes to school in Boston" Lily asked.

Maya was thankful to not be diving directly into broken hearts and homes. Maya nodded along with Hanna.

"Hanna you ended up at Tufts" Lily continued.

"Yep," Hanna said.

"Nice!" Maya exclaimed.

"And you?" Hanna asked.

"Cambridge, I—"

"Harvard? Wow, smarty pants here," Lily said, taking a sip of her cider. Maya didn't detect anything other than genuine interest in her voice. When Maya looked at her questioningly Lily rolled her eyes and said, "Please do not hit us with the 'I go to a school in Cambridge' spiel. God, why are women so humble? Own it girl, that's badass!"

Maya felt her face heat. She didn't have an issue with saying she went to Harvard because she was afraid to tell people she was smart. No, it was always what usually came next. The daunted expression followed by, "Oh, really? How did you manage that?", or the smile in understanding followed by a misinformed affirmative action joke. Then she had to get into her credentials or uncomfortably laugh off the attention. She dealt with it enough on campus; she didn't always have the energy to deal with it off campus. *Fuck 'em,* her mother would say. If only it were that easy.

Hanna turned to her and Maya braced herself, sure she was going to have a moment that outlined the different ways in which Maya experienced the world, versus someone like Hanna.

"That's awesome, what are you studying?" Hanna asked.

Maya felt her gut unclench and then felt a little guilty at her assumption.

"I'm studying business for practical purposes, but double majoring in writing for sanity.. Also doing a minor in sociology and really love it."

"No surprise, you're an overachiever," Lily teased, but again, Maya didn't detect any malice in her voice.

"Well, maybe, but while I'd like to think I am brave enough to take a stab at being a writer, I also need to eat, so hoping business helps with that. And sociology was a happy accident. It's challenging, but fascinating."

"Yeah I'm taking a bunch of soc too, because of my minor. I'm majoring in public policy—and I'm premed."

"Well shit, I am surrounded by some smart women. I *love it.*" The way Lily said it, Maya believed her and felt herself blush.

"Yeah I want to provide medical care for underserved communities, especially now, given everything," Hanna said.

Maya and Lily nodded in understanding.

"Soulful, love it, and here I am using my brains to feed myself," Maya said.

"I mean, being able to feed oneself is important, as my parents like to remind me all the time when I tell them about my plans," Hanna laughed bitterly.

"They want you to..." Lily asked.

"Go to a top med school and become a top surgeon and make top dollar," Hanna laughed. "Sometimes I think it's ironic I was adopted, Asian parent stereotypes and all."

"Well good luck with that, has to be tough," Maya said.

"Yeah, I mean, I feel like I owe them because they're my parents but *even* more so because they're my *adoptive* parents. Who knows what my life would look like without them?"

"That's kinda true for all of us, no matter what," Lily added, and Hanna momentarily looked lost in thought.

"Yeah well, maybe, I only know what it's like to be me," Hanna said eventually.

"I think Lily is just saying, that's a lot of pressure on yourself," Maya said, but because she didn't want to make Hanna feel like she was on an afterschool special, she added, "Hope it goes well with your own clinic."

"Thanks, maybe we could hang out some time," Hanna smiled.

"Whoa, I'm jealous!" Lily mock-pouted.

"No you're not," Hanna said, rolling her eyes.

"You don't know that?" Lily quipped.

"Wait, do you go to school?" Maya turned to Lily.

"Oh well," Lily's face flushed slightly, "I'm meant to take over the business, so I have a job waiting for me after graduation. And it is totally a privilege, but I got to study what I like–art. Ceramics mostly, though I do some design work for shits and giggles, and some extra cash."

When they entered the treehouse, Maya had picked up on the standalone ceramic sculptures Hanna had deemed "highbrow art" situated around the space.

"Did you make everything in here?" Maya asked, impressed.

"Yep, though a lot of what's in here is from high school. I give away a lot of my finished pieces to different organizations who engage youth with art and whatnot."

"Okay philanthropist over here," Maya said smiling, trying to throw some of Lily's quips back at her.

"Oh no way, it's so I get a good reaction on all my first dates," Lily said smiling and then slightly biting her bottom lip.

"Oh yeah? And does it usually work?" Maya asked, glancing down at Lily's lips and then back up to her navy blue eyes.

"It does! And if they're lucky, I take them on a second date to my workshop and do the whole, let me hold you from behind *Ghost* thing." Maya knew she was joking, leaning into the cheese.

It made her even sexier.

Maya laughed, "Well for what it's worth, if those are from high school I'd love to see what your work looks like now. Those look awesome."

There was a pause before a blushing Hanna said, "Wait you seriously *made* all those pieces?"

"Yep, all the *highbrow art* in here was made by yours truly," Lily said grinning, but Maya saw she was also blushing.

"Holy shit, Lily, they're dope, I had no idea you were into art in high school," Hanna said, looking at Lily like she was seeing her for the first time.

"Yeah they are really beautiful! I would love to see more." Maya took another sip of her cider.

"Thanks, I'm more into the process of my work than the final product, but I do keep a portfolio of sorts on IG. You'll have to follow me, maybe send a DM or two?" Lily winked.

"Rich kid, must be nice," Hanna said, moving her body forward as if reminding them that she was there, as if Maya could forget. Hanna may not have felt it, but based on body language alone, Lily was including Hanna in her flirtations, her body turning toward the pouty-lipped beauty. Perhaps Lily was making sure not to put all of her eggs in one basket.

"It is," Lily agreed. "Not going to sit here and act like it's not. Can't stand that. I mean, I go to Sarah Lawrence, tuition is over sixty grand a year. Come on."

"Ah I toured Sara Lawrence," Maya said. "For the writing," she added when Lily looked surprised.

"Yeah well, it's great, just definitely has a fair share of folks who like to drive to the thrift store in a Beamer."

"Doesn't everywhere," Hanna said, and Maya agreed.

"Yeah well, if you two play your cards right, maybe I'll show you to the workshop."

Maya took a sip of her beer, smiling as she watched Hanna's face flush and her dark eyes go intense.

*Interesting.*

By their fourth round of ciders, a couple of hours later, both fair-skinned women were sporting flushes that Maya found adorable, and Hanna kept making lost puppy eyes at Lily, though Maya wasn't sure if Lily noticed. She hadn't known what to think of both women, but the feeling of them clicking into place only seemed to grow as time went on. Lily was funny, a bit crass, and assertive. She seemed like the type of person who took the world for what it was, which Maya found to be refreshing for a self-proclaimed "rich kid," though she supposed if she weren't so down to earth, she'd never acknowledge that fact about herself. Maya found her unbelievably sexy. No wonder Hanna couldn't stop staring.

Hanna was sharp and had a bratty energy Maya appreciated. She was sultry, and when she spoke, her eyes had an intensity that Maya never wanted to look away from. Maya guessed that she was often underestimated, but had no problem ending up on top, in more ways than one. Maya could see that while Lily was poking fun at Hanna, Hanna was biding her time. It made for an entertaining and balanced dynamic, and the conversation flowed easily between them.

Lily let out an incredulous laugh, bringing Maya back to the present. "What? You dated Jeff for like two years! And you just what? Dumped him?"

Hanna's flush deepened. "I mean it was like a high school thing, we went to college."

"In the same city," Lily chided, raising her eyebrow and dipping her head towards Maya, as if asking her to see her point. Maya held her gaze for a beat, and Lily actually winked at her. It should have been corny, but Maya was beginning to think Lily was one of those people who could make most things seem sexy and felt her cheeks burn.

"In the same very big city," Hanna countered.

"God this is so good," Maya said, taking another sip of cider, and relished the look she saw Lily make watching her swallow. Most ciders seemed syrupy, but this was sweet and refreshing all at the same time. Like each bottle contained a cold, fresh, crisp apple.

They were talking about their high school days, since Maya had asked how they knew each other and if they were friends. According to both, they'd orbited each other slightly, but otherwise ran with different crowds.

"Jeff was my boyfriend; he was nice, and then I decided to be single for college."

"Jeff and Hanna were like, end-game," Lily said as Hanna shook her head.

"I get that though. I broke up with my high school boyfriend too, before college. Though to be fair, he showed his true colors to be, well, dick, and not in the good way," Maya said, shrugging her shoulders.

"Yikes, but *that* makes sense!" Lily said enthusiastically, like she'd won her point.

"It also makes sense to want to be single," Maya said, glancing at Hanna. "I mean my boyfriend and I had a good time, but what with his use of the word "exotic" in describing me I couldn't shake this feeling that while he was into me, he also was dating me to be..."

"...Edgy?" Hanna filled in, and Maya shook her head, understanding passing between them again.

"Yeah, edgy, I mean I don't know that his parents loved that he was dating a Black girl. I think they were so afraid I was going to get preggers and 'trap him'."

"Gross," Lily said, taking a hit off her cider.

"It's fine, there are plenty of fish in the sea, and for a pan girl like me, I mean *plenty*," Maya said.

"Pan, huh? I was wondering," Lily said, a smug look on her face.

"Wondering?" Maya asked.

"Wondering, I always like to think I know a fellow queer when I see one."

"Cheers to that," Maya said.

"You don't know everything, Lily," Hanna mumbled, loud enough for everyone to hear.

Maya smiled to herself, no, she suspected that Lily didn't. But then again, she had caught a few glances Lily had been throwing Hanna's way when the latter hadn't been paying attention. Maya, however, had caught every single one of the looks of appreciation Lily had thrown her, though she didn't think Lily had been trying to hide them.

There was definitely a tension building in the air. *Something.*

"Well, since we are all getting to know each other, shall we play a drinking game?" Lily said, smiling.

*Something indeed.*

## 5

## LILY

Whatever the vibes were, Lily chalked it all up to the power of the treehouse in fall. The smell of the wood, the blankets, and soft lighting had the power to make any moment cozy. Somehow Lily had found herself alone in her treehouse with not one, but *two* beautiful women. And it was clear Maya thought she was attractive, which Lily was on board with, and while she always thought she'd never have a chance with Hanna, it felt like Hanna had a plot twist to share. There was something else happening here too, and there was no part of Lily's prowess that wasn't going to explore it.

"What is this, a sleepover?" Maya said at Lily's suggestion of Truth or Dare. "Are we twelve?"

Hanna grinned and opened a fresh cider.

"I think it's clear we aren't twelve, but this could be a sleep-over if you want it to be. Maya, you're already staying here–Hanna? No one in this room can drive you home," Lily replied. The cider had her slipping a bit of flirtation into her retort, testing the waters. She thought of the many times in high school she had brought girls up here who were only looking for a "private place to study" to seal the deal.

"Are you..." Maya's voice went up an octave playfully, "seducing us?"

Hanna choked on her cider. "What?" she was able to stammer out, looking between the two women.

Lily lifted a blonde brow. "Oh come on, it's just a game,"

"Oh no, no you don't. If you're going to fuckboy, lean into it," Maya said, chuckling.

"Excuse me?" Lily said incredulously, but she liked Maya's energy. Maybe they'd be getting there a lot faster in the end. "You think I'm laying the groundwork to seduce you both? Hanna over there is probably still broken up over Jeff."

Hanna rolled her eyes. "I'll text my mom."

"Really? I've been picking up on, at minimum, curious vibes," Maya said, looking over at Hanna. Hanna blushed, and then took a long swig of her cider.

With a resolute look in her eyes she looked up at Lily and then turned her gaze to Maya. "I'm a baby bi," Hanna said.

Lily looked at Hanna as her mind tried to process what Hanna had said. Not because it couldn't be true, but because Hanna said it so confidently, like she *knew* that it was true. Lily expected her to be blushing, but instead her shoulders were back, and she looked between her and Maya with confidence. Lily felt the back of her neck heat slightly in excitement and then at the unnerving revelation that if Hanna knew this, someone might have shown her. Someone who hadn't been Lily in that very treehouse in high school.

*Missed opportunities.*

Lily didn't like that one bit.

"Right on," Maya said, clinking her cider bottle with Hanna's.

"Oh no, here we go," Lily started.

Hanna pursed her lips and set her jaw. "What?" she asked, sounding irritated, and this only ratcheted up Lily's growing jealousy.

"Did you have an 'experience' in college? Some Renee Rapp girl intrigued you?" Lily said, all but rolling her eyes, trying to play off her intensifying emotion.

Hanna's face flushed. "Fuck you, you know bisexuality is a real thing, not just an 'experience'."

"I'm not saying it isn't a real thing, just that—"

"Just that what? I can't be bi?"

"Well how do you *know*?" Lily was growing impatient waiting for the answer she really wanted. She knew how she was coming off, but it was like she was possessed by the jealous ghost of her old high school crush.

"I mean she said it, she knows," Maya said defensively.

Lily knew she sounded like an ass, but how a person knows whether or not they're bi wasn't really what she was after. What she wanted to know was the *who, what,* and most importantly, *when,* of it all. So help her if Hanna discovered things with *someone else* back in high school. *But she had been with Jeff,* Lily tried to soothe herself with reason.

"Lily, are you saying I can't be bi? Because I have had enough bullshit from people trying to tell me I am not," Hanna said, her annoyance (*rightful,* Lily was aware) picking up steam.

Lily took a deep breath and briefly reflected on how this was the second time today she had found herself in a conversation with Hanna where she was for sure in the wrong. "I am not saying that you can't be bi, of course you can be bi, I'm just curious how you figured it out and when," Lily said carefully.

*Please don't say with some other girl in high school.*

"Like what her journey was like?" Maya asked.

"Yes, like I always knew since I was a kid, but I guess things were always going to be more visible for me because I'm only attracted to those who identify as women."

Maya nodded and said, "Phew, I really thought we were going to have to have a 'bi and pan people exist' conversation."

"Same," Hanna said, but her voice was still cool. "I have had enough people ask me if I am sure or how I know? I mean, I have never hooked up with a woman, but not for lack of trying." Her eyes dropped and she looked embarrassed.

"What?" Lily asked, first grossly relieved that another woman hadn't gotten there first and then surprised because Hanna was a *snack.*

"I know what you mean," Maya started, "it is really hard to date women if you are not 100% a lesbian."

"Yeah! Like aside from this lingo everyone seems to know, or be practiced in, the few times I have clicked with a woman she's weary of me using her for some kind of experience to satiate my curiosity or I've simply just been told, 'I don't do bi.'"

"Yeah, I've been there. And once guys know they think you're automatically down for a threesome or some shit," Maya said, turning to pull and hand out another round of ciders from the cooler.

"So fucked up! And so yeah, then you end up only dating guys and then every woman is like 'Aha! I *knew it,* you were always going to go back to men,'" Hanna said.

"As if you ever left them," Maya was nodding, the two women animated by their shared frustration, "as if there's this competition of what you like better. I like it all, you know? It depends on the *person* it's all attached to."

"People haven't accepted bisexuality like ever, so I imagine being pan is just as hard." Hanna and Maya both opened their new ciders and clinked their bottles together.

"Well," Lily started, "that was certainly illuminating."

Maya raised an eyebrow as she drank.

"Care to elaborate?" The bite was back in Hanna's tone.

"No I mean, everything you both said was valid. I didn't mean what I said in general but more so, like about you, Hanna." As soon as Lily said it, she knew she'd said the wrong thing.

"And why me? I can know I like women without having been with one," Hanna said.

"Yeah I mean but if you've always known," Lily realized nothing was coming out of her mouth correctly. She could blame the cider, but it really was likely due to the reviving ghost of her unsatiated crush.

"Yes..." Hanna urged her on, as if daring her to say what she had to say next.

"I just wouldn't have guessed it is all," Lily said, trying to organize her thoughts and figure out a way to get the conversation back on a fun track and not one where she was a complete ass. She decided she was going to have to give some more context here. "I mean, maybe I had a little crush on you in high school." Hanna seemed momentarily stunned and then frustrated. "Why? Because I didn't let you fuck me in high school, even though you hooked up with every other 'curious' girl? Just because you like girls and I like girls doesn't mean we were going to hookup, Lily." The sting in Hanna's voice was unmistakable and shocked the room into a brief silence.

"Damn, I feel a bit out of place here," Maya said cautiously, but with a smirk on her face.

Hanna again was speaking straight *facts,* and to avoid digging herself into a deeper hole, Lily asked the question she really wanted to know. "Did you want me to fuck you?" Lily asked with a frankness she mastered long ago, but found herself nervous for Hanna's answer.

"Maybe," Hanna said quietly, and Lily felt the room tilt slightly under the weight of the revelation.

Lily's former crush was now a fully revived crush.

"I mean to be fair, I picked up on that three ciders ago, there is def something between you two," Maya said, shrugging her shoulders.

There was another beat of silence before Hanna said, "I thought...I mean, you clearly have been flirting with Maya."

"It's true, you have been," Maya nodded in agreement, "but for what it's worth, Hanna girl, you are beautiful."

*What the fuck was happening here? Did Maya have more game than her?*

"What is happening here?" Lily said out loud.

"Oh, come on, you were laying it on so thick before," Maya said.

"I didn't think, well, I thought maybe—" Lily started.

"That I'd get uncomfortable and you'd get to have Maya in your cabin of 'love'?" Hanna said, her voice still laced with annoyance, and Lily thought, jealousy?

"I was planning on just seeing where this all went. I don't know," Lily muttered and shrugged, trying to not let on that her mind was still trying to process and catch up.

There was another beat of silence before Maya spoke again. "Where do we want it to go?"

"What do you mean?" Hanna said, her voice losing its edge and coming out breathy.

"I mean, let's just put the cards on the table here. We've been pussyfooting around for like two hours in this obvious sex pad," Maya said.

Lily felt herself nod slightly before saying, "And we have been presented here with an opportunity where we are all into each other."

"We are?" Hanna asked incredulously.

"We are," Maya said back.

Lily's heart hammered in her chest. She had been sure Hanna would eventually leave and she would be able to kiss sweet Maya. But both?

*Holy shit.*

Maya set her cider aside and then leaned forward onto her knees so she could get closer to Lily and Hanna.

"I'd like to make out with both of you. Is that ok?"

"God, yes," Lily breathed out before she could really think about it.

"Make out? That's it?" Hanna said, her face flushing.

"Good point, anyone have any hard boundaries?" Lily said, her mouth beginning to water. Her body responding to what her mind was still trying to process.

"None," Maya said, "Honestly this break is already going way better than I thought."

"I want to try everything and anything," Hanna blurted. When Maya smiled at her she added, "It's why I broke up with Jeff."

"Ah," Lily heard herself say.

"So what do we do, um, how do we..." Hanna trailed off.

"Get on my lap," Lily said to Hanna. God she had been dying to get this girl in her lap for some time.

Hanna moved to straddle Lily, and Maya sat behind her. She placed her brown hands on Hanna's shoulders, hooking her thumbs under the straps of her tank top.

"So first time with a—with women, we should take care of you," Maya said, and she lightly kissed Hanna's bare shoulder. Lily heard Hanna's sharp intake of breath and her eyes focused on the spot where Maya's lips met Hanna's skin, and then her gaze lifted in sync with Hanna's till they were looking at each other.

The next thing Lily knew, Hanna's lips were on hers fully, her generous breasts taking up the space between them as Hanna bent down and took her mouth like she had been waiting to do so all this time.

Lily had kissed many, many girls, but Hanna was the first to kiss her like she was starving.

She heard Maya utter a soft, "Fuck," and Lily was lost.

# 6

## HANNA

Hanna could feel the spot on her shoulder where Maya's soft, full lips caressed her skin burn. Heat spread from the spot, fanning out until it felt like every hair on her body was on end. Her eyes met Lily's.

"So—" Before Lily could ruin the moment, Hanna kissed her, and along with the prickling feeling across her skin, there was a low swoop of warmth in her belly.

"Fuck," she heard Maya mutter, and then felt her fingertips in her hair, against her scalp as Maya shifted Hanna's head just so. She assumed it was so that Maya could get a better look at Hanna's kiss with Lily.

What she had wanted to do for so long. What she'd hated had never been asked of her. She thought about the halls of their high school full of excited whispers of girls having the best "study sessions" of their lives. How they knew what their bodies wanted. She poured all of her frustration and envy and tolerance into her kiss.

She was here to take. To receive. To both conquer and surrender.

Lily's lips were tart and sweet from the cider, but underneath there was a taste that was unmistakably her, and Hanna wanted to drink it down until she was so drunk with it the room spun.

It didn't take long.

Lily seemed to recover from shock or perhaps she had been letting Hanna get oriented, but she was kissing her back now. Her tongue met Hanna's every thrust. Hanna felt Lily's hands around her face as she pushed forward, pushing Hanna back to where Maya was waiting.

Lily broke away from Hanna's mouth to slowly nip and lick down her jaw till Lily reached the softness of Hanna's neck, which forced a gasp from her lips. Hanna's eyes flew back to meet Maya's heated brown ones. She was aware of Maya's breasts on the back of her head, and leaned into her.

"I was feeling left out," Maya said, looking down at her as she cradled Hanna in her arms while Lily explored her neck.

"Come here," was all Hanna could muster as she felt whatever knot was left in her loosen.

Maya leaned forward and kissed her, upside down, Spider-man-style.

Hanna was delighted by the difference of Maya's mouth versus Lily's. Both were hot: Lily, challenging and setting out to prove something, like she needed Hanna to feel her presence, her very essence. Maya, though, was gentle and thoughtful. She let Hanna take charge and followed her tongue and lip movements with a smooth confidence — like she *knew* Hanna's mouth belonged to her.

They kissed like that for a while, until Hanna heard her gut demand, *more*. It was like Maya and Lily had loosened one knot inside her, only to realize that she'd been doing so by tightening another. She ached to be touched, to be held, to be stripped down.

And that's when they began shedding her clothes. First, Lily and Maya took their time undressing her. She lay dazed, looking up at them. Both stared across at each other, and when Maya leaned forward to pull at Hanna's shirt hem, and Lily to pull down her shorts, they kissed, lightly, lovingly, as if they were coming home from a long day. Maya took a second to cup one side of Lily's face, as if to say, "Ours."

It was domestic and simple, like they were sharing something. *Me*, Hanna thought, *they're sharing me. Right now I am theirs, but they are also mine.*

It was perfection.

It was perfection when Lily pulled down her shorts to reveal her blue cotton panties and whimpered, whimpered. Hanna felt that whimper down to her bones.

It was perfection when Maya took off her shirt and then her bra, all while never taking her eyes away from Hanna's, a question of consent in every movement.

It was perfection when Lily sucked one of Hanna's nipples into her mouth, her back arched and Maya petted her hair gently.

It was perfection when Maya asked, "Do you like?" and Hanna nodded blissfully. Jeff had never asked that. No one had. Not that that mattered anymore, Hanna decided, she was light years away from anyone else. She was beginning to buzz with whatever energy those girls had radiated in the hallways of their high school when whispering about Lily.

It was pure elation when Maya bent over and took her other nipple in her mouth, and Lily began to move down her torso.

"You ok, Han?" Lily asked, sounding blissed out and drunk with lust.

"Yes," Hanna muttered. "God, fuck yes."

"I don't know what God you speak of Hanna, but I am about to worship you." And with that, Lily took Hanna in her mouth.

# 7

## MAYA

Maya's world came into focus along with sunlight and bird song. The former danced behind her eyes a little too aggressively, and the bird song unnerved her: where was she again?

Right.

She was in a treehouse, entangled on a mattress with two beautiful women. Last night had been...unexpected and welcome. She was being held loosely by Lily from behind and Hanna was curled up beside her on the other side. They'd slept naked, and the heat of their skin pressing into each other created another layer of warmth that made Maya smile. These two small-town girls who knew each other, and here she was fitting perfectly between them.

A threesome hadn't been something she'd ever done and she still couldn't believe last night: the eagerness of Hanna, the dominance of Lily. But *threesome* didn't feel like the best way to describe the way they'd all clicked. Sure, sometimes a girl just wants to get laid, but there had been something more. Hanna had seen her, truly seen Maya. She could tell by the way she'd looked deep into her eyes as she worked her fingers into her.

And Lily, maybe Lily saw more than she let on. Maya had been wary of being fetishized or seen as an "exotic" hookup back in Boston. Lily was hot, there was no question, but truthfully Maya had continued to explore things last night because she wanted Hanna to have whatever she'd been asking for the whole time. After Lily wrapped her fingers in Maya's curls as Maya made her come undone with her mouth, her vibrant navy eyes looked down at her like they were screaming "I see you."

Uneven breathing filled the room, and the morning was bright and still. The crisp fall air seeped into the space, but only made the small nest of blankets they'd managed to wrap themselves in cozier. Maya could see how this had been Lily's favorite spot. There was a homeyness she felt that surprised her, given she'd only just left her actual home.

"So, who wants to talk first?" Maya said to the room and felt a muffled chuckle from Lily, but Hanna went stiff. "You okay, Hanna?"

Maya felt Lily roll closer into her body. Lily's light powdery and floral scent enveloped her, and Maya loved that it seemed to mingle around them. Maya knew it was the only way Lily could see Hanna. Maya rose slightly on her arm and felt Lily do the same. She looked down at Hanna, who looked contemplative.

"Hanna?" Lily said from behind her.

Hanna's eyes snapped to Maya's. "Yeah," Hanna said as she sat up and turned on her stomach. Her dark hair spilling around her shoulders, her clean scent brushing up against Maya's nose.

"It's just, wow," Hanna said, before she burst into laughter.

Maya laughed too, but Hanna was simply cracking up. "I'm sorry," she finally said, "it's just that I have been waiting for some time to come up to this treehouse, and have my 'queer experience', and I had not one but two!"

Maya felt Lily lean into her neck and nuzzle right behind her ear, like they were both revelling in Hanna's joy together.

"And it was," Maya asked, looking at the still-giggling Hanna.

Hanna took a deep breath and then turned her head so she could look at Maya and Lily. "It was—perfect. It was, you both were perfect. Was I..." Hanna's voice trailed off.

"You were great," both Maya and Lily said in unison, and then began to laugh.

"Fuck, I sucked, didn't I?"

Maya laughed harder and Lily said, "No, no way, didn't you hear both of us call your name?"

Lily gave a small nudge to Maya. "You were great, your enthusiasm alone...I will be feeling for the rest of the day."

All three of them laughed.

"Oh my god, stop," Hanna said, and now she was pretending to smother Maya, breasts flying.

They rolled around for a moment, Hanna pushing Maya down onto her back. Maya looked over at the hovering Lily, who beamed at her. Then Lily cleared her throat and moved toward the speaker and turned on some music.

"So what now?" Hanna said cautiously, her eyes focused on Maya as if looking for direction.

"Well, I mean, it's like 8am, and it pains me to get out of bed before 10am if I'm not working," Lily said, getting back into the blankets and snuggling into Maya, who wrapped an arm around Hanna's waist.

The melodic voice of FLETCHER filled the room, and Maya smiled up at Hanna, who tentatively lowered herself back down into the blankets.

"I can't believe I'm up here with Lily Miller," Hanna said.

"Hey, am I chopped liver?" Maya said, smirking.

"No! Just, wow, that's all. I'm sorry, my baby bi mind is a bit blown. It's one thing to fantasize and another to experience being with a —I mean, women," Hanna explained.

This seemed to peak Lily's interest because she slid one

of her legs between Maya's and leaned over her towards Hanna. Her body was warm and Maya felt the heat and wetness of her arousal on her thigh. "And what do you mean you're up here with 'Lily Miller'? Did you have thoughts of me back in high school, Hanna? Hmmm? Thoughts of coming up here?" Lily's voice was a purr. Her long blonde hair was tousled in a manner only sex and sleep could muster. Her navy blue eyes fixed on Hanna, and Maya turned to see Hanna blush.

"Well, Hanna?" Lily pushed again, and Maya could hear Hanna's breath catch, and felt her own heart rate quicken. *They were still naked and it was still early...*

Maya started to make small circles at the small of Lily's back with one hand and felt Lily lean further into her thigh, seeking friction. Maya turned to Hanna, her other arm around her neck, and began stroking the same circles into her hair. Hanna's eyes closed at the touch.

"If it makes you feel any better," purred Lily, "I thought of you. Everything I did to you last night is only a fraction of all the things I thought about doing to you in high school. With your good girl attitude. I wondered," Lily paused, and Maya felt one of her hands glide over her abdomen to Hanna, who sucked in a deep breath at Lily's touch, "I wondered what it would take for you to let yourself *go*, let yourself fall apart underneath me. In my bed. In my mouth."

Hanna was panting now. "Yeah?"

"Yes," Lily responded and Hanna took in another shuddering breath. "Hmmm," Lily crooned. "Fuck, still wet for us?"

That was it, Maya couldn't stand the tension any more. She pulled Hanna close and dropped a kiss on her forehead. Hanna moaned at the movement of Lily's hand.

"Tell me," Lily said, as she leaned slightly back so that she could bend and take one of Maya's earlobes into her mouth.

Maya gasped and felt heat flutter throughout her body, spreading from between her legs.

"I wanted you to," Hanna moaned and began to writhe, "I wanted you to touch me."

"Hmmm good girl, yes, yes you did, just the way I am right now?"

Maya watched Hanna nod — god, being in this with them was so hot. It was beyond getting to watch, to listen; she knew she was a part of it. She felt her nipples harden and an ache began to build in her.

"But you didn't just want me to touch you, did you? I saw you last night, I *felt* you last night. You were eager to touch, too," Lily said.

"So eager," Hanna whimpered.

"So fucking eager," Lily coaxed, "Now show me, show me on Maya where you were eager to touch me. How you wanted to touch me. How you wanted to make me *feel*. You want that, Maya?"

"God yes," Maya responded and need was clawing at her.

Hanna let out a breath and then turned quickly, as if she'd just been waiting to be given permission, further into Lily's touch but also now so that she could place a hand on Maya. She pulled on one of Maya's breasts and pinched a nipple. Maya curled under the touch.

"Fuck, I need," Maya began.

"We know what you need," Lily said, her voice becoming breathier.

Hanna took her hand and dragged it down. Maya could feel goosebumps erupting in its path, till Hanna slid her fingers around her clit. Maya saw stars.

"Right there, right there is where you need her, right?" Lily said, and she began to rock her hips into Maya's thigh.

"Yes, there, please don't stop," Maya choked out. It was all so much, the bed still smelled like them: Lily's floral scent, Hanna's clean scent, Maya's citrus, all together in the blankets with a layer of sweat and pleasure. It was intoxicating.

Lily's hips rocked into her in earnest, and Maya pressed back slightly, hearing Lily let out a low moan. Hanna was panting next to her, her fingers moving on Maya faster and faster. They were all close, rocking and moving together in the light of the morning.

"I'm coming, fuck I'm gonna come," Hanna breathed out next to Maya and that's all she needed to allow her own release wash over her, her back arching upwards and her mouth open in a silent cry of pleasure.

As if seeing the two of them go overboard, Lily's movements quickened, and then her body jerked several times to the beat of her release as well. She fell back, all three women panting.

The room around them seemed to dial back into focus for Maya, and she continued to pant as she came down from the high, basking in the glorious heat of the two women on either side of her, the room filled with soft and crooning music.

# 8

## LILY

When their breathing evened, nobody said anything. Lily kept her arm across Maya's stomach, her hand resting on Hanna's thigh. She watched as Maya went back to twirling her fingers in Hanna's hair and shivered slightly with pleasure as she felt Maya's hand do the same in her hair, her fingertips making soft circles across her scalp. No one had touched her like that since she was a child, not since her mother or her aunt.

Lily smiled to herself as she leaned her head into the crook of Maya's neck. Hanna was looking at her. Hanna was *staring* at her—no, *into her*. It wasn't uncomfortable though, so Lily stared back into her as Maya ran her fingers through their hair.

The music, the morning light in the room, the smell of them all in *her* bed, was making her *feel things* she normally didn't. Which was silly, Lily knew that, but it had been a long time since she'd been held like this, or held anyone like this. It had been almost never that she had been touched the way she was last night. There was something in the air that made Lily feel like everything was in reach, and all she had to do was grab it. Not wanting the moment to slip by, but unsure how to hold onto something she'd never had before, she kept Hanna's gaze as she turned and kissed the skin below Maya's shoulder. She heard Maya take in a breath and turn, her soft curls shifting underneath her, and then felt Maya's lips on her own hair.

*Safe,* was the last feeling she remembered before she fell all the way into it and was asleep.

"WHAT TIME IS IT? I should text my mom." The grogginess in Hanna's voice told Lily that she hadn't been the only one to fall asleep.

"It's 9:37 in the morning," Maya's voice reverberated in her chest underneath Lily's ear.

*Fuck why did they insist on getting active again before 10am?* Lily groaned and rolled on to her back, and felt Maya sit up.

"Does your mom expect you to be home before noon after sleeping over somewhere or something?" Lily asked, rubbing a hand down her face.

"Well, this was an unplanned sleepover, and she just likes to know what's going on," Hanna replied defensively.

"Mmm," Lily responded, as if it was totally normal for a twenty-one year old to have to check in like they're sixteen.

"Wonder how our moms are doing?" Maya asked.

"I can guarantee they aren't doing how we are doing," Lily joked. "My mom probably tried to cook and then caved and ordered in. Bet you she made your mom watch one of her weird docs on horticulture."

"Mmm," Maya responded, and Lily finally turned to find her sitting up and looking over at Hanna, who was now furiously tapping on her phone.

"Everything okay?" Maya asked, beating Lily to it.

"Yeah, my mom is just trying to figure out if I am still able to help her with church stuff tomorrow."

"Ooof, you're going to church tomorrow?" Lily asked.

"Yeah I do every time I am home, it makes the parents—well, my mother—happy."

"Protestant?" Maya asked.

"Yep, the wonder bread of Christianity," Hanna said. "But I get it, the church really helped my parents raise the money they needed to, well, to get me. It's a nice community, they've always made me feel welcomed."

"Are you going to go to church too?" Maya asked Lily, and Lily felt herself burst into laughter.

"Not unless I want to burst into a ball of flames, especially after last night." Lily added that last part somewhat bitterly. "My mom isn't big on organized religion, she is more spiritual and raised me that way too I guess."

"The church here is nice, I mean, it's pretty liberal? I don't think they'd care that you're gay or that I'm bi," Hanna said, but she didn't sound sure.

"My mom said she isn't making us go. My grandparents apparently made her go." Maya added, "She said she can't deal with the whole 'she ran off with a Black man and then got divorced' thing."

"Yeah well, I will admit that while no one is outwardly judgy, there is a lot of emphasis on being a 'good Christian,' and fitting a kind of image," Hanna said quietly.

"Somehow I think all the premarital sex and now three-somes I'm having wouldn't fit well either," Lily said, giving in and sitting up.

Maya laughed and then said, "Yeah well, I think threesomes *are* all they're cracked up to be, especially with you two."

Lily watched Hanna blush as she finished tapping something on her phone and finally put it down.

"I head back up to school tomorrow night so..." Her voice trailed off, and she blinked at Lily and Maya as if re-realizing she was still in the room with them, *naked. Post sex. Lots of sex.*

After a long pause she said, "I've never had a one night stand before, so I am not sure how to—I mean, this isn't awkward, is it? Am I being awkward?"

"Are you asking us as veteran sluts?" Maya asked, but there was a lightness in her voice.

"No, I mean, I don't know?" Hanna said, and her face started to flush.

"Relax, Hanna Banana," Lily said, stretching and noticing Hanna looking at her breasts as she bowed her back. For good measure, Lily ran her hands through her blonde hair and relished in the heat in Hanna's eyes. Lily was pretty proud of her rack.

"Hanna Banana?" Hanna finally said.

"Whatever, you're not awkward, you're hot as fuck, are we going to lay back down?" Lily said, collapsing back beside Maya.

Maya chuckled, "You're not being awkward...Banana."

"Is that what you two are going to call me from now on? Feels low-key a little racially insensitive..."

A silence fell into the room as realization clicked into place.

"Holy shit, I didn't—" Lily started, and she sat up on her elbows again, alarm etched on her face.

"I'm kidding," Hanna said and beamed over at the two of them. "I know how you both see me, I know you *see me.*"

Lily watched as relief flooded through Maya, who scooted back down next Lily. Now all she needed was for Hanna to lay back down.

"But we will need to call Maya 'Papaya Maya' for me to allow it," Hanna added, smiling.

"Do I get a fruit name?" Lily asked.

"Hmmm," Hanna said. "Wait, isn't your full name Lilith?"

"Wait, like Lilith, Lilith?" Maya asked.

Lily shook her head, "Yeah my Mom's name is Diana, like the goddess, so she named me Lilith." Lily shrugged. "I don't hate it."

"You're going to just be Lilith because that name is badass," Hanna mused, and after looking between Lily and Maya, she slid back down into the blankets as well.

"Okay, and where are all these names going?" Lily asked.

"Group chat!" Maya declared, and the energy in the room shifted slightly.

"As in," Lily paused. They didn't know each other, and hadn't really known each other beyond yesterday. Sure, she went to high school with Hanna, but they hadn't talked or even been acquaintances. She literally just met Maya yesterday. Sure, they had *gotten* to know each other. They'd slept together, had sex, but Lily had had sex with lots of women and never called them again. She figured she may come up in a couple group chats on campus, but she wasn't meant to be a part of those conversations.

No, usually her mornings were full of small talk and good-byes that held true. *But she hadn't had a morning like this before, or a night like she'd had last night before*, she argued with herself. She prided herself on not fitting the "U-Hauling" stereotype, but in this moment she could almost see the appeal of it. The feeling came back, like there was something just within her reach.

"Okay so group chat," Lily said, and then added, "please send nudes."

## 9

## HANNA

Hanna reached under the covers and gave Lily a small flick.

"Ow," Lily said, even though Hanna knew it hadn't hurt.

"Ladies," Maya said in mock admonishment.

A serious silence fell over them, and while it didn't feel uncomfortable, there was a bit of a tension that Hanna could feel. She squeezed her hand furthest away from Maya to keep herself in the moment. Part of her was anxiously waiting to try and process the night before and the morning. She couldn't believe that she was here, in Lily's treehouse with not one but *two* women she really enjoyed, in more ways than one. She had to remind her anxious self that she was *still* in the moment and couldn't afford to not be present.

"So," Hanna said eventually.

"So," Lily responded with a raised blonde brow.

"Are we going to do the thing now?" Maya asked, sounding amused.

"Do what thing?" Hanna asked, but she knew.

"Do the, what's after this, yaddi yadda, conversation?" Lily said, and Hanna felt like the fuckboy Lily had come back. "You know, outside the group chat, IRL?"

But it sounded like Maya wasn't having it. "Yes, I suppose we can because we are adults," Maya said, and Hanna watched the fuckboy facade slip off Lily's face, and Hanna's crushes on them both continued to grow.

"I really had a good time," Hanna began.

"Understatement, I think, speaking for me," Maya said, smiling.

"No complaints," Lily replied.

"Maya, you're, I mean we go to school close by..." Hanna mumbled.

There was another silence, then Hanna watched Maya turn to Lily.

"Are you jealous," Maya teased, another type of smile on her lips.

"Wow, and I get called the fuckboy," Lily said.

"Because you are, apparently," said Maya. "Yes, I would love to meet up again, especially if you want, you know, more practice." She turned towards Hanna, winking.

"Practice?" Lily repeated. "Okay, yes, I am jealous."

"Sarah Lawrence isn't that far away, it's on the train line," Hanna found herself saying, because while she loved the idea of *practicing* with Maya, she loved the idea of Lily *also* being there even more. The interest that she had formed around Maya and the renewed crush she felt herself dusting off for Lily were equal in their weight and curiosity. They also felt intertwined now, a part of each other. "I mean you could easily take the train," Hanna started but stopped when Lily laughed slightly. Hanna's face flushed at her apparent foolishness.

"A whole train to get laid," Lily laughed, and it was a statement, not a question. Then Lily's eyes met Hanna's, and as if seeing the effect of her words, she said, "I mean, you two are *totally* worth it, and I don't mind Boston."

"That makes one of us," Maya said, and continued,"But perhaps we can be more strategic about when we meet up."

Hanna smiled at Maya. She appreciated the assist, as she wasn't sure how she felt not having Lily there. Whatever had happened last night, it had felt like the three of them sliding into place.

Lily pursed her lips. "Should I be jealous that you both will be in Boston, though?"

"Should I be jealous that there is undeniably some tension and history between you two that I have no context for?" Maya countered.

After a beat, Lily shook her head. "Fair, okay, but to be clear, we aren't U-Hauling times three, right?" Lily said, and Maya snorted.

"I just, I just want last night again. To share that," Hanna said quietly.

"I mean there's always the option of a video call," Maya said conspiratorially.

Truthfully, that had been the best sex of Hanna's life, a life plagued by lots of mediocre, if not plain bad, sex. She didn't see how anyone could blame her for wanting it again, and again, and again. Hanna also knew that there was some kind of chemistry between the three of them that made it feel even more *right*. A feeling she knew she'd want to continue to chase and hoped Lily would let her. That Maya would let her.

"So are we really making plans to do this again? When is everyone home again?" Maya asked.

"Leave it to the business major to help us get down to business," Lily mused.

"I am home for a bit over winter break, though I usually try to figure something out so I am not home the whole time.

Maybe we could go somewhere? My parents have a house outside of Miami."

"I would love to but I do have to come home a bit, I feel like my mom is going to need me longer than a weekend. I have already talked to my dad about it and he agrees. I am all for going somewhere though, maybe somewhere close by? Or here?" Maya said.

"Actually, I have the perfect place. My aunt runs a crunchy retreat up north, we can have our family cabin all to ourselves," Lily piped up as if energized by the idea.

"Rich people," Hanna said smiling, but she was serious. She knew that if this is what Lily described as a 'treehouse,' whatever she was referring to as a 'cabin' was something much grander than the modest ranch-style home her parents had in Florida.

"I mean yes, and if we can all take advantage of it..." Lily trailed off.

"Not complaining, but let us know how we can contribute or help or—"

Lily cut Maya off, "Don't worry about it. You both would be my guests. I just need to check on some things. I usually work up there over break for a change of pace, so in addition to nudes, I'll be sharing more details in the group chat."

Hanna smiled at Lily, and Lily melted slightly.

"Sounds good, Lilith," Maya said, also smiling. "Any chance you have food in this place or should we make our way to your house?"

"I need to get going and get ready to take on the day with my mom," Hanna said, sitting up again and looking around the room for her clothes for the first time. This was perhaps the most time she had spent naked, especially naked with others, and she'd loved it. It was like they were all just being their true selves with one another.

"Let's go up to the house, see what our moms have been up to," Lily said.

THEY DRESSED QUICKLY, and then Lily folded up the blankets along with Maya, reassuring them that she would be back to do laundry. Hanna was pretty sure *someone* would be up to do laundry. They made their way down the wooden steps into the cool morning, the sun well and high in the sky now, bathing the entire property in light, the fall leaves aglow. They walked in comfortable silence through the trees and Hanna took the time to breathe in the fresh air, as though she were walking on a new path. *Maybe this is how mind-blowing sex makes you feel.* She smiled to herself.

Just before they reached the main house's back door, Hanna suddenly felt a pang of anxiety. What if Maya and Lily were just humoring her, what if this is just what you did when you had a one night stand, maybe you just pretended or leaned into the overly optimistic idea that something would continue. Before Lily reached for the door, Hanna blurted out, "So this can happen again?"

Lily turned to her and smirked. "You bet your sweet ass," she said, and then opened the door just as Maya slid a reassuring arm around Hanna's shoulders and squeezed her close as they entered the house.

Hanna felt relieved and already warm with the idea of having her hands on them again. She'd meant what she said; she'd had the best sex of her life. She wasn't under any impressions of romance and love at first fuck, but still, last night had felt like something more.

Like something inside her had soared, and wouldn't be coming back.

# 10

## MAYA

HANNA BANANA

LILITH

That's not a nude...

LILITH

....the glee I felt seeing this message pop up
and the disappointment I now feel. Please make
this right.

PAPAYA MAYA

I am on a train, so...

LILITH

I mean I feel like a Harvard student should be
able to figure this out.

HANNA BANANA

best I can do right now, I am watching TV
with my parents.

LILITH

FINE

PAPAYA MAYA

When I get back to my apartment I will MAYBE send nudes.

LILITH

Don't tempt me with a good time!

HANNA BANANA

Wow, I was just trying to say hi and see how your train ride is going Maya. I am sorry we couldn't make it work and head back together.

LILITH

I'm not...

HANNA BANANA

WOW

LILITH

I get FOMO

PAPAYA MAYA

#needy 😳

LILITH

If you saw how I saw you two, you'd be needy too.

Maya burst into laughter at Lily's antics, her chest warming with how quickly they'd begun texting each other. She hoped it would last. Maya was sure she wasn't the only one worried that perhaps their one-night stand had just been that, but somehow, she didn't think so.

Maya sat back with her head against the window of her train. She loved train rides through New England during this time of year; it was like a front row seat to a fall-themed Pinterest board. It also gave her some long needed time to herself before getting back to the swing of school and the city.

Her mind flitted to her mother, Maggie, who had truly looked distraught when Maya had said goodbye earlier that day. After the night in the treehouse, she had spent the following night lying next to her mom, like she had done as a little girl, only this time she had stayed awake, fluctuating between rubbing her mom's back as she cried softly in her sleep and escaping to what it had been like to sleep between Lily and Hanna.

Her mom was not okay, and Maya felt guilty leaving her. But she had checked in with her dad to let him know that her mother was not okay, but that she hoped she would be okay, and he promised to do what he could. All in all, Maya could tell her father loved her mother deeply, and her mother loved him — which is why she couldn't piece together what had happened to cause them to fall apart, caused her mother to withdraw so completely. She also knew that it was her parents' position that it wasn't her right to know. With a sigh, Maya reassured herself that she'd check in with her mother as soon as she got back to her apartment, back to her life in Boston.

It wasn't like she didn't have friends and a life there, but Maya continued to feel like she was always on the outside looking in. She had been walking back from the library one night and happened to be walking by another Black woman (a *rarity*) whom Maya realized was likely faculty. Before she could ask—beg really—what classes she taught and how Maya could sign up, the woman met her eyes, smiled knowingly, and whispered to her, "Keep going, it'll be alright." Maya had been so shocked that by the time she found her voice again she and the woman had long passed each other, the moment to find a sliver of belonging slipping through her fingers. That woman's words had sounded like both a plea and a promise.

*Keep going, it'll be alright.*

She had one more year left, and then she would need to figure out what she was doing next, perhaps find a place she belonged. The thought made her mind go back to what it was like to be held in that treehouse, listening to the steady breathing of both Hanna and Lily, enveloped in their warmth.

It had stirred a feeling in her that had been fleeting since her parents' marriage began to implode: safety and belonging. Maya couldn't wrap her head around how one night had given that to her, but she also didn't feel the need to push it too far. She simply decided to hold on to it for as long as she could. As a constant outsider, that was all she could do.

# PART II

MELT THE SNOW

# 11

## LILY

It was awkward; there was no way around it. Lily fought the urge to pick at her nails, something she hadn't done in ages. She had envisioned things...differently. Currently, she was standing in the kitchen of what her family lovingly called the "cabin" in northern Vermont, a large house that sat at the edge of a winter retreat property her mother owned along with her Aunt Julia. It was really Julia who ran operations as her mother ran the orchard.

The property included recreation areas, an activity center, actual cabins, and came with a full staff. The staff tended to stay year-round as there wasn't really an off-season. There was never a short supply of wealthy travelers wanting to "escape into the wilderness"—with electricity, plumbing, and amenities, of course.

She drummed her hands on the counter. The house was pretty dark, save for the light of the kitchen, with nothing distinguishable beyond the floor-to-ceiling windows of the living room that faced a fair amount of trees. The house was kept pretty impersonal, since VIP guests sometimes stayed there. It looked as if a northern Vermont preset design from Crate &

Barrel threw up in the place. Lily did preen at the fact that her Aunt Julia had some of her old ceramic pieces in the space here and there. But that didn't matter right then.

There were *two hot naked* women in the cabin. But Lily was standing in the kitchen, drumming her fingers on the counter while Maya and Hanna both showered off their long car ride. Lily had felt relieved when they made it clear they were showering separately—though she wouldn't admit to herself why. They had arrived and briefly caught up enough for both Hanna and Maya to share that they had each barely survived the holidays being at home. This was especially true for Maya since it was the first post her parents' divorce. The day after New Year's, Hanna had picked Maya up, and they'd driven straight to the cabin. They were going to be dead on their feet post-shower, and so Lily had shown them each to separate guest bedrooms, where they all agreed that after their showers they would need to crash and begin again tomorrow. Lily thanked herself that she'd mentioned to the staff that they were arriving; they'd made up two beds in addition to the main bedroom.

When they had all agreed that a week of their overlapping winter break should be spent at Lily's family's retreat property, Lily had been abuzz with an energy akin to winning a game everyone expected her to lose.

She'd gotten there a few days before, spending Christmas at the cabin with her mother and Julia. Her mother had left after New Year's, and Lily had spent the interim trying to speed up time by going grocery shopping to supplement the essentials the staff had stocked the fridge and pantry with. Maya loved raw vegetables (Lily could not comprehend) and she bought a veggie tray complete with dip, though she doubted Maya would use it. Hanna and she would need it to get through them though. And Lily knew Hanna *needed* chocolate and cheddar popcorn (though not at the same time). Lily, of course, bought herself plenty of sour gummies. She also made the obligatory rounds, talked and said goodbye to her Aunt Julia who was leaving to travel, spoke to some of the other folks on staff she was friendly with, and subtly but not so subtly let everyone know there was no reason to disturb the house while she stayed with her friends. She had been embarrassingly dizzy with anticipation at their arrival.

She hadn't seen either Maya or Hanna since that magical night back over fall break. Well, not physically, anyway. There had been a few—more than a few—interesting video calls. Once with Lily on the phone while Maya and Hanna were sharing a bed. After that, and Lily had wondered if this was for the sake of fairness, the rest had been from each of their respective beds.

They'd become almost habitual. No, they *had* totally become habitual. Lily had changed, and everyone on campus noticed. Lily still went out, she still flirted with the women who wanted to know if the rumors were true (they were), but she always went home alone. This was incredibly confusing to her circle of friends, who started asking if she was seeing someone seriously.

The question had brought Lily up short but then a realization sunk in: it had been a while since they'd seen her go home with anyone. And that was because it had been a while since she *did* go home with someone, physically at least. This was unusual, and so of course they would notice.

The truth was though, Lily didn't quite know. Sure, they texted throughout the week in a group chat about mundane daily detailsand spiced things up over video calls, but things remained how she was used to them: stringless.

Lily had squashed her friends' suspicions by telling them she had nothing worthy to report. And there wouldn't be anything except a steamy romp over winter break, Lily was sure of it. Sure, she hadn't been out on the prowl lately, but classes were really hectic for her and she needed her sleep. Besides,

Maya had had a difficult few weeks due to more fallout from her parents' divorce, and she and Hanna were trying to be there for her.

OK—she had a bit of a fixation on what had happened over fall break. But that was likely because it had been her first impromptu threesome, *and* it had included Hanna McAvoy of all people. Lily just figured she needed it to happen *again*. She would use this break to get both girls out of her system.

Lily walked over to the fridge, opened it, and pulled out one of her family's ciders. She cracked the lid off and took a long swig. She wasn't an awkward person, but she felt a little out of her depth. Normally, women came to her. Normally, she had all the moves down. Normally, she didn't go to bed alone unless that's what she wanted. And tonight that's not what she wanted.

"Fuck, I feel drunk."

Lily spun around at Hanna's voice and found her moving into the kitchen. Her long black hair was wet, her pale skin was still flushed from the heat of the shower, and her curvy body was outfitted in a stretchy cotton tank and a pair of stretchy shorts. Hanna was also braless, Lily noticed.

"Want help with that?" Lily said, holding up her cider.

"Ugh, actually, that will probably help me double down on the sleep," Hanna said as Lily moved to hand her a cracked cider.

"What will?" Maya entered the kitchen, her lean frame outfitted in a matching pair of fuchsia and purple striped silk pajamas. Of course Maya wore matching pajamas. Maya's voice sounded so tired, and Lily was just thinking that the drive must have been long when she noticed the dark circles under Maya's eyes and her slightly pale coloring. In fact, in the relief of the kitchen light, Lily thought Maya looked whatever was a level up from exhaustion. She felt a slight pang in her chest at the thought that the drive with Hanna had likely not been the only reason.

"Ohhh cider." Maya's voice was almost monotone and her brown eyes hardened as she scrutinized the bottle in Lily's hand. "I better not, I am already so tired." As if coming back to herself, she added, "But after sleep I know I'll be way more excited to be here. Right now I can't get excited for anything other than bed." She chuckled.

"Same, so excited for this break," Hanna said, way more upbeat. She held her cider up and Lily followed her gesture before turning to grab a glass, filling it with water, and handing it to Maya so she could join in. Maya smiled weakly at her, and they clinked a cheers.

"To a steamy break so hot the snow melts," Hanna said mischievously.

"Says the girl sleeping down the hall," Lily said as she took her sip, the flavor of apples bursting over her tongue.

"Well, after that drive I do need *some* sleep," Hanna said, smiling.

"And temptation is a no-go right now, when I have nothing to give but yawns," Maya said, taking a long drink of her water. "Hanna, be careful with that stuff, we're already tired," she cautioned, which Lily found odd. Maya sometimes mother henned, but she didn't mother hen that hard.

Hanna frowned, caught off guard, then playfully rolled her eyes. "Chill Mom, I'm a big girl."

"Don't we know it," Lily added, trying to defuse whatever small tension Maya had injected into the moment.

They sat in silence, sipping their drinks, glancing at one another like kids with crushes in high school. Surprisingly, the silence wasn't uncomfortable, at least not to Lily.

"Got it, got it, sleep now, play later," Lily said finally.

"And play we shall," Hanna said.

"But sleep now, I'm going to bed before I can't make it there," Maya yawned out.

"Same," Hanna agreed.

"My room is the closest," Lily said, part playing, part hopeful. She knew they wanted to sleep but she had been waiting so long for them to arrive, the thought of waiting a whole other night before she could have her girls was suddenly so disappointing.

"Sleep now," Maya pushed on, moving towards her guest room.

"Play later," Hanna said, following her.

"Fine, fine, let me know if you need anything, but you should have everything in your rooms. Each has its own bathroom," Lily disappointedly called after them.

"Rich people are so ridiculous," she heard Hanna mumble and then Maya softly laughed.

"I'm not rich yet, but I will let the older Blake women know how you feel!" Lily joked—but she wondered if this was something Hanna and Maya had talked about on the way up, if they'd been talking about *her*. Lily tried to shake the thoughts from her mind before they could take root, but that was hard to do now that she was once again in her kitchen, alone.

But, she tried to cheer herself up, while she was going to be alone tonight, she doubted she would be for the rest of break.

And that was just fine. She shut off the kitchen lights and made her way to the main bedroom, feeling confident that by the end of break, the girls would have had their fun, and so would she.

# 12

## HANNA

Hanna woke up on her stomach, face down, head under the pillow. It was glorious. She could feel an ache in the balls of her feet, as if she'd been on them all day, but really it was just how her body experienced fatigue. She yawned and let the space between sleep and waking stretch over her and wrap around her lazy meandering thoughts.

The holidays had been the same as they were every year: dull. She couldn't even begin to comprehend why she found the dullness so exhausting. But the minute she'd had to jump in her car to get Maya, it was like life sped up again and became more vivid, like a dial had been raised on the colors around her.

She wasn't sure if she could say the same thing for Maya. While the world seemed to dial up around Hanna, Maya's energy suggested her world had dialed down. She was always pretty even-keeled, but now Maya seemed dimmed. The warm energy and light that she seemed to exude had faded, and she looked tired—there was no other way Hanna could describe it. Hanna wasn't surprised when Maya had asked if it was okay for her to sleep for the first hour, then slept for a full two before stirring, not even when Hanna had been so engrossed in her true crime podcast that she'd almost missed their exit and had to get creative on the road. *Safely, of course.* Hanna knew Maya had been going through it with her parents' divorce, mainly because of her mom, and made a mental note to pry a bit while they were together, though Hanna also didn't want to stress her.

Hanna turned her head to the side in the bed and relished the way her neck cracked. Faint light was filling the room already, so she guessed it was still early. She stretched again. The double bed was a thousand times more comfortable than the bed she had at home, let alone the one in her dorm. Yes, she was a senior, but her parents wanted her to dorm on campus, and so she did. They were footing the bill and she didn't feel the need to argue, like always. She'd been to Maya's apartment in Cambridge once and was envious not so much of the posh apartment, but of the independence she had. Based on everything Maya had shared with her about her parents' divorce, she wondered if her independence was more for her own sanity than anything else. Still, her parents gave it to her.

Hanna's parents—well, her mother was smothering, and her dad went along with whatever her mother did. Hanna knew it had nothing to do with not trusting her; it was all because they deeply loved her. She knew they'd struggled with conceiving for years; her mom had several miscarriages before they'd found Hanna. They knew just how precious life was when you wanted it. It was a complicated thing for Hanna, who would always ask them, if they'd had biological children would they not be a family, and her dad would just smile sadly and say, "But we didn't, and so we were brought to you."

The only reason Hanna's parents were even allowing her to come up to Lily's cabin was because 1) They were still technically in Vermont, though it was practically Canada; 2) They knew Lily's family, having lived in the same town all her life, even if Hanna suspected her mother didn't like Diana Blake; and

3) they had no idea what the three of them had been getting up to.

Hanna could barely believe it herself. She had determinedly sought Lily out last fall break, intent on having the bi-awakening she deserved. She had never been ashamed of her bisexuality, but it wasn't like moving to Boston hadn't presented her with options. Most of her callers were white boys who always made sure to share that they had their eyes set on studying abroad in Asia sometime soon. The women she had chased all were either coupled up already, or they seemingly spoke a language she did not. Amongst the sapphic crowd, she felt like she was a step behind, always trying to prove herself. Trying to prove she wasn't some straight girl fulfilling some bi-curiosity. The only women into fulfilling that treated her no differently than the boys who chased after her.

Plus she'd settled on Lily Miller back in high school, her fixation spreading through her to the point that for a while she hadn't been sure if it was women she wanted or just Lily. Maya had confirmed her desire, though. She *wanted* Maya—did she ever want Maya. She had *needed* Lily. Like a petulant child she wouldn't have been satisfied until she'd gotten her way. And hot damn had she. Being with Maya *and* Lily had been like a dream.

Lily with her confidence, her blonde hair and bottomless ocean blue eyes. Hanna had worried that her fixation on Lily may have come from a desire to *be* her: conventionally attractive, accepted, confident in a way only white women seemed to be able to be. But Maya had arrived, and she was not like Lily, brown skinned with dark, thick, curly hair that Hanna couldn't understand how she got to smell so good—like lavender and jasmine. She wanted them both. She wanted them so badly that when she finally got back to Boston to start classes, she worried that she'd gotten a taste of something she'd never get again.

And how could she? You didn't walk up to hot people and

ask for threesomes. Or maybe some people did (*probably Lily*) but those people were not Hanna. It wasn't that she was shy so much as she just didn't connect with most people. It was a hard thing to do when you grew up never feeling truly seen or accepted. That was something she knew she shared with May and was grateful for it. Maya may have been the first true friend she'd made.

She knew her daily striving for perfection, for 'normalcy' was self-imposed, something she wore like a shield. But she'd worn it for so long it had become like a security blanket. Maya had no such thing, and Hanna found it exhilarating to be around, to get to touch, like Maya's existence allowed her to dare to to take it off every now and then. Hanna thought the feeling was akin to the rush folks experienced flashing the crowd at sporting events.

That night back in Lily's treehouse, she had felt like the three of them fit somehow, that they had been hers. Her people. She had found them for the first time in her life, and she was certain she was going to have to let them go once school began. But that hadn't happened. They'd started a group chat and regularly kept in touch, talking about silly things in life with some serious things every now and then. They made it seem so easy, as if they'd been lifelong friends the whole time.

Hanna's body began to buzz with the thought of being so close to the two of them again, physically close. They'd gotten *creative* and hooked up a few times over video, once partially in person. It had felt like an unspoken rule that they would limit their time together since Lily wasn't in Boston with them. But that had been the last *taste* Hanna had gotten.

In her post-wake-up haze, she let her mind drift. *Just a taste.*

It had been one night when Hanna had gotten brave and asked Maya to meet up for a movie. For some reason, it didn't feel right to ask Maya directly; instead she'd put it in the chat.

Even though she knew Lily couldn't join, she still wanted her to feel included. Hanna had meant at a theater, but when Lily had lamented that she felt left out, Maya had invited Hanna over to her apartment, saying that they would FaceTime Lily and she could watch along on her end. A virtual "Netflix and Chill," Lily had joked.

Hanna had mentioned to Maya that she'd never seen *Jennifer's Body*, which Maya felt was a crime, especially coming from a baby bi. So it had been settled. They were about to deal with watching the ridiculous sapphic tension of two hot women.

The kiss between Needy and Jennifer had destroyed Hanna.

"Wait, how have I not seen this movie?" Hanna had said, pausing and instructing Lily to do the same.

"You live under a rock, Banana," Lily said through her phone, using the unimaginative nickname she had for her, and it had warmed Hanna all over.

"This scene was meant to be used as bait to get guys to see the film, but actually, sapphics everywhere rejoiced," Maya replied, pulling herself to sit flush beside Hanna on her couch so that they could both be in frame for Lily.

"I def had a raging boner leaving the theater," Lily had laughed into the screen. She was leaning against her headboard in a white t-shirt, from what Hanna had been able to see. Her blonde hair was in a high pony tail.

"Goddamn I bet, I can't believe this was out in the world and just, I think I would have—" Hanna began.

"What would you have done, Hanna?" Lily had asked through the phone, her eyes fixed on Hanna. Hanna didn't think she meant for the stare to be enticing, though you never knew with Lily.

"Well, maybe I would have ended up jumping you sooner," she said, and Maya had laughed beside her at that.

"Oh yeah? Banana, all horned up off of a movie would have jumped me?" Lily teased.

"Well, I for one am glad I was there for your first times," Maya had added, lifting her arm around Hanna's shoulders and resting her hand in Hanna's loose hair, right across her scalp. The movement expanded the shiver Lily had given her and she closed her eyes at the touch.

"Hanna..." Lily had murmured.

"Hmm?" Hanna said, opening her eyes and knowing she was in trouble. Lily's face was slightly more flushed, her only tell, and her gaze was still fixed on her, but her eyes seemed to darken with lust. Lily's eyes reminded Hanna of those pictures of crystal blue oceans with a sinkhole. There was something so unnerving about the depth, but also something exciting. Hanna wanted to dive in. Maya had started making slow circles on her scalp.

The air had become electric, and while Lily wasn't there, Hanna could feel her presence like she was in the room.

"Can you let your hair down?" Hanna had found herself saying to Lily. Lily had taken it down, moving forward to let her hair fall over her shoulders.

"That," Lily said then, her voice turning husky, "is the last order you give tonight."

A SOFT KNOCK on the door startled Hanna out of her trip down steamy lane, her hand grazing over her underwear, her waking arousal.

Hanna grabbed her phone and was unsurprised to see that Lily and Maya had been talking in their group chat. She was surprised to find that it was much later than she thought. Another knock came from the door.

"Hanna?" Maya's voice said from the other side of the door.

"Yeah, sorry, I'm up," Hanna called, scrolling through their messages.

"Cool, Lily made coffee and I'm getting ready to scramble some eggs if that works for you?"

"Sounds amazing," Hanna said, and it did. Not the egg part, but the fact that Maya and Lily were on the other side of that door. She didn't have to live in the memories of Maya's hot breath against her ear, Lily's instructions on what she wanted Maya to do, what she wanted Hanna to do. She had no need to conjure the ghost of the desire she had felt that night.

She needed to get out of bed and go see her girls. She needed to have the real thing.

# 13

## MAYA

"Okay, from here we can pretty much see everything," Lily said. They'd finished breakfast, then Lily insisted on showing them around because she was "only giving the tour once, and I don't want it to interrupt our fun." Maya and Hanna had dressed quickly, Maya in her olive green super warm wool coat, dark jeans, and brown leather boots, and Hanna in her classic black all-weather insulated coat, dark jeans and duck boots. Lily provided extra scarves and gloves.

"Ugh you know me too well," Maya said as Lily popped a sour gummy into her mouth. Maya loved to eat healthy, but she was a sucker for a sour gummy. She sucked on the rough candy as she looked over the retreat. She was glad to have this chance to hang out, given Thanksgiving hadn't worked out–Lily had been up here with her aunt, and besides, Maggie had needed Maya for their "first holiday not as a family".

The air was sharp, cold and refreshing. The ground hard, but there was only a light dusting of snow on the grass that covered the property. Taking in the site, Maya relished using her tongue to melt away the rough sour powder, revealing the sweet and juicy candy. Fitting that Lily had put it in her mouth–it was very much like kissing her, a woman ready to melt under you if you show her you're worthy.

They were currently standing in the center of the retreat, Lily, their guide, looking classic Lily in a purple long puffer, light jeans, and her own duck boots. The center was a patch of grass with a light dusting of snow between the large building that served as housing and the facility center for the retreat's guests and a patch of trees.

Maya had been glad that Lily had insisted on doing a walk-around. She wasn't exactly sure what she had expected. But they all hadn't seen each other physically since fall break. And while they had continued to text and had quite a few steamy video calls, Maya was getting worried that their *thing* was growing into one that existed only virtually. Those were dangerous in that they often continued to evolve in the realm of idealism, too fragile to withstand the external stresses of reality.

Not that a posh winter retreat was reality, but they had all been in the same room for the first time in a couple of months, and nothing had felt forced or awkward. If anything, the feeling they'd left back at Lily's house was the tension that comes from *anticipation*. Maya was sure they were all feeling the same thing: wanting to touch and feel, but at a loss for how to get started. Each time they'd fooled around on video, save for one time during a movie night, they'd explicitly known why they were all there. What they needed from each other.

And Maya needed it now. Not just the sex, to feel grounded. The first round of holidays post her parents' divorce had been tough. She didn't think it would be worse than the emotional tiptoeing her parents had done during the last year before they finally told her they were divorcing—but she had come home to find her mother in an empty house, a shell of herself. As if something more had *happened*. Maya worried it was because she had left her mother alone in Maplewood. A part of her was thankful to have the separation, but another part of her wondered if it would have been better for her mom to have stayed in Boston. She felt guilty for not applying to any Vermont schools for grad school. She would just have to wait and see how her mom did, and if she even got in.

The three of them fell into easy silence as they followed Lily towards another "recreational site." Maya was thankful for the silence, she needed to get her head into the day, into the trip, and she was *close*—she just needed a minute to sort through what she had left back in Maplewood, her mother in the same bathrobe she'd worn the whole time, oily hair, a despondent look in her eyes. Like something or someone had died.

She was devastated for her parents, for her mother, but relieved that she no longer had to dance around the circles they drew around themselves. Maya didn't know everything, she knew that. She couldn't even say *what* had caused the divorce. She had asked each of them separately. No one had cheated, gambled away money, or lied. It took them only a year to legally untangle the layers and layers of over twenty years together. At the end, she wasn't sure either of her parents had found the answer either. All of the tension, all of the avoidance, the pressure in her house for four years of high school and three years of college, and there had been nothing, no reason.

Sure, her Dad moved to Manhattan, and she and her mother moved to Maplewood, but that's where she had found Hanna and Lily and had immediately felt settled in a way that surprised her. Not only because it had been unexpected but also because it had been something she hadn't allowed herself to crave for most of her life.

"Through those trees is a path that leads to the lake, which is definitely frozen this time of year, hence, I am taking you skating," Lily said, pointing.

Lily's voice brought Maya up from her introspection and then the realization of what Lily was saying clicked.

"Uh wait, what, we are skating *on* the lake?" Maya said, a prick of anxiety warming her neck.

"Where else would we skate?" Hanna asked, her big brown eyes wide with genuine confusion.

"Like...in a rink, indoors, a rink built specifically for skating on? Something not left up to nature?"

Lily's pink mouth quirked on one side into a sly smile. "City girl through and through, huh? Well Banana, we are going to show her how us regular folk do it." She said the word 'folk' sarcastically and only teasing, Maya knew.

"Is it safe?" Maya asked.

"I'm sure it's fine, besides people work here to ensure safety, right Lil?" Hanna said, and Maya could see she was fighting back a smile for the sake of Maya's ego.

"I did have this scheme to ruin my aunt's business and name by having two lovers drown on her property, but I don't know, I'm having second thoughts," Lily said, laughing. She rested a hand on Maya's shoulder, and Maya leaned into her touch: she had called them *her lovers*.

*Interesting.*

Before Maya could give that more thought, Lily slid her hand down Maya's shoulder, and grabbed Maya's hand, pulling her forward. Hanna grabbed her other hand and smiled up at her, "It will be fun," she said reassuringly. Maya swallowed her fear.

"There's a bunch of games and stuff, a basketball court and whatnot inside. Plus a heated pool and hot tubs. Over there is where you can pick up a shuttle to take you about forty minutes to the mountain for skiing and stuff," Lily continued.

"Do a lot of people go skiing? I thought this was supposed to be a wellness and yogi-like retreat," Maya asked.

"Yeah, it's about leisure more than community or anything

too regimented. It's basically rich people paying to feel crunchy and get away for a bit. My aunt building this near the ski resort was really smart." Lily reached to open the glass door to the single story building. "Shall we? We can grab skates here, and don't worry, we don't have to—" Her voice broke off as they were fully inside.

Inside was a bunch of different winter activity equipment: sleds, skis, and, Maya could see behind the counter, ice skates. Behind the counter stood two women: one with pale white skin and fiery red hair, spiral curls spilling down her back, and the other with deep brown skin with red undertones, her black hair cut into a chic pixie. The redhead wore green glasses, a purple patterned top and jeans. She had the most interesting rings on her fingers, Maya noticed, and she was flushed with the heat of the building. The black-haired woman wore no glasses and had a beauty mark below her left eye and a corresponding one on the right side of her chin, right underneath her lips. As they got closer to the counter, Maya caught her eye. She was striking, with obsidian eyes that seemed to pierce into her soul.

"Sruti, you work here now? With Fe?" Lily said, her voice asking the question with a twinge of nerves that Maya wasn't used to hearing.

Before the woman Lily was talking to could answer, the redhead said, "*Felicity*, and yeah, I mean I like an equipment shack same as the next girl."

"As you well know," the black-haired woman, Sruti, said, not taking her appraising eyes off Maya's. Her voice was low and sultry, a slight accent punctuating each word.

"Some of us actually *work* here, Lily, or did you forget that, too?" Felicity said, crossing her arms over her chest.

Finally, Sruti broke eye contact—her gaze was truly magnetic—and turned her head slightly towards Lily. Maya tracked her movement, noticing a silver cartilage piercing in her ear.

"It is good to see you, Lil, your aunt gave me a job here recently, so I'll be staying for a while," Sruti said, her voice even and calm.

"A lot has changed since last winter, since you didn't come up all summer," Felicity said, and Maya didn't miss that there was definitely an embedded accusation in the statement.

Maya heard Hanna scoff just as her stomach began to drop.

"I know that look," Hanna muttered, and walked right up to the counter. Maya knew that look too. And now when her eyes flitted back to the dark-eyed beauty's alluring face, she pictured Lily experiencing the same pull, experiencing the desire to lick each one of her beauty marks. The thought turned something inside her so tightly she found herself momentarily unable to speak.

"Hi!" Hanna said at the counter. "Whatever drama aside, we are looking to get some skates. And can you also definitely confirm that other people are skating and are *fine* for my friend here?" Hanna indicated Maya.

Maya knew that Hanna was trying to inject some levity into the situation. Neither of them had any right to be jealous, but Maya *was* jealous. It wasn't that Lily had a sex life, it had been made super clear that Lily had a very healthy sex positive mindset, and Maya loved that for her. No, it was that this retreat was supposed to belong to her, to them. She didn't leave her mother in bed and travel hours to practically Canada to watch Lily get distracted. Maya had never been possessive before, not with any of her past lovers, but she was so close to screaming most days that she needed this *thing*, whatever it was, to be *only them*.

"Your new girl is not used to skating out here in the wild," the redhead said, nodding her head over to Maya as she looked at Lily, and Maya felt her face flush.

"Fe—" Lily started, her voice dropping an octave.

"Felicity, only my *friends* and *lovers* get to call me Fe, and you haven't been one since you stopped picking up your phone," Felicity said, and Maya could hear the bite in those words.

Maya's jealousy took a pause to feel a pang of disappointment, so Lily was the type to love them and leave with no explanation? She momentarily thought of her mother in her bathrobe back home. She opened her mouth to share that she was not 'Lily's girl' when she caught the way Hanna was switching her gaze between her and Lily, as if trying to work something out and not liking the result. Maya's stomach dropped even further because she knew that Hanna would also be put out that Felicity, whoever she was to Lily, had assumed it was *Maya* who was Lily's girl, not Hanna. Not that either of them belonged to each other.

"Can we go skating already?" Hanna said, turning and pushing past Lily. "Unbelievable," she muttered and walked out.

# 14

## LILY

"I got you, come on," Hanna said as she skated backwards, a nervous Maya holding her hands in a death grip.

"Wait, you have skated before?" Lily asked, skating easily alongside them. Lily remembered then that Hanna had done some skating in high school–of course the princess had.

"Yeah, it's not the skating that has me on edge," Maya said as she looked around at the dozens of other people skating on the lake. She took a deep breath, and Lily saw her relax her hands in Hanna's. Lily took off a glove, reached into her pocket, and pulled out the bag of sour gummies. She grabbed one and popped it in her mouth, leaned forward and took Maya's mouth in hers. Maya took in a sharp breath but didn't push her away. Lily slipped her tongue across her lips and when Maya opened for her, she slipped the gummy into her mouth. She pulled back, popped another in her mouth, and turned to give it to Hanna, but Hanna had already started skating away.

"Whoa Banana! I had one for you, too," Lily said, turning to catch up. She turned her head towards Maya and said, "Come on." If Maya had been surprised before, it didn't show; her face was flushed, her eyes were soft, and they were trained on Hanna.

*Of course they were.*

Lily caught up to Hanna and pulled her arm to slow her down. "Hey, let Maya catch up, superstar. I forgot you skated in high school."

Hanna turned towards an approaching Maya, looking slightly guilty. "Yeah well, that was a long time ago."

"What was?" Maya asked as she finally caught up to them. People skated around them. It's what was nice about the retreat–Aunt Julia never overbooked it, so there was plenty of space and breathing room.

"Banana here used to figure skate in high school," Lily said, after Hanna failed to answer.

"Whoa really? Can you show us a thing or two?" Maya asked.

"It was a long time ago, but yeah, I used to skate. I can do a couple of things. I'll show you once we've skated around and I've gotten a feel for the ice."

They began to move again, slow and steady and in sync.

"That makes me feel better then, if you think the ice feels good so far, or safe I mean," Maya said. She was between Hanna and Lily and grabbed their hands. But the look on her face, Lily noticed, made it clear the hand grabbing was more about safety than affection.

"If you fall in, I'll jump in and save you," Lily said, and Maya rolled her eyes.

"Like I saved us from your *whatever* back there?" Hanna said, and her sarcastic laughter unsettled something in Lily. That had been a bit of a surprise: Sruti and Fe working, in equipment, *together*. Sruti usually worked in equipment in the main lodging area for sports.

Lily felt Maya's hand tighten in her grip, as if bracing herself for a fall, even though they were skating just fine.

"Yeah, what *was* that exactly?" Maya asked.

"Oh I think we know, right *Lily*?" Hanna emphasized Lily's

name in a way that she did not like. "Just notches in your bedpost?" She shrugged as if it was not a big deal, but Lily could tell it was in fact, a very big deal.

Lily's mouth dried as she tried to think of the best way to explain.

Maya added, "Oh, well, Sruti was it? The pixie cut? She was alluring, and well, you have that thing for redheads, right Lil?" Maya said. Her voice was calm, but there was still a bite to it.

*Were they both annoyed with her?*

Before she could stop herself, her defenses were up and her playgirl took over, "I mean, who doesn't?"

*Definitely the wrong thing to say.*

"Jesus Lily," Maya muttered under her breath, but didn't let go of her hand. Lily decided that it was because she was more afraid of falling flat on her face than holding onto her at the moment.

*Definitely annoyed.*

This is why she didn't *do* attachments, and by attachments, she meant multiple hookups. Look at how icy Fe—Felicity was treating her. She couldn't help who she'd been with before. She certainly couldn't help that they'd run into not one but *two* of her old flings. And that's what they had been, flings. Sure, she and Felicity had been a bit more consistent, but it's not like Lily was ever going to U-haul up to Northern Vermont and put a ring on it.

"Doesn't matter, they both clearly had eyes for you, so tell us Lily, old flings?" Hanna said.

"Not going to lie, it gets lonely up here." Lily was annoyed now; she didn't really owe them an explanation. She had been looking forward to bringing Hanna and Maya up here to spend some time with them somewhere that wouldn't be too expensive for them. She had broken her rule because there was *something* about Maya and Hanna that made her want to give in. The closest she had ever experienced to this desire was Felicity, and that was a disaster now. Lily wondered if now the rest of the trip was ruined.

Hanna scoffed.

After a pause, Maya blew out a breath and said, "It's cool, I mean, it's not like–" Maya took another breath and then something like defeat edged into her voice. "Whatever, let's just have a good break, ok? I really need a break."

The last part, that plea from Maya, immediately slammed into Lily's defenses. Lily could feel them slowly crumbling.

"They're two old flings from a while back. I just didn't expect to see them here, together, is all," Lily offered, because that's all she could really say in this moment. She was desperate for the activity at hand to get back on track somehow.

"Yeah well, it's cool, we know we aren't the only ones, and, of course, you have good taste," Hanna said.

Thinking briefly back to the fact that two past lovers were now working together in close proximity, Lily wondered if they were in there exchanging notes or if they'd already gotten through the entirety of the *Lily Miller Experience.* That's what Lily had overheard it referred to. It did wonders for her prospects at the retreat. She didn't work hard to make them last, but the other women didn't usually work hard to make it last *either.*

Not *wifey material,* let alone *girlfriend material*—but no one had ever really asked. Not that she was interested in being tied down; she'd seen what heartbreak had done to her mother. Diana had been in love with her father, Gavin, and he appeared to be in love with her. Turned out all those business trips Gavin took for his "top client" were really just him visiting his second family on the other side of the country. How someone could act and lie so convincingly–that's what had devastated Lily the most, and then there was her mother's devastation. She didn't speak to her father—aka sperm donor—to this day, nor the family he ran to after the divorce. He didn't reach out, ever. It was like she had just been an experience to him, too.

"Earth to Lilith," Maya's voice cut through the haze of ugly thoughts.

"Sorry," Lily muttered, and her eyes landed on Maya's brown eyes, sturdy and strong. They centered her. "Wait, where's Hanna?"

Maya turned and pointed to Hanna, who was spinning to the delight of the few children skaters on the ice.

"Show off," Lily said, but she was smiling.

"She's fantastic," Maya said.

"That she is. You think she'd want hot chocolate? I wanna get you both some." Lily didn't really wait for Maya's answer. She needed some space to knock the previous thoughts clear out of her head so she could enjoy her time here in the now with not one, but *two* hot as fuck women.

Lily skated over to the designated guest area where they had left their stuff. With the practiced ease of someone in their element, Lily slipped off her skates and put on her boots. She walked over to the small kiosk whose sole purpose was to provide a place for whoever had booked it to sell their hot chocolate. Today it was some teens from the local youth center. There was a small line, and Lily got behind a family of five. She remembered coming here with her parents before Julia had purchased more land and built the retreat.

"I never grew up with this," her father had once said, as they spun and laughed on the ice. "Thank you for being my amazing daughter, my family," he'd said. And Lily had believed him. She had no reason not to. Now, she realized, he had been thanking her for the *experience,* not for truly being Lily, his daughter. She was wondering if he was somewhere else skating with his new family, or if he was off experiencing other things when someone cleared their throat behind her. She turned and as soon as she saw the fiery red curls, she knew who she'd find.

"Hey Fe, I mean Felicity," she said, meeting the mossy green eyes that used to drive her crazy.

"Fe's fine," Felicity said dryly. She wasn't one for long drawn-out speeches or apologies, so Lily took it as the peace offering that it was. She'd put on her signature beanie and the dark green only drew out the color of her eyes.

"Okay, hey Fe," Lily started again. "Taking a break?"

"Getting some hot chocolate for me and Sruti."

"Ah, I see," Lily said, but she really didn't, so she looked at Felicity, hoping she'd fill in the blanks.

"Yeah we've had some staffing changes, given the growing business. Julia had me shuffle the staff—one being Sruti—to new posts, so I'm training her out here."

Okay, so Felicity was going to make Lily work out some things on her own. "Wait, you hired someone?"

"Yeah I was promoted to being one of the managers, helping Julia out since I'm around all year and it allows her to step away from the business more."

Felicity had been working for her aunt since she was in high school and went full time soon after. That had been six years or so now. The fact that she was a manager had more to do with her having always done the work, and Lily knew her aunt trusted Felicity completely, hence why she wasn't currently present on the property.

The line moved and they followed a few paces forward.

"I was surprised you didn't come up for the summer," Felicity said after a moment.

Lily looked into her green eyes. Felicity was tall, about 5'10, all long lines. Her almost waist-length hair made her seem even taller.

"Yeah well, my mom needed me on the orchard," Lily lied.

Truthfully she had been avoiding Felicity, and Lily had a suspicion that was what Felicity was getting at. The question was if she was going to let Lily get away with it.

Felicity scoffed.

*So that's a 'no' then.*

"Wow, so the thought of coming up here during the summer was so terrifying that you opted to stay on the orchard with Maggie."

"Whoa, what does that mean?"

"You hate the orchard during the summer, managing the staff. Unless there's a newbie who makes you want to stay."

Lily grimaced. "Fe, I don't spend my time chasing the staff members of the orchard and the retreat. Jesus you make me sound so—" Lily couldn't find the right word. Yes she liked to play, but she rarely shat where she ate. Sruti and Felicity had been exceptions and clear examples of why they shouldn't have been.

"Okay, so what, you're here with friends? Your new winter snow bunnies?" Felicity said, looking over from the line at the people skating. "Or are you the third wheel? Afraid to come up here alone?"

Lily turned her head to follow Felicity's line of sight and saw Maya and Hanna skating together—to her discomfort—towards them. They were arm in arm, and Hanna was helping them along, Maya laughing. Lily could see the ease in their features, the level of comfort they had with one another. Was *she the third wheel?*

She made eye contact with Hanna, who gestured to Maya. They started skating towards Lily in earnest. To Lily's relief, they didn't remove their skates, but waited for Lily at the edge of the ice. Clearly watching the exchange. She wondered how much they could hear, being only about six feet away.

"Fe," Lily tried to untangle her voice in her throat. She shot tentative glances at Hanna and Maya and saw that each of their gazes were fixed on the scene before them.

"No I get it, just thought we were beyond avoidance and at least you could talk to me, to my face. Maybe at least a phone call or text message. Apparently not." She huffed out a breath and added dismissively, "But hey, I get it."

"No you don't," Lily began to protest.

The line moved again and Lily was up next. She ordered three hot chocolates.

Lily handed over some cash and told the teen behind the counter to keep the change. "I just—"

Felicity cut her off. "Sruti is really nice, a pretty cool girl, and she's, well, you left her on read, too?"

The anger in Felicity's voice momentarily surprised Lily. Was Felicity mad on *Sruti's behalf*?

*Interesting.*

"I don't really see how that's any of your business," Lily retorted, feeling her defenses building.

At that moment, the teen handed Lily three cups in a cardboard carrier. They looked about sixteen, and their pale face turned red at Lily's words.

"I gotta go," Lily said quickly, flustered and truthfully not prepared to have the conversation. Not that there was much of one to have; they hadn't been together, even though Felicity was probably the closest she'd had to a relationship in her whole life. What was more, Hanna and Maya had witnessed everything they probably needed to know about her and romance and for some reason that unnerved her.

"I bet you do," Lily heard Felicity say as she hurried back towards Maya and Hanna.

# 15

## HANNA

"That hot cocoa was really good," Hanna said as the three of them finished cleaning up the kitchen after dinner later that evening. Maya and Lily were at the island, Hanna on the other side.

"Must be if you're still thinking about it, Banana," Lily said, smiling as she dried a plate. They'd made lasagna—well, Lily and Maya had made the food once they'd realized Hanna couldn't cook. In Hanna's defense she had offered to chop the onions, but as soon as Lily saw the way she was holding the knife, she'd taken over. Hanna liked to think she was great company though, and kept their wine glasses full.

"You know how she feels about chocolate," Maya said teasingly, and Hanna was relieved at the small break in the tension that still hovered around them. Dinner had been somewhat subdued as they made forced conversation, which likely led to the wine being drunk faster than normal. Lily had made attempts at humor, while Maya seemed just—sad, but Hanna wasn't sure the current vibe conditions were ideal for checking in with her.

"So your grad applications are in?" Lily turned to Maya,

taking a sip of her wine and keeping the conversation safe and neutral.

"Yep." Maya didn't elaborate.

"So where did you apply again?" Lily pushed.

"Doesn't matter, let's see if I get in," Maya said. She picked up her wine, looked at it, and then set it down without taking a sip.

"Sociology right?" Hanna piped in, trying to help the conversation gain momentum.

"Yah," Maya said again, without elaborating. Instead she focused her gaze on Hanna and asked, "And med school?"

Hanna felt her face heat. "Applications are in!" she said, perhaps too brightly. She'd applied, but these days she wasn't so sure if she wanted to go straight to med school or focus more on the medical policy aspects of her studies. Or perhaps say "fuck it" and volunteer on a vineyard in France.

"Look at me here with two future doctors, and me, just an artist," Lily mused, once again trying to inject humor into the room.

"Well, some of us have to worry about bills when we graduate," Hanna said, and immediately regretted it. "Sorry, I didn't mean—"

"It's all good, you're right, I'm a trust fund baby who gets to pursue a passion that will most likely pay me nothing. But," Lily added, her voice wavering with something like shyness, "it's my passion. It's the only way I feel like I can really say anything *right,* you know? I'm better with my hands than I am with my mouth." Realizing what she'd said, she laughed.

Maya laughed too, full belly, and Hanna couldn't help but join in.

The laugh wasn't enough to break the tension, but it did seem to coax it out of its hiding place.

Hanna thought of the two women they'd seen earlier, and the exchanges she and Maya had watched between Lily and the redhead (who she *knew* Lily had a thing for). It had looked intense in a way that suggested more than a fling had happened. Was it still happening? Was that why Lily has brought them up here? As a fun distraction, a sure bet with two women she'd already slept with? Hanna also couldn't help the way she felt Maya *fit* with the two women they'd met earlier that day. Both were cool and collected, confident and sexy. Maybe that was Lily's type, and the only way Lily thought she could get Maya on this trip was the way she had before: with Hanna in tow.

"I can practically hear the wheels turning in there," Maya said, stepping to Hanna and sliding a thumb between her pinched brows. Hanna relaxed them and looked up at Maya, who had a careful and thoughtful expression on her face. Hanna reached for her hand and squeezed it.

"You ok?" Maya asked quietly, but it felt like an assertion, *you're ok*, and she squeezed Hanna's hand back.

"What are you two whispering about," Lily asked, moving closer. Hanna turned from Maya.

"So Felicity, is she like an ex?" Hanna asked. She felt her face turn slightly red. Hard things weren't discussed in her house, and she didn't have much practice, but holding Maya's hand made her feel safe.

"Pfft, no, I don't—" her voice slightly faltered, "I don't have exes," Lily said. Hanna thought she didn't sound proud or ashamed.

"Well there was something going on," said Hanna.

"*Was* being the operative word there, Banana. You don't have to worry, you have all of my attention these next few days." Lily moved even closer. Despite wanting more information, Hanna's body began to warm, and she had to wrestle with wanting to lean into the direction things were moving physically and wanting answers.

She thought about what Lily had previously said, about

being able to show and tell better with her hands than what she was able to say.

"All of it?" Maya said, sliding her free hand into Lily's hair, massaging her scalp before tugging slightly.

"I'm sorry, I meant an equal share of attention for both of you," Lily amended, her voice going husky. "Is that what you wanted to hear?" Lily asked, and Hanna nodded. "Mmm," Lily said.

"Not what I only want to hear," Hanna said. "Show me, show *us*."

The atmosphere changed in the room with the shift in tone in Hanna's voice. She could feel it.

Maya slid behind Hanna and kissed her right where her shoulder met her neck. Hanna heard Lily take in a sharp breath.

"Show you?" Lily asked.

"You said you are better at showing with your hands than your mouth," Hanna replied.

Lily's eyes locked on Hanna's, and she smiled conspiratorily.

Hanna could feel Maya's careful breath behind her and knew she was gazing over at Lily, watching and waiting for how to proceed. Hanna felt the control of the situation, and saw in Lily's eyes that she was giving it to her, was giving her something.

"Tell me what you need, babe," Lily said quietly. As if she truly would be willing to give Hanna whatever she needed.

And Hanna did know what she needed. She needed to feel like Lily was hers, even if just temporarily. She didn't like thinking about the other two women from earlier today, and needed to know Lily wasn't thinking of them either.

"You, I need you," Hanna began.

Lily smiled down at her.

"On your knees," Hanna said.

Lily's smile faltered slightly, just for a second; a flicker of a decision danced behind her eyes. Her face became all serious lines, as if deliciously resigned.

Then she kneeled.

"What else?" Lily said, now looking up at Hanna. Her blue eyes were pools of desire. "Maya?"

"Right now, we are going to take care of Hanna, and then," Maya said as she kissed Hanna's neck, "because I am at my wit's end, I am going to ride your face until I forget my own name. Then, and only then, can you come."

"Done," Lily said, and Hanna relished watching the one who was normally so dominant handing over control to her and Maya. And they deserved it, after today.

Hanna pulled Maya's arms around her. Maya enveloped her and then moved one hand to lightly glide over her exposed collarbone. Pleasant tingles prickled her skin, and she took in a sharp breath as Lily's hands skated over her middle, working her jeans open. A moan escaped her when Maya lightly pinched one of her nipples over her clothes. Hanna turned her head, exposing her neck to Maya further.

"How?" Maya whispered against her skin, and Hanna had forgotten what they'd been saying. As if reading her blank mind Maya continued, "How do you need us babe?" *Babe.* Hanna loved it when Maya switched to that pet name, too.

Lily pulled down Hanna's jeans and helped her step out of them. Hanna turned to look down at her, and while looking up at Hanna, Lily took one finger and dragged it across the front of her cotton underwear.

"Mmm, I missed this." She pushed her finger deeper between Hanna's thighs, sliding under her underwear and Hanna closed her eyes and gasped at the sensation. "Maya, she's so warm. I can feel she's getting wet for us."

Hanna felt another finger join Lily's and moaned again:

Maya had moved to feel for herself, her hand starting to undulate as she lightly stroked Hanna.

"Good girl," Maya cooed, rewarding her with added pressure to her stroking.

And Hanna learned she had a bit of a praise kink—she maybe would unpack that later. Maya began to circle the now pebbled nipple through Hanna's shirt and the sensation had an orgasm barreling towards her. "Wait, not yet," she gasped.

"No?" Lily said, leaning forward to kiss Hanna on top of her underwear, in between Maya's strokes. "Don't worry, this is the first time you come tonight, not the only time."

"I wanna come, but not like this," Hanna said desperately.

"No?" Lily repeated.

"What do you want?" Maya asked into the crook of her neck, easing off from stroking her.

Hanna took a few deep breaths. She had trouble saying what she wanted and usually, even from afar, Lily took charge. Maya gave her a small kiss on her neck as if to encourage her.

"I want to feel you all around me," Hanna said, pressing her back into Maya.

"And me?" Lily asked, still on her knees, at their mercy.

"I want your mouth on me, I want you so full of *me* you can't fit those other two anywhere in your mind tonight," Hanna said in a desire-laced rush. Her face heated, but she'd said it, and she'd meant it.

"Fuck, that's hot," Lily murmured, and she pulled down Hanna's underwear, "but you don't have to ask me twice, I missed your taste." She kissed Hanna's slit. "You two are all I can think about." She gave Hanna's slit another kiss, harder this time, and Hanna felt her clit throb at the pressure. "Both of your pretty pussies tightening around me as I rock my fingers in you, my name on your lips." Lily pulled on one of Hanna's legs and Hanna lifted it so that it was over Lily's shoulder. And with that,

Lily leaned forward and slid her hot tongue into Hanna's slit, moaning as she went.

Like back at the treehouse, it didn't take long for them to find a rhythm: Lily bobbing and slowly lapping, her expert tongue navigating through to what seemed to be Hanna's very core as Maya slid her hand under Hanna's bra and shirt, tugging at her nipples.

Maya then licked up her neck, her breath hot, and Hanna knew Maya was going to need to be touched soon, and she couldn't wait. Maya licked her neck once more and then bit down in the spot she'd licked, and Hanna saw stars.

# 16

## MAYA

Maya was nestled between Hanna and Lily and, because she woke up first, she had the chance to really be present and *feel* them next to her. Like the two nights before, after the first time in the kitchen, Lily licking Hanna and Maya rocking her fingers into her, then riding Lily's face till she'd blissfully been able to forget the tension of the day —they slept naked. It was like an unspoken agreement between them now and Maya couldn't get enough of it. She didn't normally sleep naked with her partners, but with Lily and Hanna, it was like they couldn't get close enough to one another. They'd come into her life in such a wild manner, and she couldn't be more grateful. These mornings so far had been so soothing, she could feel the stress of winter break so far lifting. Just like they'd lifted her anxiety of being new in a small town.

Back at school she was always going and going, and nowadays when she was with her mother, she was always up early so she could get a handle on the day before being her mother's entire emotional support system. "Thank you for coming home this break," her mother said to her every morning before kissing her on the temple and grabbing the mug of coffee Maya prepared for her. While sometimes Maya missed her mother and felt the strain, her mother had taken care of her growing up, had always been there for her. This time she could be there for her mother. She was exhausted, but she knew if her mother didn't think Maya was waiting for her in the kitchen, she wouldn't leave her bed.

Hanna stirred slightly in her sleep, and Maya moved closer to her to tighten her arms around her, relishing the skin to skin contact, until Hanna was still once more. While Maya woke up first, she knew this would eventually pull her back to sleep: Hanna in her arms and Lily's deep, steady breathing behind her, the comforter warm and smelling like *them*. These moments untainted by whatever was beginning to form around them.

The last two days had passed with laughter and hot sex. They had not run into Felicity and Sruti again, but Maya couldn't help but feel like something had shifted between all of them. The laughter came with considerable work from Maya as Hanna seemed to be permanently annoyed by Lily, and Maya suspected it was due to jealousy. But Hanna's attitude had been a little too curt to suggest she was just jealous over the Sruti and Felicity run-in; she seemed to also bristle at Maya, though Maya couldn't figure out why.

The new dynamic was starting to gain steam like a hurricane in warm air, putting a strain on Maya, who couldn't take on any more emotional shit.

So, last night, she had uncharacteristically agreed to Lily's suggestion of some physical activity other than what they'd been getting up to between the sheets. Today, Lily was taking them on a walk—or a "walk" to Lily and Hanna, but what Maya suspected was actually a hike. A view was involved, and so while the two native Vermonters didn't consider the elevation they were setting out to achieve to be a big deal, it was a hike to Maya. She hoped that whatever was going on between Hanna and Lily, they could somehow find a way to work it out on the hike. After everything Maya had been through with her parents, she was all about being out and open with *everything*. There was more harm in letting things go unsaid when it came to matters of the heart —or in this case, body.

She turned into the back of Hanna's neck even more and breathed in her scent: jasmine and wood. Before she could stop herself, she parted her lips slightly and sucked on the back of her neck. Hanna let out a small moan in her sleep.

"Well aren't you two cozy?" Lily's sleepy voice said from behind.

Maya wasn't sure if she detected a bit of annoyance in her voice, or dismissal. With Lily, Maya was beginning to learn, they could sound the same. Maya didn't pull away from Hanna, but instead grunted out her acknowledgement and then said against Hanna's neck, "Come over here and find out."

It wasn't long before Lily was pressed up against her back, her clean and powdery scent enveloping Maya. Lily put an arm around her and slipped her hand onto Maya's bare stomach, dragging her fingers in circles on her skin, something Maya knew Lily was realizing drove her crazy. Lily nuzzled the crook of her neck and Maya could feel the tickle of her hot breath on her baby hairs. Maya let out a slow and audible breath.

"Banana awake?" Lily asked, and then kissed below Maya's ear, another thing Maya knew Lily was learning drove her crazy.

"Not yet," Maya breathed out.

"Mmm shame," Lily said.

Maya rolled over to face her, sliding one of her legs between Lily's. The wet heat against her thigh sent a shiver through her body, even if they had all been at it for hours the night before.

"Good morning," Maya said, smiling slightly, feeling herself being pulled into Lily's magnetic blue eyes.

"Morning," Lily said, her mouth moving into a crooked smile.

Maya brought Lily's face to hers and kissed her good morning. This was something new for Maya as well; normally morning breath was a huge turn off for her, but for some reason, with Lily and Hanna, it never bothered her. They kissed deeply for a few beats before Maya pulled back, keeping her hand on Lily's face.

"What was that for?" Lily asked, blonde eyebrow raised.

"For being here, and being you," Maya replied, and then added a quick kiss to the tip of Lily's nose.

"Whoa no fair, you both are getting started without me? While I'm still asleep...next to you?" Hanna's voice came from over Maya's shoulder along with a long yawn.

"Ooooh baby Banana is up," Lily said, and Maya could *feel* Hanna's eye roll. Lily had started calling her that in the morning because well, it was true, Hanna was *not* a morning person and it showed.

"Mmmm fuck you Lilith," Hanna groaned and Maya felt her shift behind her so that she was now spooning Maya.

"Didn't you have enough last night?" Maya said as Lily playfully hissed at the use of her full name.

"Never," Hanna said, rubbing her nose between Maya's shoulder blades. Maya laughed. Since Hanna had started sleeping with women, she was insatiable, and Maya felt lucky to be among her first.

Maya rolled onto her back and looked between the two women. "Okay so level with me, this isn't a walk right? This is a hike?"

Maya watched Hanna look at Lily and Lily look at Hanna, something silently exchanged between the two women.

"Fuck, it is," Maya said, and she put her hands over her face.

"Well, yes and no," Lily said.

"Fine yes, it is a *small* hike. Like really small Maya, we believe in you," Hanna said, not doing anything to hide her laughter.

Maya removed her hands from her face and looked between the women. "Wait, did you both conspire to get me to go on this hike?" When both women began laughing she added, "When? We planned this in the chat, don't tell me you two secretly DMed each other?" The thought actually settled her. For one thing, if they were close enough to DM, then maybe there was a way to work out the tension that was building between the two. The previous sex certainly hadn't, although the tension *had* made things a bit more intense and interesting. That part Maya wouldn't complain about, but it was outweighed by the bigger issue.

"No, no, Papaya Maya, we talked about it here," Hanna said, laughing and running her hand over one of Maya's hipbones under the covers.

"'Papaya Maya! Don't try to butter me up!" Maya said incredulously.

"You love it," Hanna retorted, and Lily snorted.

"I feel like this is your fault, Lilith," Maya said, turning to Lily.

"Hey if you both get to use my full name, then nicknames are fair game. Besides I like Papaya Maya," Lily began and then her voice dropped to a husky rasp, "it's juicy." And her hands joined Hanna's, both of them falling into a rhythm of once again drawing small circles on her lower belly. Maya felt her body begin to warm.

"Do I have to go on this hike?" Maya said.

"Yes," both women said in unison.

"If I go, what do I get?" Maya said. Her eyelids were becoming heavy under the heat building inside of her, but she was relishing this united energy between Hanna and Lily, each circle the women drew getting lower and lower.

"We will just have to get going and you'll see," Lily said, temporarily stopping her hand, "besides this is a good time of year because most people won't be on trail. It isn't the fall foliage or the beautiful greenery, but it is peaceful and quiet, and private."

"Hmmm so none of you ex-lovers will be going with us then?" Hanna said, also stopping her hand.

"Well I can't make any promises, Banana, you've had me, you know what it's like," Lily responded, her voice turning into her fuckboy persona.

Maya felt Hanna's body tighten slightly and watched Hanna's face redden as she slow-blinked. Maya was recognizing that as a way Hanna gave herself time to carefully choose her words.

When Hanna opened her mouth to respond, Maya cut her off and playfully said, "Hmmm, I think I like payment upfront, but I could settle for a deposit."

# 17

## LILY

Lily popped a sour gummy in her mouth and breathed through her chewing, letting the cold air focus her senses. She adjusted the rolled-up blanket she had strapped around her for them to sit on, should they decide to linger. They were all now sated, showered, and bundled up again for their hike—walk. Lily wasn't sure, if Hanna hadn't gotten them moving, that she would have been able to convince her body to leave that bed. If she was being honest, part of her mind was still there, still nestled in between Maya's legs while Hanna worked inside of her...

"Lily? We doing this or?" Maya's voice brought her mind reluctantly back to the present.

"Look who is eager to get started," Lily teased back.

"I'm eager to get this over with," Maya retorted.

"Oh stop, it's going to be beautiful at the top, you'll see," Hanna said, starting them forward on a clear footpath into the woods away from the water.

"How would you know?" Maya asked Hanna, falling into step between them.

"Because we're in picturesque northern Vermont? Also, I

doubt Lily would make you go somewhere ugly, not when we could have just stayed in," Hanna said, a slight chuckle in her voice.

"Right you are," Lily huffed out, and popped another sour gummy in her mouth. The truth was that Lily was surprised she was taking these two women on the walk. Mainly, because she was going to take them to one of her favorite spots overlooking the property, during her favorite time of year when everything was crisp and still, when they were less likely to be interrupted. But she hadn't exactly realized what the reality of them spending so much time together would mean beyond rolling around naked. Really she needed something to pass the time, because when they spent time idly (not in bed), the tension that still loomed in the background threatened to surface. Ice skating hadn't gone well, and there wasn't a whole lot to do out here this time of year.

The snow covered grass crunched underneath their boots as they walked and when Maya gave a small grunt of what Lily identified as displeasure, she handed her a sour gummy.

"Are you bribing me with gummies again? How many of these do you have?"

"Not a bribe, just an incentive, and I have...enough," Lily said, smiling.

"The movement is going to keep you warm, Papaya," Hanna said.

"Mmmhmmm sure, warm," Maya said, but there wasn't any real annoyance behind it. "So how long is this hike?"

"The *walk* is about thirty minutes, not too long," Lily responded.

"And what do we do when we get there," Maya continued.

Lily couldn't help but smile at how genuine the question was.

"We look around," Hanna said.

"And then we..." Maya pressed on, and Lily actually chuckled. Maya was being too cute.

"Come back," Lily said, popping another sour gummy into her mouth before continuing, "like people normally do."

That last remark earned her an eye roll from Maya. "So we are going to walk for forty minutes, just to, what, have a look-see?"

While it was hard not to find the whole exchange endearing, Lily's stomach made a small flip-flop. This is why she should have planned better. Sure, they had gotten all hot and heavy over video calls and exchanged texts about their day-to-day every now and then, but what did they really *know* about each other?

"So Lily, do you take this trail often?" Hanna asked, shaking Lily from her spiral.

"Yeah, I mean I come up here sometimes when I'm here for the summer and helping my aunt."

"And *hanging out,*" Hanna said the last bit in air quotes and there was a touch of ice in her voice. "Do you bring all the girls up here?"

"Hanna," Maya said cautiously. Lily was appreciative of Maya's attempt to quell things, but also noticed the note of impatience in her voice. Perhaps Maya was doing so for her sake.

"And what if I do?" Lily bit back, with way more heat than she'd meant. "Possessive much?" Her defenses were rising and she was over the tension between them for reasons she didn't think she'd rightfully earned.

Hanna scoffed. "You are so full of yourself."

"I'd rather be full of you, Banana, you just aren't paying attention." Lily felt a hand slide into hers and squeeze. She turned her head slightly to look at Maya, who kept her gaze forward but Lily could see her face was tense, maybe even pleading. "I don't take anyone up here, ever," Lily said quietly, and it earned her another squeeze from Maya, this time gentler.

"Sure, I'll pretend that I believe that," Hanna quipped.

Lily heard Maya suck in a breath.

"What makes you think I'd lie?" Lily felt her patience continuing to wane. By the strong grip on her hand returning, she didn't feel she was the only one.

"I don't know, maybe your need to be 'smooth,'" Hanna emphasized the last word.

"Hanna," Maya started. She had been putting a warning tone in the way she had said Hanna's name over the past couple of days, since Ex-lovergate. Lily briefly wondered if it had been something the two of them had talked about when she hadn't been around, like in the shower or something. Either way, Lily knew *something* passed between them every time Maya said Hanna's name like that. It made Lily feel a twinge of loneliness.

"Hanna you don't know everything about me," Lily said, turning on the two women while pulling her hand from Maya's. She was annoyed and she let it show; she had no idea why she was being put on the defensive with Hanna. "What is the issue, *your* issue? Seriously?" Lily looked into Hanna's almond brown eyes, wide with surprise; Hanna looked at her for a few beats before the stare transformed into a glare. "Right," Lily snorted.

But before she could go on, Maya put both of her hands on her head and let out what could only be described as a growl.

"Really? This is what we are doing?" Maya began, and there was no mistaking the anger and frustration in her voice. "Hanna what is the issue? You have so clearly had something to get off your chest and when Lily asks, you have nothing to say?" Maya didn't let Hanna respond, not that Hanna had looked ready to do so. Hanna's face had gone red and she was sputtering slightly, as if processing this abrupt outburst and trying to figure out what to say at the same time.

Maya turned her attention to Lily, took a deep breath and said, "I'm just so—" and then Lily's heart sank at the sight of Maya's face cracking wide open. Maya took a deep breath as tears spilled onto her pinking cheeks.

Lily stood there stunned. Sure things had been tense, but she hadn't expected tears. But Maya *had* seemed a little on edge this whole time.

"I'm so fucking tired," Maya breathed out, and then she put her head in her hands.

"Papaya," was all Lily was able to get out before Hanna walked in front of Maya and put her hands on hers, pulling them from her face while cooing softly, "Hey it's okay, hey, shhhh."

"This is supposed to be *fun* and you two, Hanna," Maya choked out, "You're—"

"Shhh," Hanna said softly, and then turned to Lily. Lily didn't find another glare, but she did feel like she was now an onlooker to a very intimate moment, a moment that seemed to confirm that she was a guest shared by Hanna and Maya—an *experience* they shared.

"Can you give us—" Hanna began, and Maya shook her head as if she was going to say something, but Lily didn't need anymore confirmation.

Instead she nodded in understanding at the dismissal then turned and continued up the path. She needed her spot more than ever and the path was wide and clear. They could easily find their way back to the cabin, without her.

In Lily's annoyance and if she were being truthful with herself, hurt feelings, the remaining fifteen minutes or so went by quickly. She was hot under her coat and scarf as she followed the path's curve. It opened up to a small clearing looking over the retreat property. It wasn't that high, but in winter no one ventured up here, and Lily needed to be alone more than ever. She sat down on the frosted grass, dropped the blanket but left it rolled up, and unwrapped her scarf slightly, relishing in the cool air touching her heated skin. She undid her jacket to let more air in. It was like she could feel the heat escaping her, both in the literal and figurative sense. What the fuck had Hanna's problem been? This was the opposite of what she'd envisioned, and now it was everything she feared: they still had three more days together. Was it going to be awkward? She had been shut out. Hanna had dismissed her and she was sure Maya was about to, too.

Right?

Sometimes, when her parents were still together and she was stuck at home for a weekend, she would attempt to spend time with both of them. But the secrets they built around themselves, her mother's heartbreak and her father's affair, made her full house impossibly lonely. She always felt shut out. So when she couldn't stand it anymore, she went to the treehouse. That had been her refuge, her home that she could fill with lust and longing, if not love. Lily hadn't lived with that in a long time. It was something she joked with Maya about– how Maya was lucky her parents' marriage fell apart when she had a means of true escape, a life to live outside of their house and not just a treehouse. There was no treehouse here, just the home she'd brought Hanna and Maya to. Maybe they would leave, and all she would be left with was longing.

Or maybe Hanna and Maya would save her some grief and just be gone when she got home. That's how her father had left. She just came home to find a half-empty house, her mother and a bottle of wine at the dining room table they only sat at for special occasions. Lily had always thought it was better that way, judging by the vacant look on her mother's face when she told her her father wasn't coming back. Lily thought if she had watched him go, she would have that look on her face too.

Sitting there in the cold, she let three hot tears drop on her cheeks and then began trying to push the feeling down, but her body trembled and a sob erupted past her lips. The sheer size of the hurt surprised her, unsettled her. But between her run in with Fe and Sruti and confirming that she was once again the outsider, she felt a familiar sting she spent most of her romantic feats avoiding. This was exactly the reason she had distanced herself from Fe, so why hadn't she done the same thing with Hanna and Maya? She felt stupid for even inviting them up. Perhaps they would have rather spent the break together, but Lily had offered a getaway they couldn't pass up. An *experience* they couldn't pass up. She dropped her head into her hands and let the sobs roll through her.

No one was going to hear her anyway.

AND NO ONE HAD. Lily had long stopped crying by the time she needed to re-zip her coat and heard footsteps crunching behind her. Each crunching step seemed to bring her back to the world around her, but also froze her in surprise. She'd cooled down physically, knew her eyes were no longer red, but she could feel the heat burning in her cheeks as Maya and Hanna approached her from behind.

"See Maya, this view is totally worth it," she heard Hanna say, not too far behind her.

Lily knew Maya was giving Hanna a look, but decided not to push it. They'd come to get her. The realization warmed Lily, despite the cold, spreading from her chest, down her limbs, to her fingertips and toes. She felt her eyes burn hot again with the threat of tears that she quickly squashed.

Maya grabbed the rolled-up blanket and began to unravel it next to Lily. Lily sat quietly, waiting to see where this was going to go.

# 18

## HANNA

Hanna had been a straight ass. She knew that, without Maya freaking out. It had been unexpected, and even though Maya was the one clearly in pain, she had pushed it aside to focus on Hanna, lovingly telling her to "grow the fuck up."

*Sweet Maya.* Hanna had started to tell her that nothing was going on, but then knew she owed her more than that.

"I just, I don't know, I just feel like, maybe this was a mistake and I don't know why. I feel like this is a game to her. I don't like being reminded that we might just be one—two of many?" Hanna had finally confessed to Maya. Who thankfully hadn't pushed her to explain why that was the case for her, but pushed Hanna to either be honest with everyone or to cut the attitude.

Hanna was self-aware enough to know that growing up in a household with two God-fearing Protestant parents who never raised their voices or showed any hint of conflict had made it so she didn't know how to navigate and express her feelings properly in this situation. She never lashed out, mainly because she never allowed herself to. And yet, when it came to Lily Miller, she hadn't been able to stop herself. It also unnerved her how freeing it had been to simply express *how* she was feeling, even if she hadn't expressed *why*. Still, Maya's warning to be truthful stuck with her.

"It's not fair to Lily, me, or you," Maya had said, looking worn down.

Hanna hated that she'd pushed her to that point. She wanted to be able to change immediately and say something like, *Sorry, something about you flares up this insecurity in me and I lash out*, but that would require her to be way more emotionally well-adjusted than she was at the moment. That probably required therapy.

But she did know, hopefully, how to gloss over a bad spell.

She sat down on the blanket facing Lily's back, Maya sitting on another corner.

"I know the view is great, but you've already seen it and besides," she grasped at an attempt to be coy, "the view over here isn't bad either." She cringed at her poor attempt at lightness. She heard Lily sigh, but then she lifted her legs and spun around so she was on the blanket too.

"Well?" Hanna said, trying to smooth the unease from her face.

After a long pause Lily said, "It isn't bad," and ended with a weak smile.

Despite the recent exchange, a comfortable silence began to spread out between them, like their tension was dissipating. Finally Maya said, "So what were we going to do up here?"

"I don't know," Lily said softly.

"Well what do you usually do..." Maya shot her a look that said *careful,* and Hanna changed directions, "...when you're up here?" Lily looked up at her, her blue eyes so piercing in the surrounding grey and white of winter. In them Hanna thought she saw something she'd never dared imagine: vulnerability.

Hanna held Lily's gaze for a beat longer, and then Maya said,

"So you know, we have spent more time *physically* together these last few days than ever before."

The math in the statement had Hanna blinking away from Lily and turning to Maya. "Can't you just say that we don't know each other so well?"

"Yeah or just literally put that any way else," Lily added, and Hanna warmed to the moment of alignment.

"Yeah, yeah okay, my point is we don't know each other so well and like, we can't spend this whole trip fucking."

"Is that a challenge?" Lily's voice was even and low; whatever Hanna had seen in her eyes earlier was gone.

"Okay, Ms.'we need to go for a hike,'" Maya retorted.

"Oh my god was that a hike?" Lily asked, finally cracking a smile.

"To be fair, we aren't even up that high," Hanna said, continuing to lean into the current alignment with Lily. She hoped if she leaned far enough into it, Lily would see she didn't want to fight. She wanted to be on the same side.

"Whatever, Vermont ladies," Maya said, rolling her eyes but smiling. "Why don't we do something fun together to get to know each other? I wanna play twenty questions."

"What are we, twelve?" Lily asked.

"It is on brand for us, we did have a sleepover the first time we met," Hanna added.

"Sure, take her side," Lily said, but shot her a mischievous smile that let her know they were okay. They were on the same side.

"Oh come on," Maya said, "I came all the way up here."

"I should have packed hot chocolate or a bottle of something maybe," Lily said.

"Here, come here, everyone open their coats." When Maya gave Hanna a look, Hanna added, "Trust me, my cousins and I used to do this."

"Uh," Lily started.

"Oh get your mind out of the gutter, this way we all can stay warm. Here, I'll lie this way." Hanna moved everyone so that she and Lily were on either side of Maya, their coats open and wrapped together to create a little blanket over Maya, whose coat was also open. All of their body heat was pressed together, trapped by their winter coats. It wouldn't last long, but Hanna could feel heat collecting between them.

"Okay, so I may have also snuck this up here." Maya shimmied and produced a small flask. "Cinnamon whiskey," she said, peering up at both Lily and Hanna.

Hanna turned to Lily and then back to Maya. "Where did you get a flask?"

"I found it in Lily's house, I don't know. There were like three in one of the cabinets so I nipped one. I wanted to do a cute little day-drinky toast to celebrate our hike." Maya smiled, her brown eyes turned skyward, the daylight pulling out the light amber hues in them. Hanna wanted to kiss her, but Lily beat her to it, planting a smack on Maya's cheek.

"I knew there was a reason I fuck with you," Lily said, taking the flask.

"And your family just keeps flasks around?" Hanna asked instead.

"I mean, yeah," Lily supplied, and she started to take a swig.

"Wait," Maya interrupted her, "what are we celebrating?"

"To this wonderful walk," Lily said.

"To this wonderful walk," Hanna repeated.

"To this wonderful *hike*," Maya corrected, and the three of them laughed. Lily took a swig.

Hanna took it as a promising sign that Lily then handed the flask to her. Hanna took a sip. The burn of the whiskey was immediate, but the syrupy cinnamon flavor helped keep her from coughing. She handed the flask to Maya, who took a swig.

"That's no cider," Maya declared, and the three of them laughed.

"So, twenty questions?" Hanna said, because truthfully, she wanted to know about both women. She snuggled in closer, Maya's lean body beneath her, Lily's pressed against her side.

"Fine, now that I have some booze I guess," Lily said.

"Okay, hmmm, if you could travel anywhere in the world, where would it be?" Maya asked.

"Whoa, okay, thought we could start with like, favorite color or something," Lily said.

"We only have twenty questions!"

"I mean it *is* cold, so this needs to be over rather quickly," Hanna said. Curiosity nipped at her. "But what is your favorite color?" she asked, turning to Lily.

"Green," Lily said immediately, "like an obnoxious lime green or even better, limerick."

"Limerick?" Hanna repeated.

"Trust the art major to know that one," Maya said, smiling up at Lily.

"What's yours?" Lily said to Maya.

"I was going to just say purple but I better be more specific and say magenta, like a dark magenta."

"Ooooh sultry and sophisticated, makes sense," Hanna said, and then because she was the only one left she said, "I just like blue. All kinds of blue," and the three of them laughed.

LIGHTER ON THEIR feet than they had been on the way up, they made their way down the path towards the house for a late lunch or early dinner, depending on how you looked at things. Hanna walked between Lily and Maya, smiling as they continued their game of twenty questions, having been chased away by the cold at around question ten. She learned Maya was a Sagittarius, December; Lily, a Leo (because *of course she was),* July; so two fire signs, which would prove interesting to navigate considering she was an October born Libra.

"We really could use an earth sign to ground us," Hanna said.

"God what is it about us queer folk and astrology?" Lily laughed.

The air around them was lighter then too, but as the questions went on, the more in depth they were becoming. Lily and Maya shared about navigating their parents' relationships. Hanna learned that Lily's father had a whole other life now, which was heartbreaking. The man was also an idiot, because the Blakes made for great women from what she could tell.

"Yeah well, I'm not a Blake, am I?" Lily said, and there was a pause before Maya asked if she ever wanted to change her name. After a long moment Lily said, "It's the only thing I have left of him, the last reminder that it had all been real once."

Hanna stopped, and so did Maya.

"Let's not make a thing out of it," Lily said as she kept walking.

Hanna looked at Maya, and Maya shook her head slightly before moving to catch up with Lily.

After that, Hanna attempted to lighten the mood with silly questions about sex positions and the silliest things each woman had ever done. Hanna could tell Lily was trying to keep on that theme as they neared the house.

"When was the last time you missed being together, the three of us?" Lily asked, a hint of flirtation in her voice. "I'll go first, the night before you both got here I def had to rub one out so I didn't jump both of you as soon as you got here. I was thinking about our last video call and couldn't fall asleep."

"I couldn't sleep either, I was just excited to see you both finally," Hanna said.

"That's all you're going to give us? Come on Banana," Lily said, turning to Maya, who was looking down at the ground. When Maya didn't look up she said, "You, insatiable Banana? All you did was be excited and go to sleep?"

"Yep, some of us can hold out and wait," Hanna said without thinking. She hadn't meant anything by it, but she had spent most of her life waiting. Wanting. She knew how to do without. Lily's smile faltered for a second but before Hanna could try to smooth over what she said, Maya looked up.

"New Year's," Maya said seriously.

"You mean you wish you could have smooched us?" Lily asked.

"No–I mean sure, but no, New Year's Day," Maya said. "I had just cleaned the house and gotten my mother's laundry done. She was still in bed, and I realized I hadn't gone out. I spent the night trying to distract my mom that her "new beginning" was happening without my dad. I thought I would be relieved once they divorced, when I didn't have to walk on eggshells at home. Getting them to talk to me was like pulling teeth, getting them to talk to each other was impossible. I felt like I was this broken light system trying to guide them through a storm. I had this moment where I stood in my kitchen that morning and realized how exhausted I was, just emotionally tired. So fucking tired, so bored, so lonely. And then, I thought of the treehouse and how I felt wrapped up in both of you and I got the urge to call you both."

"Why didn't you," Hanna said. They were nearing the house now.

"I figured you two had gone out and maybe–well, either way, I closed my eyes and I thought of waking up in the morning with you two, and then I made breakfast."

## 19

### MAYA

Maya hadn't meant to bring the mood–that Hanna and Lily had so obviously been trying to rescue and revive with levity–back down. A heaviness settled around them. Back at the house they showered to warm up, and Hanna insisted on making grilled cheese sandwiches once she discovered the pantry contained tomato soup.

After a relatively subdued dinner, they realized they had some hours left before bed. With the current mood, it was a chunk of time that loomed over them. "We can watch a movie?" Lily said, moving them into the living room and picking up the remote. Maya nodded and Hanna mumbled her agreement. "Oh *Bridesmaids*, just what we need," Lily said, selecting a film.

"Wait," Hanna said, looking around the space. "That couch looks comfy but, how cool would it be if we built a movie fort?"

"A what?" Lily said, turning to look at Hanna.

Maya felt a smile relieve the tension in her face. "Oooh I like that idea, this way we can all sit facing the TV."

"If we grab a laptop we'd have to snuggle," Hanna said.

"Or we can just watch TV? I'm still unclear as to what you're asking," Lily said, and she sounded genuinely confused.

"You know, when you were little, didn't you ever build a little fort and watch movies or play games or read in it?" Maya asked, but then realized too late that was a stupid question.

"My parents tiptoed around the fact that my dad was actively banging someone else..." Lily responded.

"Right, so," Maya said, turning to Hanna, "we are going to have to just show her. Lily, where do you keep the extra blankets?"

Maya and Hanna took the lead, and took the extra blankets Lily brought to them and began building a fort, using pillows and extra chairs from the kitchen so they could build a makeshift roof of sorts. Lily just watched, her blue eyes tracking their movements as if she was trying to put together a puzzle.

"Ok," Hanna said, "hand me your laptop?"

"We also have an iPad somewhere," Lily added.

"Too small," Maya and Hanna said together. While Lily was a ceramics major, she also did design work on the side and had a laptop with a large screen. She momentarily left the room to grab it and then reappeared with a bottle of wine.

"No glasses?" Hanna asked teasingly.

"We've shared a bottle, besides I'm not sure glasses are conducive for, in there," Lily said, gesturing towards the fort.

"Okay so in we go," Maya said, grabbing the laptop and ushering the other two women inside. Hanna and Lily settled on either side of Maya, so much like the way they always slept together. Maya didn't mind, she needed the contact.

The comedy helped a bit, with occasional laughter peppering the air, but the mood still felt heavy, still felt like they were constricted by words unsaid. Maya admonished herself for being "that girl." She hadn't meant to get so real and gloomy; it was just something about being with both Hanna and Lily. She felt comfortable in a way she hadn't for some time. Lily was lonely, Maya could see right through her fuckboy persona. She was terrified of being hurt. It was a truth Maya could see so clearly, and it made her want to hold Lily's hand and let her know she would always have at least a friend in her. And Hanna, such a brat at times but really, she was just as afraid of rejection as Lily. Maybe that's why they butted heads; they were so similar and yet dealt with their fears differently. The fact that Maya could see this so clearly made her comfortable. She *understood* them, and perhaps that's why she felt so safe with them, these two women who worked so hard to hide the fact that all of their cards were face up on the table.

Hanna and Lily laughed at the bloopers at the end of the film, and Maya's chest warmed. The room had darkened considerably with the day, and peeking from inside the fort, Maya saw that fat snowflakes had begun to fall.

"It's snowing," Maya said, to no one in particular.

"Oooh let's go out and see it real quick," Hanna squealed.

"You're a native Vermonter, what do you care?" Lily said.

"It's romantic!" Hanna breathed out, her lips stained red from the wine.

"Could be cute," Maya said, humoring Hanna. She was willing to do anything to lift whatever spell of a mood she had placed on them.

"This is why I shouldn't have given you two wine," Lily said, but there was no real bite behind her words.

They left the fort and piled into the front doorway. They hadn't bothered with coats; instead Maya grabbed one of the blankets off the top of the fort and wrapped it around them as they poked their heads outside.

"Ah it's beautiful here," Hanna said, as they looked out down across the dark property. Lily's Aunt Julia had installed solar-powered fairy lights to illuminate different pathways and areas of the retreat. The effect, Maya had to admit, was quite romantic. The dark made it impossible to see everything, but that only added to the mystical effect the lights had on the property. The fact that they were seemingly the only ones witnessing the swirling snow made it feel like it was a scene laid out just for them.

Hanna bounced slightly on her heels, and Maya smiled as she looked out across the property, an inch or so of snow already on the ground. It must have started shortly after they began watching the movie.

"Guess a hike is off the table tomorrow," Maya said.

"It was a walk, Papaya," Hanna said from between her and Lily, and Maya's chest warmed at the use of the nickname.

"Traitor," Maya mumbled, and Lily laughed.

"It's beautiful," Hanna said, and Maya agreed.

They sat in silence for a moment, looking at the dark grounds, the occasional gust of wind causing little snow swirls that were picked up by the lights.

"You could have called, you know." Lily's voice was serious. "I get it, I lived with that kind of stuff for years."

It took a second for Maya to remember that there had been something hanging over them. "I know, I just...I didn't, I don't know."

Hanna, shorter than her and Lily, had to look up at her slightly. In the faint glow of the lights outside, Maya could read genuine concern on her face. "I—we could have been there for you, I didn't realize...it sounds like that was a lot, Papaya."

"Or at least texted us to let us know what was going on, babe," Lily said, and Maya's stomach flipped at the pet name. The use of it made something inside her come undone, and a small tear escaped from her eye before she could blink it away.

"It's just been like, I don't even really know how my dad is managing, but my mom needs me so much. She wouldn't even get out of bed. If I didn't cook for her, I'm not sure she would eat." Maya began to cry. "And I feel guilty being up here with you two, but I really needed this, and then you both started fighting and–" Maya cut herself off with a sob.

In what seemed like a swift single movement, she was wrapped up in both Lily and Hanna. Lily held her from behind and Hanna from the front. They slowly began to rock, back and forth. "We're sorry," they said, continuing to rock back and forth, eventually moving in a circle.

They stayed like that for a while; the movement was so soothing and combined with the release of what she'd been carrying, Maya began to calm, to relax a muscle she hadn't even realized she'd been clenching. "Thank you," she said. "It has been a lot taking care of her," Maya admitted, wiping her eyes.

"I know babe, so let us take care of you," Lily said from behind her into her ear. "We got you."

"Yeah, we've got you," Hanna repeated.

THEY MOVED IN SILENCE, though the tension had lifted. In its place was a tenderness Maya hadn't known possible between the three of them. They kicked off their shoes and moved back into the house, all while still wrapped up together. It was like neither Hanna nor Lily wanted to let go of her, and Maya was grateful. When Lily started to move towards the living room, Maya asked, "Wait, we're going back to the fort?"

Lily laughed and said, "We spent all that time building it!"

Hanna also laughed and said, "Admit it, you secretly liked it," and Maya knew Lily did. The way she'd watched them putting it together. Maya smiled. She could give this to Lily. It didn't really matter where they were, she just wanted to be close to the two women. The urgency of that desire had her urging Hanna in the direction Lily had started in.

"Come on, it will be like another sleepover," Maya chuckled, and Hanna just shook her head.

They piled into the fort, now with an extra blanket and a half roof, but it was theirs and somehow felt more intimate than the big bed they'd been sharing. Though Maya supposed her back would disagree in the morning; Lily's bed was incredibly comfortable.

Maya settled in, still between Hanna and Lily. "Thank you both," Maya found herself saying.

"Come here," Lily said as she took Maya's chin between her thumb and index finder so that she could bring her mouth to hers. Unlike the hungry and dominating kisses Lily often gave, the kiss was slow and sweet. Lily still had all of the control, but it felt intentional and purposeful. She could feel Hanna pushing her curls to the side and kissing the back of her neck, a spot she knew drove Maya crazy. And it did, but something about it felt hot, not simply in a sexy way, but hot in the way that she was acutely aware that she was *with* both Hanna and Lily, and truly believed that they indeed did have her.

Slowly, Hanna and Lily moved away from Maya and both began to undress. In a moment of clarity, they'd put on extra sweats before going outside to look at the snow, and they peeled off layer after layer without breaking their gazes. Maya was so taut with anticipation and the need to feel each woman that she thought she would die if they looked away.

Finally, both were gloriously naked. Both fair women had full breasts, Hanna's a little bigger. Lily had a medium build, even through her hips and legs. A small patch of neatly trimmed blonde hair was barely visible in the shadow of the fort. Hanna's curvy, soft figure was only slightly covered by her long black hair. They were both beautiful, and they were hers tonight.

Each woman then began to peel off Maya's clothes. Holding her gaze, they removed first her socks and then her pants gently,

Lily taking in the sharp breath she always did when she took off a pair of underwear, like every time she was amazed by what was underneath. They kept going till they got to her shirt and bra. Then they were on her, Hanna's arms were around her while Lily captured her mouth with hers for another deep and slow kiss. Hanna kissed down the back of her neck, till she came around to the underside of her chin. Maya broke away from Lily, and turned to where Hanna's mouth was waiting for her. Lily began to kiss down her body. It was like they wanted to cover every part of her.

Lily found one of Maya's nipples and tongued it greedily, her head bobbing slightly as she worked the pebbled flesh, and Maya was gasping.

"Please," Maya said into Hanna's mouth. She couldn't stand the distance she felt like was between them, even with their clothes off. She needed them all over her, around her, inside her.

"We got you," Hanna breathed back, and she slid a hand in between Maya's legs, right to her slit already slick with want. "Oh fuck, we got you Papaya," Hanna whimpered as she dragged a finger from Maya's center to her throbbing clit. Maya gasped.

Lily slid one of her hands to join Hanna's, and Maya's body jerked with the added stimulation. Finding a rhythm, the two women began to work her together, sliding her clit between each one of their fingers before Hanna took over and Lily slid a finger inside of her. Lily turned to kiss Maya deeply once more.

Maya could feel her release building, and tried to use her hands to reach Hanna and Lily. "Not yet baby, we got you," Lily whispered with her lips against Maya's.

Maya would have argued, she loved touching them too, got off when her partners got off, but just then she could feel herself being overtaken by ecstasy, falling deep into the feeling, and so she let herself fall.

# 20

## LILY

**LILITH**

This place is too quiet without you two loudmouths.

**PAPAYA MAYA**

Just say you miss us Lilith...

**LILITH**

...mmmmmaybe if you remind me why I miss you...

**PAPAYA MAYA**

You are absolutely insatiable

**LILITH**

What?

**PAPAYA MAYA**

Hanna says denial isn't sexy

**LILITH**

Maya I know Hanna's driving so she can't send nudes

You on the other hand...

**PAPAYA MAYA**

YOU'RE SO ANNOYING

LILITH

Hmmm but you have a smile on your face no?

**PAPAYA MAYA**

LILITH

You love it

**PAPAYA MAYA**

Secretly

Hanna not so secretly

LILITH

LILITH NAMED THE GROUP CHAT "MY GIRLS"

LILITH

I am going to go bother my Aunt Julia for a while but hit me whenever

**PAPAYA MAYA**

Will do, we are switching in a couple of hours.

^From both of us

Lilith 🤍 'from both of us'

L
ily set her phone in her pocket and smiled. Dirty old man antics aside, she really did hope someone sent nudes, *soon*. She wasn't sure how she was going to make it till spring before seeing her girls—at least, that's what

they had agreed upon after not being able to get enough of each other the last few days.

Since the first time a few days ago, they'd taken to sleeping in the fort that was still partially constructed in the living room.

Lily loved it, and she didn't care that it was very apparent Hanna and Maya knew how much, since they both always snuggled closer into her when she asked if they wanted to move to the bed.

Something had definitely shifted. That first morning, Lily had opened her eyes feeling completely at ease. She'd listened to the soft breathing of both Hanna and Maya and knew they were still sleeping. Like usual, she had an arm around Maya, who was curled up with Hanna. But the sight hadn't made Lily feel lonely that time. Instead, she'd nestled closer to Maya and took a second to treasure waking up to such a sight. To a *feeling* really. They had all still been naked, and the wetness between her legs had been a reminder that the night before had been incredible. Both her and Hanna taking care of Maya like that. And while whatever had happened between her and Hanna was not entirely resolved, they had needed to put it aside to take care of Maya, the same way she had tried to take care of them. Then Maya had fucked both of them at the same time while Hanna had kissed Lily feverishly. A truce of sorts.

Hanna and Lily hadn't realized how much strain they'd put on Maya, and there had been a silent agreement from that moment on to not add to Maya's plate. And they'd kept that agreement during their last few days together before Maya and Hanna made their way south, back to Boston.

Lily had a few more days of break and expected that she'd help Aunt Julia around the retreat. Julia had returned from a trip the night before. Maybe Lily would ask her advice on whatever was brewing between her and the other two women; she had a feeling Julia would be able to lend some wisdom. Certainly, she would prefer that to being stuck with Felicity and Sruti for the remainder of her time here. Not only would Hanna hate it, but Lily wasn't ready to dive into *that* awkwardness.

Lily took one last longing look at the fort. She knew she'd sleep in the bed tonight, not wanting to sit in the fort alone, missing the two other women. She felt like she wouldn't be able to stand not waking up the next morning to hearing Maya and Hanna in the kitchen, dishes clinking and Maya insisting on weird concoctions like hot chocolate and coffee, like some domestic soundscape playlist. It was a playlist she had never woken up to and had never known she missed. It sounded like *safety*, like *togetherness*, like she was still being held even though both of her lovers were no longer in the bed with her–well, in the fort.

*The fort they'd built together.*

It's how Lily *knew* that this was *something*. Something they were all in together, navigating together, like a family. Sure they had fucked all night long, every night since the building the fort, but it certainly felt like something else had occurred too. Another unfamiliar scenario, something Lily only had a sense of.

Something that Lily couldn't wait to see more of.

# PART III

IN FULL BLOOM

# 21

## HANNA

Hanna's belly was in knots—but the good kind. The kind she knew came with anticipation, the kind she knew only her girls would be able to unwind.

It had been long, too long. The last time the three of them were together uninterrupted had been over winter break at Lily's family's winter retreat home. She hadn't seen both Lily and Maya in the flesh since then. And she couldn't wait.

Hanna pulled down the last corner of the fitted sheet she'd wrestled onto the giant bed. She hated fitted sheets. After getting the comforter on and pillows arranged, she went about removing family photos from the main bedroom — it would be too weird with her parents' haughty expressions staring down at them.

Her fingers thrummed with the anticipation of having her girls in bed: Lily, the one she'd secretly crushed on all through high school, all those years ago, and Maya, her rock. Maya had a confidence that had never sprouted for Hanna, snuffed out by feeling like she couldn't burden her adoptive parents. She was one of the few Asian kids in the Maplewood, VT school system, and the only Asian person in her home. Hanna envied the way

Maya could take up space. Her tawny brown skin was often a source of confusion in the situations they found themselves in. Maya would just say, "That's being half-Black in Boston, babe," her words loaded, but she'd roll them off her shoulders all the same. It was the type of confidence Hanna knew drew Lily in, a confidence she could not match. How could she think she was enough for Lily? Had enough changed in the four years since high school?

And now they were in Florida, spending four days in a white ranch house lined with struggling hibiscus in a quiet suburb outside of Miami. Out back was an enclosed pool, and the smell of chlorine filled every inch of the home.

Luckily, they were just outside of Miami, so not *Florida* Florida, but still, with the current state of things, Hanna wasn't sure this was the safest place for her to bring her two...girlfriends? Was that what they could be?

Hanna sat on one of the barstools at the kitchen island, facing the foyer and front door. She knew the girls would text her upon their arrival, but she wanted to know the minute, to hear the moment they arrived. A blue wooden "Sea You Later" sign hung above the door. The entire house was nautically decorated, straightforward and predictable like her parents. Mary and Evan McAvoy were good people, tolerant people, but they definitely grew up coloring inside the lines. It was a four-bedroom, ranch-style house with a pool.

"For when you, your husband, and the kiddies visit," her mother had stressed when Hanna had asked if four bedrooms were truly necessary, if it was just going to be her and her father.

*What about for me and my two female lovers?* Though, she thought, Lily's very being was gender ascendent.

She had shown the same amount of enthusiasm when Hanna had asked her to use the house for spring break. "Hanna of course! I love that you're finally using the house—and with friends! There's plenty of room, you know that! A bed for each of you." *Thanks Mom, pretty sure we will only need one, the biggest one.* Thank goodness for the Californian King in the main bedroom.

The idea gave Hanna a thrill and also a shudder. She hadn't even come out to her parents yet—a fact Lily often rolled her eyes at, even though she knew how vanilla Hanna's parents were. She didn't want to destroy the image of her they subscribed to: a wholesome, sweet, smart, and together girl. Such a brave girl, for having the life she almost didn't have back in that Chinese orphanage.

She knew her parents loved her, adored her, but there were some things she was afraid they wouldn't understand, and her saying, "Hey, I'm also into girls and have been sleeping with two different girls since last year's fall break" felt like one of those things. Plus, winter break had made things feel deeper than simply sex.

Each time they'd lain together in each other's arms, it was like something was clicking into place all around them, but inside Hanna too. What had started as a messy queer exploration and friendship was snowballing into a different kind of desire than she'd started with: the desire to have them, truly have them, to truly be theirs and for them to be hers. They hadn't ever dared talk about it–what it would mean, or exclusivity, or if they were even building something.

Were they even building something? Or did she just want to because they were her firsts?

If Hanna were being honest with herself, she knew there was a level of refuge she found in sharing Maya and Lily. She had spent all of high school wanting to be one of Lily's girls–to be taken up to her room after school to study and leave seeing stars. And Maya was just beautiful: she carried herself like a torch, drawing everyone to her light. Hanna both admired and envied how she seemed to burn so bright when as a fellow minority, Hanna had tried to hide. Hanna thought she could lie in Maya's arms for hours. Maybe forever.

*You know you want more.* It was the creeping thought that had led her to research "polyamory" and Google questions like, "how to know if you're poly." Those searches led her down the rabbit hole of a subreddit on what it means to be in a *polycule* and "how to do poly right." She came across one person saying that "throuples almost never worked" and that they "were for the inexperienced and naive." Another post said triads were "basically poly on hard mode." She'd stopped searching after that.

Lily was practically a sexuality within her own right — women loved her, and she happily loved them back, and Hanna was sure she was doing exactly that while at school. Maya was harder to gauge. *Stop thinking like a lovesick puppy.*

Hanna was googling "female queer scene in Miami" when she felt her phone vibrate. She opened the "My Girls" group chat:

LILITH

Knock knock.

PAPAYA MAYA

A car door slammed. She felt the prickle of perspiration, nerves and the anticipation of seeing her girls.

Hanna grinned, and then felt her smile slip — wait, had they arrived together? Hanna knew they were taking separate flights, Lily from Burlington and Maya straight from Boston. Hanna had been expecting Maya first, and then Lily not too long after. She had been looking forward to that time with Maya, not to mention the unwarranted twinge of jealousy she had now, the feeling like they'd started without her. *Don't be ridiculous, Lily isn't exactly crazed about you and Maya sharing a city during the school year.*

Hanna made it to the door, breathed, and then opened it to what she hoped would be the start of something new. She just had to find a way into it.

## 22

## LILY

Lily closed the car door behind her and slung her duffle over her shoulder. She hated the humidity of Florida, or any tropical place for that matter, much preferring the desert. But she was here, in fucking Florida, excited to have as much gay sex as possible. Being with her favorite ladies and having protest orgies, win-win.

She heard the other car door close. She felt Maya behind her and heard the Uber begin to pull away. Before them stood a white ranch-style house with a turquoise door. Hanna's parents clearly paid for landscapers; there was a cute petite lawn with a decorative walkway to the door.

"We made it, let's go see our girl," Maya said.

Lily turned to her, unsurprised to find a smile on Maya's full dark pink lips. She could hear it in Maya's voice. They were about the same height, 5'7, but Maya seemed to stand a whole head taller in Lily's eyes. God she was beautiful, sexy, smart, and way out of Lily's league, if she were being honest. Hell, so was Hanna, but here they were.

Maya began moving from the driveway up the walkway, her curly brown hair pulled back into a high messy bun, accentuating her neck. It had been too long since Lily had kissed the spot where her neck met her back. So yeah, they were in fucking Florida, but they were all here together, and Lily couldn't wait. She caught up to Maya and knocked on the door.

The door opened almost immediately to reveal Hanna, a few inches shorter than Lily and Maya, her dark straight hair loose around her shoulders and her red pouty lips smiling. Her big dark eyes were alive with excitement. Lily felt her own face mirror the sentiment.

"Welcome!" Hanna said, moving to the side to let them in.

"Hey! Lily was able to catch an earlier flight so you get double the fun right now!"

Maya entered the house and dropped her bag, scooping Hanna into her arms. Lily watched them for a moment, her girls, who weren't really hers and probably never would be. She saw the way Hanna melted in Maya's arms and the way Maya held her. She didn't think she'd ever get tired of the sight, but something also niggled at her. She was split between a familiar loneliness, the fear of being just a shared experience between the two and the desire to pull both women into her arms. She decided to focus on the latter. She dropped her bag and tackled Hanna and Maya.

"Okay so you want to go out tonight? Laze by that sick pool you have in the back tomorrow?" Lily asked between mouthfuls of fish taco. They'd ordered in almost immediately post hug—Lily knew she was a complete nightmare when she was hungry. Maya had tried to ply her with snacks in the Uber, but Lily called her snacks "junk food's junk food," and Maya called her a "junk food snob".

"We can, but I don't really know anywhere to go, I don't come here often and when I do..."

"It's with family?" Lily asked.

"Yeah well, yes. I mean, I looked up a few places, but all I could find were a bunch of gay bars in South Beach that seem pretty dude heavy."

"Ah yes, that's not surprising for Miami," Lily began, "but no thang right? We'll have each other. It really is about the atmosphere."

"Yeah and it will be nice to be in a space where there aren't bros thinking we're trying to put on a 'show'," Maya added, rolling her eyes.

Lily nodded. It was one thing to be out with one other woman; she still got unwanted attention. Add in another, and everyone seemed to expect that they were performing and pandering for attention. Really they were just in their own world, and Lily was so happy to be back in it. She couldn't wait for her favorite part: when they all fell asleep together in each other's arms, often with Lily as the ultimate big spoon, holding both Maya and Hanna.

During winter break, something had clicked for her. It both intrigued and scared her. Mainly she was scared of the pang she felt each morning, when she woke up slightly apart from Maya and Hanna, wrapped around each other. This is why Lily didn't typically do repeat hookups; she felt like she'd boarded a train knowing the track was out somewhere; she didn't know how soon she'd find out, and the anticipation was killing her.

"Yeah okay, so how about this place?" Hanna said, giving Lily what she needed to push her anxious thoughts aside.

Lily looked up to see a Google page for a bar, "The Tank", sporting rainbow lettering. "I'll go anywhere with you ladies." Lily swallowed, hoping no one noticed her face flush.

"Yeah, thanks for finding," Maya said, and leaned over and kissed Hanna on the cheek.

Hanna beamed, and Lily envied Maya being the source of that smile.

"Get ready together?" Maya asked the table, getting up to clear the carnage that was dinner.

"Yes please!" Hanna said, grabbing the take-out containers from Maya and heading to the trash can. Watching them, they were so...domestic. Had they been spending more time together in Boston than Lily knew about? Tufts and Harvard weren't that far from one another–closer than Sarah Lawrence, in any case.

Lily felt a warm hand slip into hers and squeeze.

"You okay?" Maya asked quietly.

"Yeah, just tired—but I'll wake up with some music and drinks," Lily hastily added.

Maya smiled back at her and brushed a kiss on her lips.

# 23

## MAYA

Maya got in the Uber with Hanna and Lily followed. They'd gotten ready in record time, listening to early 2000s hits. Maya smiled to herself. She had been a little worried about this trip. Mainly because winter break had been a lot. Watching Lily and Hanna tiptoe around the feelings they had for each other filled her with a tension similar to watching her parents tiptoe around the feelings they'd lost for each other all last year. She loved both Lily and Hanna, but they had some shit they needed to work out: they both wanted and feared each other.

Maya almost tripped, figuratively pulling her thoughts up short. She *loved both Hanna and Lily?*

Maya knew that during winter break something had slid into place for her: they fit. What was surprising to her was that they fit equally. Differently, but with almost the same intensity. Maya had loved and lost, but she had never loved at the same time. What's more, even with whatever was going on between Hanna and Lily, she'd been there in that cabin over break; she saw the way Lily tracked Hanna with her eyes, how Hanna lit up whenever Lily entered the room. The way each woman desperately clung to Maya when they fucked.

Maya had never ventured into poly, but she would be foolish to not realize they were building a polycule. And she wanted to–she just knew she couldn't be the only solid foundation. But getting Lily to open up was like pulling teeth and anytime she closed up, Hanna immediately followed.

The car slowed and came to a stop, the three of them exiting the car and making their way to The Tank's entrance. Hanna let out an exhausted sigh before handing her ID to the bouncer.

Maya smiled, knowing it was likely because Hanna had to wrestle her ID out of her wallet. She would have to set those thoughts aside. Tonight was about fun, being present. She had been itching for this–the three of them, together. The few times she and Hanna had met up in Boston, they always acknowledged how much they missed Lily.

They moved into the bar; it was moderately packed, dark and loud, with a plethora of beautiful men in various amounts of dress confidently moving about. The air was thick with the heat of the crowd and the smell of cologne, male musk and stale beer. They approached a group of men who were clearly on their way out and took over their little wall table and two barstools.

"I'll get us some drinks, beer ok? I don't want to be too blitzed," Lily half-shouted over the music so they could hear her. Both women nodded in agreement. Maya would go up later to grab waters. She didn't necessarily want to 'mother-hen', but Maya knew Lily and Hanna would be as cranky as their hangovers were intense tomorrow.

Maya didn't feel like sitting, but hovered over the barstool in case Lily wanted to. Hanna happily sat on a barstool, her head already bouncing to the bass beat that thrummed through the space. She reached around to grab Maya's ass.

Maya smiled. Hanna could be insatiable, but Maya knew this was also her way of laying claim when they were out. She was most comfortable doing it to Maya, Maya noticed; maybe she didn't think she could lay claim to Lily. Maybe that's what the issue was.

"What are you thinking about?" Hanna's voice brought Maya back to earth.

"How I can't wait to get my mouth on both of you," she replied. It had been too long, and Maya knew Hanna appreciated verbal confirmation that she was desired.

"Oooh, dirty, we gotta dance first though," Hanna said.

"Are you saying you won't kiss me on the dance floor?" Maya teased.

Hanna laughed. "Of course not!"

She felt a body behind her and Lily said, "It's me, babe." Maya wondered if she had meant to let the pet name slip.

Lily handed a beer to each woman and raised her glass to cheers. She looked at Hanna expectantly.

Hanna smiled, not understanding what Lily wanted, so Maya chimed in, "To us!"

Hanna's face lit up in realization. "To us," she repeated, and they all took a drink.

Maya hoped it had been a promise from the other two, as much as it had been from her. The heat of the bar superseded that of the Floridian night outside, with the crowd driving up the internal humidity. She could practically feel her curls and coils tightening. She continued to laugh with Lily and Hanna. They'd even danced, just the three of them, and a few times with some other patrons.

"Dance with me!" Hanna shouted now over the music.

"You two go on, I need a break," Lily said as she leaned back, all cool and confident.

Maya recognized the look in her eye, it was the look she'd

seen over a video call session, one where Lily was gearing up to watch her with Hanna.

Maya pulled Hanna to her a few feet away, just as a remix of "Dancing with a Stranger" by Sam Smith came on. Hanna wrapped her arms around Maya's neck and their bodies quickly found the rhythm of both the music and each other. As they swayed, Maya glanced around Hanna to see they had Lily's undivided attention. Lily's face was slightly flushed from the heat, but Maya knew there was also a different heat there, its intensity peaking in her eyes.

"Can't believe Lily wouldn't join us," Hanna said in her ear as they continued to move to the music. But Maya knew Lily liked to watch.

"Oh I think she's participating, in her own way," Maya said in Hanna's ear, her eyes still fixed on Lily's, a sly smirk creeping across the blonde's pink lips. Still, Maya knew Hanna was a physical creature; she wanted both of them. Maya had picked up that Hanna equated touch with reassurance.

Understanding what she meant, Hanna intensified their movements, one hand resting on the back of Maya's neck and the other sliding down to her lower back, just above her ass. Hanna plastered her body to Maya's, resting her face in the crook of her neck. Maya smiled as she felt Hanna's lips gently massage the sensitive skin there. Hanna turned them, Maya knew, so she could also make eye contact with Lily.

They stayed like that till the song changed to something Maya didn't recognize. She felt Hanna's body go slightly rigid, her lips moving from Maya's skin and her head cocking up slightly. Maya pulled back to look at her, and her eyes were fixed behind her, calculating. Maya slowly spun around her so that Hanna's back was fixed to her front, wrapping her arms around her lover so that she could get a sense of what she was looking at. She felt a wave of uneasiness crest and crash.

## 24

## HANNA

Hanna knew this would happen one day; she just didn't think it would happen in a predominantly male gay bar in South Beach. The abrupt unexpectedness intensified the break she felt at the sight of Lily talking to a redhead, a pretty redhead, her gorgeous curls flowing around her shoulders. Both women seemed to be enraptured with each other. Lily was smiling slightly, and Hanna knew that smile. Both women laughed and a red curl slipped into the mystery girl's face. Lily didn't even hesitate to tuck it back behind her ear. Hanna knew that move. The redhead grabbed Lily's hand and pressed her lips to it. Lily didn't pull away.

*Fucking redheads!*

*Triads and throuples are poly on hard mode.* The warning Hanna had seen slammed into her mind. A feeling crept its way up her spine, something she knew was jealousy, but she had no right to be jealous, not technically. Another thought dawned on her that she hadn't truly considered, maybe because she didn't want to, but poly simply meant multiple; maybe that's what she was looking at: multiple possibilities for Lily.

She felt Maya's arms wrap around her tighter, and let herself be slowly swayed out of her spiral.

"Such a flirt!" Maya's voice said in her ear, as she gently rocked Hanna from side to side. There was a hint of amusement in her voice. Hanna knew she could count on Maya to ground her. Of course Maya would find humor in the situation. Of course Maya wouldn't spiral and overreact. And why wasn't she overreacting? Did that mean Maya didn't care, and if she didn't care, what did that mean? Was Hanna the only one thinking they'd deepened things between each of them?

"Hanna Banana!" Maya had stopped swaying and was nuzzling the side of Hanna's face. She pulled away and moved in front of her.

"Do you want to get some air?" she asked, cupping Hanna's face in her hands.

"No," Hanna said, shaking her head for emphasis. No, she needed to calm down. Lily didn't owe her anything, didn't owe them anything, clearly Maya could see that and was OK with it. Hanna could be too. She just needed to detach, detach, detach.

"Let's go to the bar and get some shots," Hanna said into Maya's ear.

"Ah...." Maya said, her sultry brown eyes searching Hanna's face. Hanna knew though, Maya wouldn't say 'no' to her. And she didn't.

The first shot took the edge off, tequila burning her throat and bubbling up in that noxious way only tequila does. Maya did one with her, but said she wasn't going to do anymore. Hanna wasn't surprised because Maya hated shots, but she didn't stop Hanna. The second had helped her begin to drown out the storm of jealousy inside her. And as she took a moment to slowly blink her eyes closed, the third confirmed that the shots had been a mistake.

"Why did you let her do shots?" Lily's voice broke into Hanna's consciousness and then the sound seemed to float away, along with what she thought had been the bar. Her head was against someone's shoulder, and the uneasiness in her stomach told her she was in a car, her body between her girls.

"What was I supposed to do? She said she wanted to do shots," Maya replied in a terse but hushed voice.

"Okay, but since when do any of us *drink* drink, like have you seen her do shots before?" The world was coming back into focus decibel by decibel, sensation by sensation. She could tell through the vibrations and proximity that her head was on Lily's shoulder. Her eyes were heavy, and she didn't feel like making any sudden movements.

"Yes, actually, we went to a party once—" Maya started.

"Oh right, so you guys party together now, great." Lily cut her off. She made an annoyed scoffing sound.

"Yes, you FaceTimed with us the next morning. Remember, it was the night she had that presentation we'd helped her prep for? We were blowing off steam."

"Blowing off steam, yeah," Lily responded, and from the sound of it she had turned her head.

"Yes, blowing off steam."

Hanna wanted to tell them to stop. That she was fine now. Well not fine, but she was okay.

"And tonight? Was she 'blowing off steam,'" Lily said sarcastically.

"As a matter of fact, yes she was, you ass." Maya sounded angrier than Hanna was used to, but still her voice was quiet. Cutting, but quiet. Hanna wanted her to stop; if Maya said why she'd been upset out loud, then she'd have to really deal with it.

There was a beat of silence before Lily said, "What do you mean?"

"Are you fucking kidding me?" Maya snapped.

"No Maya, I am asking you because I know." Lily's voice was dripping with obvious sarcasm.

"The fact that you don't know would be unbelievable, but it's you."

"What the actual fuck, Maya?" Lily's voice was raised now, and her body shifted under Hanna's weight.

No, no, no, but she was too heavy to stop it, held captive by tequila and bad decisions.

"You are so fucking unbelievable," Maya said, and she sounded truly exasperated. "You two..." Maya started, but then stopped.

"Us what?"

"Nothing. I swear this is a stereotypical rom-com moment and I am not here for it."

There was a heavy silence, like the silence you notice after a loud noise, like thunder, like something was about to crack. And then it finally did.

"The redhead," Lily said quietly.

"The redhead," Maya agreed.

And though she could feel unconsciousness thankfully coming for her, it was not before her hot tears begin to fall.

## 25

### LILY

Lily hated how because of humidity, Florida was always hot, even in the mornings. She took a deep breath, the smell of chlorine stinging her nose. She was resting her head, face down, on the side of the pool. The concrete was not as cool as she'd like, baking under the glass of the pool enclosure. But you know, alligators.

The water was cool though and was doing everything to settle her weariness. She knew it was a sign of her nerves, and Hanna's impending hangover, that she'd woken up before both women. They'd gotten Hanna in bed and settled, both scooting in on either side of her. Lily had noticed then that what she originally assumed was sweat had been tears on Hanna's face.

They'd gone to sleep, she and Maya, wrapping themselves around Hanna. But like before, when she awoke, Lily was off to the side, and Maya and Hanna were curled together. She showered, threw on a sports bra and underwear, and drank her weight in water before deciding the pool was a great idea. She hadn't been wrong. She needed a moment to think, to collect herself. To give Maya and Hanna whatever fucking magic time they needed without her.

*Relax. Breathe,* Lily coached herself. *They don't need time without you; they didn't ask for the time you're giving them.* This was not how she'd wanted to start their break together. She had been looking forward to the uninterrupted days when she could finally be back with her girls. But then Marta showed up.

"Hi! Fellow lesbian?" she had said when she walked up to Lily in the bar.

Lily had arched a brow, but nodded in confirmation. .

"A bit forward, but I've lived here for over a year and you three are the first I've seen!"

And Lily understood. There were only like thirty lesbian bars in the States last time she checked, and while she had no issues at school, when she traveled city to city she often found herself wondering how queer women had even found each other before dating apps.

"I too am third-wheeling it," Marta had said, nodding in the direction of the dancing Maya and Hanna. The comment dislodged the insecurity that had been growing in Lily, making it feel like truth. Was she a third wheel? Surely if a stranger could objectively see it... And in any case, what could Lily say to counter that? No, actually, we are all together?

So, Lily had just smiled and nodded, leaning into the insecurity and falling into an old routine. Flirt, flirt, flirt. This she knew how to do. And Marta was beautiful, all wild red curls and golden tanned skin—two things you didn't often associate with one another. "My mother is Cuban and my dad moved here to be with her. She didn't want to leave her family," she had shared with Lily.

And then Marta had kissed her. Well, she'd kissed the inside of Lily's wrist, but instead of the familiar rush that often accompanied welcomed overt advances, Lily felt wrong. Her instinct had been to pull away, but then her shock at that instinct froze her in place, giving Marta time to continue to massage her lips on Lily's sensitive skin, her warm hazel eyes watching Lily.

Lily got it, she was just shooting her shot. Lily had turned, searching out Hanna and Maya. She wanted their presence, their thoughts. She wanted to gauge their comfort. Mostly, she was suddenly gripped with anxiety at the fact that she didn't want Marta if it meant not being able to have them.

But they hadn't been there. Lily had grabbed their stuff, excused herself from a disappointed looking Marta, and went to go look for her girls. Finding them dancing again closer to the bar, Hanna had grown more and more inebriated, she and Maya had argued, and Hanna had cried. Hanna was probably telling Maya why. They were probably still curled up together, sharing whatever they didn't share with Lily.

*Stop*, Lily thought to herself. These were the same thoughts that seemed to choke Lily anytime she wanted to press forward, to ask things like "Hey, can I visit you both for a weekend," or the like.

Lily took a deep breath to fully extinguish those thoughts just as she heard the sliding door behind her open. She turned in the pool to find Maya and Hanna entering, both wearing bathing suits and holding mugs. Maya was holding two, and Lily was touched when she stood by the edge of the pool and handed it to Lily when she crossed through the water.

"Thanks," Lily said, and took a long sip. Hot chocolate and coffee. Something Maya had made for them over winter break because she swore it made you feel better after a night of drinks.

"Mmmm," Maya replied.

Hanna sat at the edge of the pool, her bare legs in the water and her navy blue one-piece clinging around her bust in a way that Lily dismissed for later–if there was a later. Maya set her mug on the side of the pool and slipped into the water to stand beside Lily. Her olive green bikini didn't leave much to the imagination—but once again, Lily didn't allow her mind to fill in any blanks.

Maya took a deep breath. "Okay so—"

"We need to talk about last night," Lily cut her off. Maya's face relaxed into something that looked like relief, and Lily continued, "We need to talk about last night, and we need to talk about us, all three of us."

## 26

### MAYA

Maya felt the muscles in her shoulders relax and a knot smooth out in her stomach, even as her shock at Lily's words had her closing her mouth. She couldn't believe Lily had just laid it all in front of them like that, but she was immensely grateful. She slipped a little deeper into the pool, leaning on the wall fully as she soaked in the relief. They were talking about last night. They were going to talk about them—there was a 'them'.

"Okay, what is there to talk about?" Hanna's voice was huskier than normal, and she still looked a little green.

Maya felt the urge to roll her eyes. When they'd gotten up to find Lily gone, Hanna had tried to talk to Maya. But Maya just couldn't. She'd woken up with the determination to sit the three of them down and facilitate a conversation. She hadn't been crazy about coming to humid Florida in the first place, and she certainly wasn't spending the remainder of the break navigating through Hanna and Lily's tension. She wouldn't be able to stand it. Not in this heat.

"Hanna, come on," Maya meant to sound encouraging, but her voice came out pleading.

Hanna looked at her first with mild betrayal but then seemed to register something on Maya's face, and her expression softened.

"Look, let's not fuck around Hanna, you know I'm bad at this stuff," Lily chided.

"I'm sure that was not your first experience with a beautiful woman, Lily," Hanna said sarcastically.

Maya wanted to throttle her. Hanna wasn't typically this passive-aggressive. She was often way more direct. Maya was a bit floored and annoyed by this change in her typical behavior.

"No, it was not, but it was the first time I experienced you going off and drinking yourself into a stupor, only to end the night crying about it," Lily said.

"I didn't—"

"Oh for fuck's sake, Hanna!" Maya didn't quite shout, but her voice left no room for games. "I cannot, I will not. You know what I went through last year—" She took a deep breath, thinking of all the brokered peace talks between her parents. "We are going to lay it all out on the table. Lily is trying, you try too."

Maya watched Lily and Hanna turn and exchange a glance that looked like guilt. Yep, she was not above playing the "my parents had a messy divorce" card.

Hanna grew resolute. "Fine," she started, "I didn't like it–like, at all," she let out another breath, "but what right do I even have to be pissed? It's not like, it's not like—" Her voice trailed off.

"We're together," Lily filled in.

"Yeah it's not like we are together," Hanna said, her voice steely.

"No, that's not what I meant. I meant, *we are together*," Lily said, and Hanna's expression showed surprise at the admission.

Maya was shocked too. "We are?"

"I have this friend, she's got waaaay more 'fuckboy' energy

than you two accuse me of having. But she always says if you sleep with someone more than three times, you're in something with them," Lily said.

"Okay, then," Maya said, a smile creeping across her face. It was part relief and part incredulity that Lily was facilitating this conversation. "So let's talk about what we are, then," she said.

There was silence between the three of them, the slight swish of pool water the only noise.

"I looked up polyamory," Hanna finally said sheepishly.

"Of course you did Banana," Lily replied, and Hanna seemed to relax at the sound of the nickname. Lily moved in the water so that she was now on the other side of Hanna's legs.

"And what did you find?" Maya scooted even closer to Hanna, so she was cozily sandwiched between her and Lily.

"Really just some definitions and...warnings about, well about how triads are hard and often not advised. That they usually start with people who are naive and don't know any better." Hanna said that last bit with disdain.

"We *are* new. And naive. And I guess...well, are we poly?" Lily said, as if she were thinking out loud.

"Well, are we a thing? That's where we need to start."

Maya had been about to ask the question, but Hanna, surprisingly, had beaten her to it. Maya beamed, proud to see her Banana back.

"We are a thing, we've established that," Maya said. "We just need to understand what this thing is. What does everyone want?" After a lack of immediate response, Maya said, "Ok, I'll go first. I like the energy between us, but the dynamic of me having to resolve things or fix things is exhausting for me. We are all adults."

"You don't have to—" Lily began.

Maya cut her off. "And if I don't, then we just have this

awkward thing that grows between us. And I just want us to be chill and together."

"I want that too," Hanna said quietly.

"Okay, me too," said Lily. "Fine. It's just, how? I mean fuck, Hanna, you'd never even kissed a girl until last fall. How do you—"

"Oh my god, you're not going to make me have the bi-validity and bi-erasure conversation Lily, are you? I've had this conversation with people before and it sucks."

"Okay but you and Jeff—" Lily started, and Maya knew that was going to trigger the shrill growl that came out of Hanna.

"Jeff and I dated in *high school*."

"And okay, you've had years at school and what? No other willing girls tickled your fancy?" Lily replied.

Maya could feel the prick of anxiety creeping up her spine. She needed to regain control of the conversation. "Maybe she was waiting for us," Maya said confidently.

Lily scoffed.

"What? Maybe I was! I don't know Lily, I just know how I feel now and fuck you for trying to question it. That's your shit."

"It is," Maya agreed. "What are you worried about? I'm pan, are you worried about me?"

"It's different," Lily mumbled.

"How? Because I'm a 'baby bi'?" Hanna asked.

"Yes," Lily said quickly.

"Oh fuck you," Hanna said and she made to get up, but Maya placed her hands on her thighs.

"We are getting through this," she said, "and once again, I feel like I am playing mediator, which believe it or not, sucks. Fuck Lily, what are you so worried about?"

Lily lowered her head and sighed. She then turned so her body was leaning against Hanna's thighs and under the water she rested a hand on Maya's hip. Maya leaned into the touch.

"I'm sorry, you're right. I am afraid, I'm afraid that this is some kind of experiment and that we don't know what we are doing. I looked it up too, you know, poly stuff. Triads almost never work."

"Every triad isn't us," Maya said.

Lily chuckled sullenly. "Said every ambitious naive trio of lovers ever."

"I want to be with both of you," Hanna said, and Maya and Lily both looked up at her. Her face was serious, all hard lines. "I don't care if it's easy or hard or whatever. There's a lot of hate in this world and it'd be nice to be in this with the both you, extra love and all. Maybe we are naive or too ambitious, or whatever. Besides, I feel, you both, you both feel like—"

"Home," Maya said.

"Home," Lily agreed.

"I hate that you both are in Boston and I'm not," Lily breathed out, "and I hate how that makes me sound needy."

Maya squeezed her shoulder. "You're not needy. I hate that you aren't in Boston."

"I hate that you aren't in Boston too. I miss you like crazy Lil," Hanna said.

"Really?" Lily asked, and she sounded genuinely surprised.

"Really," both women agreed.

Hanna added, "It feels like a part of us is missing when you're not around. But for the record, Maya and I don't hang every weekend or whatever. Anytime we are together we're hitting you up or talking about how we miss you too."

Lily pushed up on her toes at the same time Hanna leaned down to kiss her. Progress.

"I think we have to accept we can't be together physically all the time, but only till the end of this year," Maya said, "which, it's not like we're in our dorms twiddling our thumbs. We are all multi-hyphenated with plenty to keep us occupied."

"Yeah, not long," Lily repeated, looking at her and giving Maya a quick kiss on her lips.

Maya smiled at the idea of one more year.

"And shit, we are just going to have to figure this out. Like if two of us fight or break up or whatever, we have to talk about it," Hanna said, like it was all simple. But maybe it was and wasn't at the same time. They'd still need to figure it out either way.

They were quiet for a moment, but this time it was a comfortable silence. They were on the brink of something new, but the trepidation that hung around them was dissipating.

"Whatever this is, let it just be ours," Maya said, leaning in closer to both women.

*Ours.*

"Now, can we get to the copious amounts of gay sex? You know, as a big fuck you to the current status of the Sunshine State?"

Maya laughed, a full laugh that rumbled her belly.

*Lily.*

"Of course, copious amounts, for advocacy reasons," Maya agreed.

"Okay but first I need grease, and I need to hydrate," Hanna said.

"Hmmmm but first we need a make-up kiss," Maya countered and leaned in.

They all leaned in to press their lips together playfully, laughing at the initial awkwardness of the three-way kiss, and in that moment, even over the scent of the chlorine in the water, all Maya could feel and smell was them.

# 27

## HANNA

"Just what I needed," Hanna said, drinking down the last of her second coffee and hot chocolate to wash down the spectacular breakfast sandwich she'd just finished. To be honest, she wasn't even sure what combo of egg, meat, and cheese Maya had ordered; all that mattered was that there had been plenty of grease. She felt the world steady around her as her hangover haze began to recede.

They had all showered and were currently sporting swimsuits, poolside. They'd each swum in the pool while they waited for the food Maya ordered because Hanna was "not yet fit for society". Hanna had pulled out lounge chairs, and they'd arranged them so they were all facing each other next to the pool.

The sun was high in the sky now, as the afternoon rays shone down on them through the glass. Thank goodness Hanna's parents had opted for the UV blocking option and temperature control, though Hanna wasn't sure it was particularly environmentally friendly. At least the house wasn't used that often, outside of family vacations and some Airbnb bookings to pay for the property taxes.

"Feeling better, Banana?" Lily asked, as she stretched her arms out behind her on the lounger.

"God yes," Hanna exclaimed, turning her attention to both Maya and Lily. Maya was wearing a lime green bikini that looked incredible against her skin and hair, while Lily wore a pair of black swim shorts, a white cap (*backwards of course)* and a purple sports bra. Hanna had opted for a blue low-back one-piece. She loved not wearing a bra and the assurance that all was still contained without one. Plus, judging by the way Lily appreciatively gazed back, she knew she looked good in it.

The conversation of the morning still hung in the air, but it wasn't tense; it was more like an airy cloud that settled around them.

"What time is it?" Hanna asked.

"Oh wow, it's almost one," Maya responded, looking at her phone.

"Time flies," Lily began, "when you're nursing your bratty lover's hangover." She laughed along with Maya.

"Excuse me? Bratty?" Hanna said incredulously.

"Bratty!" Lily said. "You are such a brat."

"I am not!" Hanna countered, her face heating as she watched Maya and Lily exchange a look.

"It's okay, we have decided not to vote you off the island," Maya joked, and Lily smirked.

"Is that how it'll work? We have a democratic system, do we?" Hanna asked. She was thankful for the calm and easy vibe they had going on, but there was a part of her that also needed to understand the mechanics of their newly decided relationship.

"Hmmm I think we need to make a beer run first, I was promised drinks by the pool!" Lily said, standing and moving to re-enter the house.

"You are such a frat boy," Hanna called after Lily's disappearing figure.

"Yeah let's get some clothes on and grab some drinks. We don't have to get only beer," Maya said lovingly to Hanna, and kissed the top of her head.

"Did you just kiss me on top of my head like a child?" Hanna asked, walking behind Maya into the blissfully cool house.

"Ah, Hanna don't make it weird, you are no child," Maya said over her shoulder as they made their way to the largest bedroom. "I just know we have to make sure our brat is taken care of and our brat doesn't always want beer." They entered the bedroom, where they found Lily.

Topless.

Momentarily distracted, Hanna said, "I am no brat," but her eyes didn't leave Lily. Lily smiled devilishly. Hanna was swiftly discovering she was definitely a breast woman, and it appeared that Lily had noticed.

"Ah, what do we have here?" Maya finally asked. "We don't need to change if we are just going to come back and hang by the pool."

"I know," Lily began, "but I remembered that I was also promised something else." She cocked a brow.

"Oh?" Maya responded, her demeanor softening.

"Yes, after our brat was fed, I was promised copious amounts of gay sex," Lily said, and she bent and pulled off her shorts.

"Well then," Maya said, her tone showing interest.

"Stop trying to distract me from the fact that you're calling me a brat!" Hanna said, but she felt her heart rate increase.

"Hmmm I don't know," Maya said and moved behind Hanna so that she was able to bend her lips right at Hanna's ear level. "You sure behaved like a brat last night, no?"

Hanna opened her mouth and then closed it again. Maya's

breath tickled her ear and the low voice Maya had used began to cause heat to pool in her abdomen.

Finally Hanna said, "Not really, I was upset, I—"

Hanna stopped as she watched Lily smile and pull back the comforter. She got on the bed, pulling the cap off her head and tossing it on the floor as she moved like a cat over the sheets. Her blonde hair spilled around her shoulders, her naked body on full display. As she moved, Hanna's eyes were drawn to the way her muscles flexed under her skin and the way her hips rolled with every crawl till she was in the center of the bed. She turned towards them and leaned back, propped up by her elbows.

Hanna closed her mouth again, unsure of what she had been saying. Daylight filled the room, and while she had seen Lily naked plenty of times, she realized in that moment that she hadn't ever seen her on display like this. Her fair skin was already taking on a sun-kissed glow, and Hanna took in every detail: her thin neck that led to a broad, full chest; the swell of her breasts and cute pink nipples; her slim waist and supple stomach. The mound between her legs had a light dusting of blonde hair. Maya more often than not was fully waxed, and Hanna relished in the contrast when she had both women. Looking at Lily now, she wanted nothing more than to rub her face between her legs and breathe in her scent.

"See something you like, brat?" Lily smoothly asked.

Hanna swallowed thickly, before her brain came back online and she remembered that she had been annoyed. "I am no brat, I was upset last night and—"

"Papaya, I don't think she understands," Lily cut her off.

"Hmm you were upset last night and what did you do, Banana?" Maya asked, pushing Hanna's hair aside as she landed a light kiss behind her ear and began trailing kisses down Hanna's neck. The fire inside Hanna only grew, and she knew she was not going to get her point across, not with these two distracting her. Not with the warmth in her belly spreading lower and lower.

"I uh, I—" Hanna moaned as Maya nipped at the skin where her neck met her shoulder and then ran her tongue over it.

"You came to us and told us how you felt?" Maya teased, placing one hand on Hanna's hip and using the other to pull down the strap of her swimsuit.

"Well I—" Hanna's breath caught again as Maya kissed her shoulder, pulling Hanna closer to her body with a hand on her hip. Hanna felt Maya's small and round breasts on her bare back, could feel her hardening nipples.

"You came to us so we could all sit down and talk? Hmm?" Maya cooed and continued to pepper Hanna's back in kisses, sending delicious prickly sensations down Hanna's spine.

"I don't think that's what she did, Papaya," Lily said, and Hanna met her navy blue eyes that were so carefully fixed on her and Maya.

"I—I went and —" Hanna took in a sharp breath and closed her eyes as Maya dragged the hand on her hip up her stomach and chest, brushing over one of her nipples.

"You are going to have to help out our bratty Banana, she seems to have trouble with her words," Lily said, and she carefully relaxed her legs so they spread slightly.

"You're distracting me—both of you—" Hanna choked out.

"Hmmm let's see, Banana," Maya said, ignoring Hanna's pleas, "you got upset and instead of coming to us, you went to order shots. Isn't that right?"

Maya enveloped Hanna in her arms and placed her lips behind Hanna's ear as she began to slowly rock. While Hanna missed her touch, she relished the chance to come down from her growing high and refocus.

"I got drinks because I was upset and—" Hanna started, but Maya interrupted her.

"You got upset and you acted out? Isn't that what you'd call it?" Maya nuzzled behind her ear, and Hanna realized she couldn't really argue.

"That's right, bratty Banana," Lily said from the bed. "How did that make you feel?"

"Make me feel?" Hanna repeated the question.

"How did it make you feel to be able to act out?" Maya added and licked behind her ear, arms still wrapped around Hanna, drawing circles on her skin with her fingertips and swaying her slightly.

Hanna wasn't sure, she had been so mad in the moment, but then when she thought about it, there was another feeling, too. Something like *glee* at lashing out.

"I lashed out, yes," Hanna moaned out the last part as Maya began to widen the circles on her skin, growing closer and closer to her inner thigh.

"Hmm yes, you lashed out," Maya replied.

"Ah so you are seeing it now," Lily added, steadily watching the scene before her. "What should we do, Papaya? We have a brat in our midst."

"Hmmm, I'm glad you got a chance to lash out, our girl, our Banana always so controlled," Maya said, and stopped swaying and unwrapped Hanna from her arms. She brought her hands up, one to Hanna's bare shoulder and the other to the remaining swimsuit strap. "Did it feel good to let go? To let yourself get lost for a moment?"

*It had.*

"Yes," Hanna breathed out.

"I bet it did," Lily said from the bed.

"You lashed out, you let go, and what did you want?" Maya said, slowly beginning to pull down Hanna's other strap.

"I wanted—" Hanna paused.

"Be honest, babe," Lily said from the bed.

"I just wanted you–wanted you both to do something," Hanna said, breathless, panting with need. She had wanted them to do something then and she wanted them to do something *now*. Her body was at full awareness and heat throbbed between her legs.

"You wanted us to react?" Lily said from the bed.

"Of course you did," Maya cued. "The thing is baby, if you want a reaction, to get a rise out of us, you'll get one, right Lilith?"

"Hmmm yeah I don't know, what do you think, Banana? Do you think that's the best way to get our attention?"

Hanna let out another gasp as Maya bit down at the base of her neck. "I—" She was beyond trying to have a conversation. She wanted to give in to the weakness building in her knees and fall onto the bed with both Maya and Lily.

"Listen bratty Banana, we can't just let you act out without putting our brat in their place," Maya said as she pulled Hanna's swimsuit down. The air on her naked skin made her even more desperate to be touched.

Maya stood, her soft curls brushing deliciously across Hanna's skin. She placed a soft kiss behind Hanna's ear and said in a low and sultry voice, "So get on the bed like a good girl."

## 28

### LILY

Lily watched as Hanna shivered at Maya's words, and then watched as the dark-haired beauty got on the bed, taking her in fully as she moved. She thought Hanna's body could be described by no other word than "glorious". She was shorter than Maya and herself, with a build differently from Maya's slim frame or her own athletic one. Hanna was curvy, soft in all the places that Lily loved to hold on to as Hanna said —no, screamed—her name. She had full breasts with dark pink nipples, a soft and feminine stomach, and thick thighs on top of shapely, stocky legs.

Hanna's body had been pleasantly straining against the one-piece, and Lily knew she would never make it out of the house before having a taste. "Come here and lay down," Lily said as Hanna moved over the bed. She sat up to give Hanna room, and Hanna lay down in her place.

"Yes, good girl," Maya cooed again, moving to stand at the foot of the bed.

Lily watched Hanna look down her body and followed her gaze to Maya, who was slowly untying the top of her bikini.

Once removed, she made quick work of the bottoms, standing naked at the end of the bed.

Lily's mouth watered as she zeroed in on Maya's pussy.

God she could eat Maya every day of the week.

Not to be distracted, Lily turned to look down at Hanna, smiling at how she seemed to flush deeper and shiver at the praise.

*Good to know.*

She had been right in terms of what Hanna needed. Maya was good at reading Hanna's heart, but Lily could read her body. Lily knew she needed to understand that lashing out was *ok,* that she was a *good girl* for them just as she was.

"Hmm Lilith baby, how should we take care of our bratty Banana?" Maya asked as she knelt on the bed at Hanna's feet.

"Take care of me?" Hanna said it as a question, but Lily also heard the plea in her voice.

"Well Papaya, baby," Lily said, trailing a finger from Hanna's shoulder down to her hip as she sat beside her, "first she needs to admit she is our brat."

When Hanna didn't immediately do as she asked–Lily hadn't expected the brat to–she slid her finger from where it had been resting on her hip and let it glide over her pubic mound, with just enough pressure for her clit. Lily smiled when Hanna sucked in a breath and tried to meet her fingers for more friction.

Lily watched then as Maya moved to the other side of Hanna, her tawny brown skin almost golden in the sunlight of the room, her perfect and perky small breasts catching the momentum of every one of her movements. Maya looked like a goddess, and Lily was taken aback for a moment by these two women, knowing they were hers.

"More," Hanna uttered, still trying to move her hips towards Lily's teasing fingers.

"I don't know bratty Banana, do you deserve more?" Maya asked, and looked directly at Lily, as if making sure they were on the same page.

Lily knew they were, that was one thing that she felt with Maya, they always *moved* on the same page.

"Yes," Hanna breathed.

"Yes? Why?" Lily asked, smiling over at Maya who moved one of her hands to Hanna's thighs.

"Why? I don't know?" Hanna said, and worry had edged into her tone, and Lily knew it was because she needed to be touched and was afraid she wouldn't have the right answer to get her there.

Lily's own want throbbed between her legs. Watching both Maya and Hanna interact, even as she watched Maya make the same circular movements she had been making on Hanna's thighs before they'd gotten on the bed, she couldn't stop getting off on knowing that they *both belonged to her.*

"You do know," Maya said soothingly, bending down so she could look into Hanna's face. "You do know."

"I do? I don't—" Hanna gasped as Lily watched Maya dip her fingers to tease Hanna's clit.

"You do, bratty Banana, what are you?" Lily asked, turning and running a hand through Hanna's hair.

There was a beat of silence except for Hanna's panting breath as Maya slowly worked her.

"Say what you are," Maya breathed.

"A brat?" Hanna breathed out, closing her eyes at Maya's continued touch. The sight made Lily burn with lust. She was quickly barreling towards the need for release as much as Hanna.

"Yes babe, a brat, you acted like a brat last night," Maya prompted, "but what are you *now?*" She turned her lust-filled brown eyes to meet Lily's. Lily's gut did a pleasant flip.

The room was full of Hanna's panting and, Lily realized, her own. Maya stared back at her, and Lily knew that Maya knew that all it would take to send Lily over the edge was for Hanna to answer.

And she did.

"A good girl?" Hanna panted.

Lily closed her eyes at the wave of need that throbbed through her, igniting sensations in her nipples and clit.

"What?" Maya breathed out. "Say it like you *know*."

"A fucking good girl," Hanna said, her voice fully pleading now.

"Yes, you fucking are," Maya said, "but you're right, you were a brat last night, drunk and all of over me and so while we are going to take care of you, you're also going to take care of us." And with that, Maya moved towards the headboard where Hanna's head was.

"Put your legs up for me baby," Lily said, and Hanna immediately did as asked.

Lily moved around so she could see Hanna fully on display for her, every fold flushed pink with want.

"Open for me," Lily ordered and knew she could no longer hold back. "You remember what I taught you and Maya?" she asked and heard Hanna take in a sharp breath.

"Fuck please," Hanna whined.

"Mmmm only because you've been so good for me. Has she been good for you, Papaya?"

"She has, but I think she can be even better." Maya straddled Hanna's face and seated herself as Hanna cried out in relief and opened her mouth to welcome Maya.

Lily heard Maya's sharp intake of breath and then Maya moaned, her face twisted in pleasure, and Lily knew she and Hanna weren't the only ones holding back, whether willingly or forced.

"You two seem ready for me," Lily said, and Maya's eyes fluttered open to look straight into Lily's, her brows lifted in a plea. "Yeah, you're ready for me."

Lily held Hanna's knees as she pushed her legs back even more, and then opened her own so that she could line herself up with Hanna. Once her clit came in contact with Hanna's slick center, her eyes nearly rolled out of her head.

"So wet for me, so ready for us," Lily moaned as she rolled her hips forward, rubbing against Hanna and making her moan, and that in turn drew a moan from Maya.

Lily began to move, steadily and intently, against Hanna, who continued to moan, Maya keeping time with her own moans. Lily relished in the fact that *she* was doing that, taking care of both of her girls.

She rolled her hips with a twist to add more pressure to her and Hanna's collision and picked up her speed. She and Hanna were both so wet, offering the perfect glide to her movements. Lily looked up at Maya as she moved, fixed by the warm brown eyes that looked back at her. Maya leaned forward, and Lily met her with her lips.

Maya opened for her and they slid their tongues together. This was Lily's favorite part when they fucked, all three of them moving together in time.

Lily could feel her release building and wanted to throw her head back and relish in it, but before she could she felt Maya's hand in her hair, holding her in place as Maya fucked her mouth with her tongue. The sensation, the desperate way Maya needed *her*, her mouth in that moment coupled with Hanna's vibrating thighs had her on the edge of her orgasm. When Hanna's body jerked in earnest and Lily could feel a flood of arousal against her own, she lost it.

Lily came hard and deep, moaning into Maya's mouth, and

Maya drank it down before succumbing to her own orgasm as their mouths broke apart.

As one, they each rode out their pleasure with heavy breaths, their bodies undulating and jerking with tremors.

Finally, Lily let go of Hanna's knees and collapsed on top of her, nuzzling into her stomach, but not before Maya moved from Hanna's face and saw Hanna's flushed cheeks and blissed-out expression.

They lay like that, breathing hard, the heat settling around them.

"Fuck," Lily heard Hanna breathe, "if that's what being a brat gets me..."

"We may have created a monster," Lily said against Hanna's stomach, reveling in the way Hanna moved a hand to play with her hair.

"Not sure I have any complaints though." Maya chuckled.

"Alright, everyone catch their breath for the next round," Lily said playfully.

"Girl," Maya said.

"I was promised *copious amounts* of gay sex," Lily mock protested.

"Who's the brat monster now?" Hanna snickered and flicked the top of Lily's head.

Too sated to protest and falling into the mutual bliss of the moment, Lily smiled. Later they would need to get up and shower and wash the smell of sex off of them. But in the moments after, wrapped in the haze of her afterglow, she savored the heat of them, the smell of them. She took in a deep breath, inhaling Hanna's scent coupled with Maya's and smiled. She knew if anyone could see her, she'd look like a sleeping drunk. And maybe she was–drunk off *them*. Their essence seemed to seep down into her very bones, her soul, etching so deep inside her she knew she'd never be able to remove it, even if she wanted to.

What they'd created was all around her and inside her, and she was happy to be fully submerged in *them.*

## 29

### MAYA

Maya sipped on her beer, thankful for its coolness, even if she was chest-deep in Hanna's parents' pool. They'd gone another round, soft and slow, before showering again, redressing in their swim gear and going for the beer run. They'd also picked up burritos, which had long since been inhaled.

Even still, Maya couldn't wait for more. She was relieved by the conversation that morning, though she knew they weren't done yet. She also knew that Hanna did best with rules and structure, and they were going to have to talk sooner rather than later.

As if reading her mind, Lily said, "Let's talk, since we're in a cool down period before more sex." Hanna choked on her beer from where she sat on a lounger, a wet towel balled up at her waist.

"What? You know you want more," Lily said from behind Maya, where she was lounging on a floaty. Hanna wiped her mouth.

"It's not the sex she's balking at," Maya said to Lily over her shoulder. "You sure are up for talking today."

"Yeah, well I don't know how to do any of this, like at all, but I don't like how upset you both were earlier, so let's talk."

Maya threw Lily a smile before turning to Hanna and giving her a smile as well. She was proud of Lily; she was trying.

"Okay, yeah, let's talk," Hanna said, getting up from the lounger. She sat down on the edge next to Maya and put her legs in the pool. Maya beamed. Hanna was trying, too.

"Hmm, wait, Papaya, can you help pull me over," Lily said from behind her.

"You can just swim over," Hanna said, bemused.

"Yes, but then I would get wet again," Lily countered.

"You're *in* a pool," Maya said, turning to face Lily.

"Yes well, I warmed up basking in the sun," Lily retorted.

Maya rolled her eyes and leaned forward, pulling the floatie to park Lily in front of Hanna's legs and next to her.

"Thank you," Lily said sweetly, smiling at Maya.

"I am starting to agree with Hanna, I'm starting to think I am in a relationship with two brats," Maya mused.

"No way Papaya, you have yet to put me in my place," Lily responded with a cocked eyebrow.

"Don't think I can't," Maya said, purposely resting her wet, cold hands on Lily's legs.

"Hey!" Lily protested.

"Could have been worse," Maya snorted. "You're lucky I didn't just flip you on your way over here, though the thought hasn't completely left my mind."

"Do so, and I won't touch your pussy for—" Lily stumbled because, what could she say? "—for a long time," she filled in.

"Yeah I mean we *are* long distance... Not a lot of opportunities for touching in the near future," Hanna said glumly.

"Maybe this is a good place to start?" Maya said, and then added, "I am really, really happy to talk about this. I mean, I'm not sure my parents ever—" but then she stopped herself, realizing she wasn't quite sure what she wanted to say. She knew that relationships required communication, total communication, and this one was completely uncharted territory: *three* people *and* long distance.

"Okay this may be long distance," Lily started, as if trying to help Maya, "but we've also kinda been doing it this whole time, no?"

Lily was right, they *had* been at least communicating and being *something* the whole time.

"So where do we start, then?" Hanna said, seemingly coming back to the world around her. Maya was happy to see her be able to get herself out of her head in this moment that she knew was uncomfortable for her.

"Basics? Like exclusive, open, or?" Maya began.

"Exclusive," Hanna and Lily said at the same time. Maya was not surprised by Hanna's answer, but she didn't expect the same answer so quickly from Lily.

"My sperm donor literally started over with a whole new other family. I don't know that I can handle open, even if it is ethically," Lily said when Hanna and Maya looked at her. "Besides, you *both* are *mine.*"

Maya didn't love possession typically, but because she understood how important it was for Lily to have something that was *hers,* just hers, like her own space back at her home, Maya warmed to the idea.

"Okay so, exclusive, I agree; I don't like to share. You're ours too," Maya added, squeezing one of Lily's legs in reassurance.

"Totally, which, I will admit, is new to me and so I may not get it right every time," Lily said, turning to look at Hanna, "but I meant it, I didn't have any desire to take on that redhead at the bar. I simply was flirting for the sake of flirting. Is flirting okay?"

"I'm not sure you can help flirting," Hanna said, chuckling, and Maya felt the release of tension in Lily's body.

"But you have to tell us about it," Maya added. "I don't want to ever feel like something is happening outside of us." Maya knew she wouldn't be able to stand it, not after seeing whatever her parents kept to themselves eat their relationship from the inside out, having seemingly just one day fallen apart. Watching it had made Maya feel helpless, not that it was her job to save them, but she had wanted to at least be given the chance to *try*. She was a part of the family too, *right*?

"Okay, and I think if things ever go beyond flirting, we all decide and we are all together," Hanna added.

Maya was surprised for a moment, but she thought Hanna was getting to exactly what Maya needed, too. "Right so, we come first, like our relationship?" Maya asked, making sure she and Hanna were on the same page.

Hanna nodded and Lily said, "I like that."

"What about one-on-one time, I mean, how do we balance the dyads in our triad?" Hanna asked, and Maya turned to exchange a look with Lily.

Lily laughed and said, "Hanna, babe, did you do more research?"

Hanna shifted uncomfortably in the way Maya knew she did when she'd been caught doing something that she felt awkward about. "I mean, I don't even know what we are doing! So yeah, I googled."

"When?" Maya asked. They'd pretty much been all over each other.

"Honestly just now, when I was on my phone earlier, just trying to understand, you know, I have never—"

"It's fine, Banana," Lily said, laughing.

"Yeah it's not like I haven't googled this relationship too," Maya added. She had, after winter break, when she had been trying to make sense of their dynamic.

"Let's just accept that we don't know what we are doing, but I am okay with that, because...well I trust you two, ok?" Lily said, so genuinely that Maya melted.

"We will talk about stuff, right Banana?" Maya said.

"I'm not always good at that, but I promise to try," Hanna said.

"That's all we can do," Maya said softly, because she realized that's what had happened to her parents: they had stopped trying for some reason. The realization was both a devastation and a relief. Devastating for her parents, but a relief that there was some aspect Maya could cling to to understand the *why,* so she could understand *how* to avoid it.

"I don't care too much about one-on-one time," Lily said, pulling Maya from her thoughts. "I know you two have your own thing, and I am just happy to have you both..." Lily trailed off but Maya knew what she'd omitted: *any way that I can get you.*

"Don't do that," Maya soothed, rubbing her hands over Lily's legs. "Don't think that you are just going to get whatever *we* give you–this has to work for all of us."

"Yeah well, not sure what I can do from New York while you both are in Boston."

"For now," Hanna said, as Maya watched her go into her thoughts.

"Why don't we keep the group chat as our ONLY means of communication for now?" Maya suggested, remembering a piece of advice she'd seen one late night on Reddit.

"What do you mean?" Lily asked.

"I mean, we keep everything in the chat. So even if Hanna and I are making plans to meet up, you are a part of them?"

"I like that idea," Hanna said slowly, as if processing their conversation along with whatever her mind was trying to work through. Maya hoped she was just mustering up the courage to raise whatever it was. She'd give her the space to do so, but would press if she didn't.

"Actually I do, too," Lily said, smiling.

"Yeah it's something I read, but it will also force us to talk about things, instead of having—as Hanna mentioned—dyad conversations about one another. And truthfully, when we need advice we should be talking to friends anyway, like any relationship. And you two are most certainly more than friends." Maya waggled her eyebrows.

"Done," Lily said.

After taking a deep breath, Hanna said, "Yeah, I think that'll be great, especially while Maya and I are in Boston." As if finally deciding on something, she continued, "I don't know how long this will go on, but I've decided to hold off on med school for a year or two."

Maya was surprised. She wondered if Hanna had told her parents, but she didn't want to stress Hanna out any more than she knew she must already be.

"Holy shit, babe," Lily said, adopting the pet name she used to note that they were in a safe space.

"I really want to work for some sort of socially conscious organization? Like Planned Parenthood or something? Since my goal is to serve underprivileged communities."

"That's fucking awesome," Maya said.

"So for now, I have been looking at jobs just kinda, around. I don't know where you two want to end up after graduation."

Maya nodded. They had shared their interests, their hopes and dreams in a hypothetical context, but they'd never really sat down and talked about their *plans*.

"You know how I told you both I applied to grad school before winter break?" Maya said sheepishly.

"Ah yes, but you wouldn't say where!" Lily said, turning to her and splashing her with a bit of water.

"And! For what?" Hanna enthused.

"Uh, well, Harvard, Princeton, Columbia, and—"

"Oh my god," Lily said, laughing, "of course." She looked up at Hanna, who was also laughing, but Maya didn't feel put off. The fact that her two girlfriends were sharing knowing looks made her feel like they got her, truly saw her, and seeing her brought them joy.

"Well, and Brown, those are where the best sociology programs are, and some really interesting MFA programs, should I ever decide to say 'fuck it' and become a starving writer."

"You won't ever be starving with me, love," Lily said, and Maya could feel she meant it.

"I have a trust fund. I can go anywhere. Diana is going to run the family business until she wants to retire, and I think that will be about the time the Grim Reaper comes to collect her, and even then..." They all laughed at Lily's dramatics. "I will have to work with her from time to time, but my near future is super flexible, I have no plan."

"Must be so nice," Hanna said without any bite.

"It is, truly," Lily said, nodding her head with a touch of smugness that Maya hated that she liked.

"So, wait, are we U-Hauling?" Hanna said, laughing, but Maya could hear the hopeful note in her voice.

"Ugh," Lily made a big deal of rolling her eyes in lament, "you both tricked and trapped me, that's what I'm telling everyone."

This time Maya lightly smacked her and Hanna flicked the top of her blonde head.

"Chill, we don't even have a plan okay?" Maya said, but she beamed at her girls.

"So let's make one. Once we have more information, we'll

talk about it," Lily said, and Maya swooned at this open version of Lily.

"Yeah we will, we'll work it out together," Maya said, and she knew they would.

# 30

## HANNA

**LILITH**

Ugh, hate that I am so far away from you two.

**HANNA BANANA**

I know, I thought there was a chance our gates would be close.

**PAPAYA MAYA**

I know, rude.

**LILITH**

…you know what would make me feel better?

**PAPAYA MAYA**

Lilith we are at the gate we are NOT sending nudes.

**LILITH**

Relax Papaya I was not going to ask for nudes

**HANNA BANANA**

👀

**LILITH**

FINE I was going to ask for nudes…it's like my thing 🙄

I bet both of you are smiling

PAPAYA MAYA

I hate you

HANNA BANANA

^What she said

LILITH

SCORE 🎉

HANNA BANANA

You're so annoying lmao

LILITH

I'm not...

PAPAYA MAYA

Ugh this is going to be a long semester without you

LILITH

We will get creative *winky face*

Like we have in the past...

HANNA BANANA

Can't wait!

PAPAYA MAYA

LILITH

Were you able to get seats next to each other?

HANNA BANANA

Sadly, no 😟

Even with Maya's scary posh vibes

PAPAYA MAYA

You love it

HANNA BANANA

LILITH

Good

PAPAYA MAYA

PETTY!

LILITH

Okay I am boarding, ttyl xox

PAPAYA MAYA

Nice, we are in about ten minutes, smooth travels babe 😚

HANNA BANANA

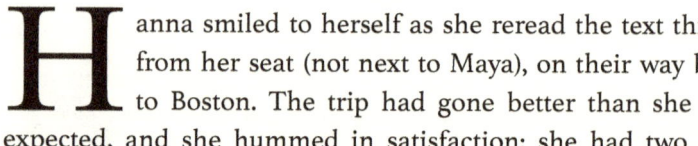

~

**H**anna smiled to herself as she reread the text thread from her seat (not next to Maya), on their way back to Boston. The trip had gone better than she had expected, and she hummed in satisfaction: she had two girl-friends. If she wasn't in public and in close proximity to a stranger, she might actually squeal.

Perhaps the most freeing aspect to Hanna was that she had acted like an ass, or like a *brat,* as Lily and Maya described her, and that had been *ok.* There was a new level of delicious plea-sure in confirmation that she was *allowed* to be everything, pleasant and unpleasant, with her girls. She knew that a small tantrum when they went out wasn't a *huge* deal to some, but it was to Hanna. She *never* behaved that way. She had fully given into her emotions, ready for her two girls to say she was *too much,* to have it all blow up in her face and break whatever they had been building. But it hadn't.

They were *hers*, and they liked it.

She had no idea what that meant, and she had no idea how she was going to tell her parents, but she also had the rest of the school year to figure things out, and she wouldn't be alone in doing so. Maya and Lily would be there for her.

Hanna was also certain that her parents were going to be way more upset at her deferring medical school and being in a nontraditional relationship than the fact that she was bisexual. Her mother wouldn't understand how to explain either to her church group. Hanna cringed inwardly for her mother's sake; she didn't want to hurt or disappoint her. No matter the odd pressure Hanna felt, she knew her parents loved her and had given her everything. That was part of the problem: they'd given her everything and she couldn't shake the feeling of *owing* them, of wanting to be *perfect* for them.

So they could never regret her.

The fact that Maya and Lily had seen her act out and still felt that she *fit* with them was everything. It was perhaps, Hanna thought, the little push she needed to understand that to love is to love the whole, not just the part. Emboldened, Hanna turned on some music and popped in her headphones.

As the plane lurched forward, she closed her eyes, smiling, knowing that through all the clouds, the sky above her was blue.

# PART IV

AN ENDLESS SUMMER

# 31

## MAYA

Maya opened her eyes in a still-unfamiliar bedroom but felt happy her mother had finally found a house. She had barely spent any time in the room and wondered briefly when it would start to feel like hers, if ever. And now she was back to packing. She turned in her warm bed, unruly curls streaming down her back and over the pillow, to look at the boxes she'd barely unpacked in the first place.

Back in Maplewood and heading to Providence, RI. Maya shook her head at her inability to get out of New England. It had been Rhode Island or New Jersey, but Hanna had gotten a job in Providence, and Lily apparently could go anywhere—*perks of being a rich kid*—so thems the breaks.

"Only you would begrudgingly give up a spot at *Princeton* for one at *Brown*," Lily had said when they'd video called to discuss how to finally all be in the same zip code. Princeton did have the better program, Columbia was out of the question for her due to recent events, and besides, Brown had a kickass MFA program if she got deep into her studies and decided to forgo her funded degree and roll the dice on being a writer.

"It just would be nice to live somewhere and not be one of

the few Black women," Maya said. Sure, she was biracial, but she had grown up being seen, and seeing herself, as a Black woman. Plenty of African-Americans were in fact, mixed—whether consensually or otherwise—with something, if their families were old enough. That was part of being Black in America, as far as Maya and her dad had been concerned. Hell, according to his DNA, her father was something like 20% Norwegian. "I mean Providence, Rhode Island in general is pretty..."

"Brown is diverse—" Lily said.

"White," Hanna interrupted. "It's white. You may not notice it everywhere Lily, but your girlfriends definitely stand out. Let's not forget senior year of high school when people avoided me because of Covid—even though I'm adopted? And from the US?"

"And that's ignorant, and plain racist as hell?" Maya interjected.

"It was so fucking awful," Lily agreed solemnly.

Hanna continued, "Providence could be interesting. Still it's so much easier to navigate new queer spaces when you're a dude, a white dude. Also, not only do you have two girlfriends, you have two non-white girlfriends." Though Maya knew that while being heckled by straight men was annoying, there was a certain amount of privilege all three of their fairly femme presentations lent them.

"Well I never like anything the easy way, and I always like to go big or go home," Lily joked.

Hanna had smiled. Maya had smiled too, but she couldn't help but know all too well what Hanna was voicing.

After a beat of silence Lily said, "Seriously though, is this something that is–are you both super worried? We can always wait and get to somewhere like New York, or..."

"No way, it'll be everywhere Lily, you can't *do* anything, but you can be there for us, which you are. We have each other, and

I get to come home to you both. That's what I want," Maya reassured her.

"Same," Hanna agreed.

Maya could see Lily's face fall slightly, that feeling of helplessness Maya had seen on her mother's face from time to time. "Besides, I seriously may pursue writing at some point. You know, an impossibly lucrative profession," Maya said to lighten the mood.

"I'll be your sugar momma," Lily had joked.

They still would have a lot to figure out, but the last two months had been great. Maya knew they were aligned in giving this whole 'thing' a chance. Every day they seemed to grow more and more accustomed to being with one another. According to all the blogs and a very informative Reddit thread, they were still headed for dicey poly territory, but they had gotten way better at communicating. Lily and Hanna especially—Hanna was sometimes still a brat, but that was okay. Lily and Maya liked her that way.

They still hadn't told their parents. It was something Hanna was incredibly nervous about–she hadn't even told her parents about her bisexuality, let alone the fact that she had two girlfriends with whom she was moving to Providence, RI. Maya and Lily had promised her that they wouldn't say anything, though it was getting a bit difficult with the amount of time they currently spent over at Lily's. Maya supposed maybe all the parents involved thought they'd just developed a really strong friendship.

Besides, Maya noticed her mother was distracted lately. Pleasantly distracted, but distracted nonetheless. Perhaps her mother had a secret lover of her own and she was working out how to tell Maya. Maya hoped so. She was afraid her mother would be devastated over her father for a long time, which is why she still hadn't mentioned that the last time she'd spoken with her father on the phone she overheard the voice of someone in the background. It had sounded...intimate, and had left both her and her father very flustered and in a hurry to get off the phone.

Maya wasn't sure what Providence would bring, but they had talked it over and each made sure that the move would still be beneficial to their individual goals. Maya couldn't wait to sleep next to her two lovers every night and wake up to them every morning.

MAYA PADDED down the hallway outside her room and made her way downstairs to the kitchen. The house her mother had purchased was cute, a classic small New England colonial, two bedrooms and two bathrooms. It was periwinkle with blue shutters, a bit of overkill in the sense that it had an *actual* white picket fence. Maya was convinced that had been the true selling point of the home for Maggie, who truly had "white picket fence" dreams. It was part of the reason Maya thought she was having such a hard time with the divorce. Maya wasn't convinced that it was the fact that she and her *father* hadn't worked out, but that her *marriage* hadn't worked out in general.

"Oh? And are you going to make it worth my while if I do?" Her mother's voice floated down the hall from the kitchen. The idea to slow her movements came too late; Maya entered, still heavy-footed from sleep.

Her mother's face flushed. "Um, let me text you," her mother said quickly and then ended her call, placing the phone face down on the small kitchen island.

*Busted.*

"Don't end your conversation on my account," Maya said, smirking at her mother.

"Oh, I just–I didn't realize you were home! I thought you were at Lily's again."

"Oh? Should I consider myself lucky that I just stumbled upon a flirty conversation and not something else?"

"It was not flirty! I was just talking to a friend." Her mother's deeper flush betrayed her. "Anyway, um, breakfast? Should we go out or should..."

Maya decided to go easy on her mother. "Mom, you do know you're allowed to date, you're allowed to be happy again," Maya said carefully. All joking aside, it had been a relief not to find her mother in a borderline catatonic state when she came home this time around.

"I know sweetie, it's just um, new."

Maya could tell her mother was not going to elaborate further. Which, considering she had yet to tell her anything about Lily and Hanna, was fair. All her mother knew was that she was going to Brown and had found roommates.

Her mother brushed an invisible crumb from the kitchen island. "Through this whole thing, I haven't really said aloud how hard this has been for you. I just want you to know I see you, and I love you, and I am the luckiest woman in the world. I could never regret anything, because it led me to you. You know that, right?" The words came out in a bit of a rush, and her mother's eyes grew glossy, making them look extra blue.

Her sincerity made Maya's throat constrict. The thing is she *did* know, but she needed to hear it. "I know Mom, I know."

Maggie smiled and then let out a small laugh. "Good," she said, wiping at her eyes, "good, because I love the shit out of you."

Maya laughed and embraced her mother. They sat there for a second before their limit on sappiness was reached.

"Let's go out for breakfast," Maya said decidedly, and her mother smiled.

# 32

## LILY

"So you think your mom has a secret lover?" Lily asked, grabbing three ciders from the cooler. She loved it when Hanna and Maya came over and they all piled into the treehouse. She looked over at her lovers, already nestled in the bed. The sun hung low in the sky, bathing the room in a fiery orange hue. They'd attempted to build a fort like they had back at the retreat, but it failed spectacularly, so now Hanna and Maya were just wrapped in a ton of blankets. Lily walked over and cuddled in between them, handing each a cider.

"I don't know, but for the last week or so since I caught her in the kitchen, she has definitely been hiding something. It's like she's happier, so I don't get why she is hiding her happiness? Maybe she thinks I won't like her moving on from my dad," Maya said, taking a sip, "which is crazy because I told you both I definitely heard someone at my dad's new place the last time we spoke."

"Maybe she's part of some secret drug ring or something far worse than love," Lily joked, turning her head towards Maya and relishing the brush of her curls on her face.

"Honestly that might be more likely than the lover, and well, she didn't make out well from the divorce. She was a stay-at-home mom, so not a lot saved up."

"Prenups man," Hanna said. "I believe in them strongly." They all clinked their bottles of cider and then drank.

Lily took a moment to really soak up the evening. They'd been spending many of them together, and if they were a precursor to what she had waiting for her in Providence, she was excited.

"It's your money, use it how you want, I trust you," her mother had said when she told her she was moving to Providence with friends. "So you're moving with..."

Lily knew Diana hadn't heard her talk about other friends, certainly not ones that she felt close enough with to move in with. After Lily offered up no additional information, her mother just shook her blonde head and said, "Well, it will be good for you to get some time to yourself before this is all yours–" She paused again. "If you want it that is. I can always speak to Julia—"

"No, I do," Lily had said, and it was true. She had always accepted that she'd take over the family orchard. She had previously seen it as a way to keep working on her art without worry. It was a privilege, she knew, but now she saw it as a vital way to help her support Hanna and Maya. She knew Hanna and Maya didn't *need* her to, but still, she had the means and she loved them.

The thought had brought her up short then, but sitting in the blankets snuggled between them now, she knew it was true. She just had to figure out how to tell them, how to say it out loud without the fear that this was just some kind of thrill for them.

"How are things with your parents, Banana?" Lily turned to Hanna, who shrugged at her question.

"I mean, they're great, same as they've always been. Though I'm not sure how crazy my mom is about me coming over here."

"Is she afraid I'm corrupting you?" Lily teased.

"Hmmm maybe. But, I don't know, sometimes I just want to scream when I'm home."

But Lily thought she knew. Hanna was so stuck on not being a disappointment to them that she continued to be the daughter she thought they wanted, rather than just doing what *she* wanted. Having spent time around Hanna's folks, Lily felt like it might be something Hanna felt more than her parents.

"Either way," said Hanna, "I am totally coming out to them before the summer is over. Thanks for being so patient, you two, I know keeping this from your moms isn't easy, especially with them having known each other and all."

"No biggie Banana," Lily said and raised up on her elbows to kiss Hanna on her forehead.

"I think we both know how weird it can be," Maya added, and she turned her body so she was completely spooning Lily, who was curved towards Hanna. Hanna was flat on her back, looking up at them with dark brown eyes full of uncertainty.

"How did your parents take it?" Hanna asked.

"I don't really know," Maya began. "I just kind of told them who I was into from time to time and sometimes that person was a chick. Not to mention I've lusted after Janelle Monae for years."

"Ooof seriously," Lily said, "why are non-binary folks always so hot?"

"Because they've ascended beyond whatever boxes we keep putting ourselves in," Maya said.

"True dat," said Lily.

"And they never said anything?" Hanna asked, bringing the seriousness back into the conversation.

"Well, I don't think my dad ever would care about something like that, and my mom– well, she never said anything, but I don't know that I really gave either of them space to," Maya said thoughtfully.

"Lily?"

"Yeah, well my dad never gave a fuck obviously, but Diana definitely doesn't care. And Aunt Julia is a proud lesbian. Took me out for cake and ice cream when I came out during a family dinner."

Maya laughed, "Nice."

"It was," mused Lily.

"Diana seems cool with everything," Hanna said, and Lily detected a small amount of longing in her tone.

"Yeah, she's cool but also borderline disinterested. Like she's always given me space to do my own thing, but sometimes I wish–well, I wish she hadn't given me so much space, you know?"

"Please, trust me, you wanted the space," Hanna began. "My parents kinda hovered for a long time."

"They love you, and this is a pretty white town. Your family was different, and they wanted to protect you," Lily said and added, "I was loudly different too, but my mom never stood in to shield me from anything."

After a beat of silence, Hanna said, "I'm sorry, I don't mean to sound ungrateful."

"No need to be sorry," Lily said.

"It sounds like they just want you to be okay," Maya said.

"Yeah, but my entire life I wanted to give them that so badly that I feel like I have been walking on eggshells. I think we all are. It's like a McAvoy requirement." She laughed sarcastically.

"Look Banana, you don't have to come out if you don't want to. We can just talk to our parents separately."

"Mmm," Hanna replied. "I need to. I don't want to be this paranoid mess. I really wish we could have gone to each others' graduations and what not...I'm sorry for making us not an *us* outside of us."

There was another beat of silence before Maya started laughing and Lily followed her.

"What?" Maya said, throwing her head back and laughing harder.

"You may have gotten lost in the sauce with that last bit, babe," Lily said, but rubbed her cheek on Hanna's forehead to reassure her that she knew what she'd meant. Hanna had been very guarded about either of them coming to her graduation, or each others', for fear that someone's parent would put things together and tell the others.

Hanna leaned into Lily's touch. "Yeah," she said, "I just meant that I want this next chapter in life to not be so restrained, or something like that."

"Or something like that." Maya put her arms around Lily and Hanna, taking a second to drop a quick kiss on the top of Hanna's head.

"Don't worry Banana, whatever you decide, we got you." Lily didn't worry about making false promises, not as she let herself sink into the warmth of her girls.

## 33

## HANNA

"I spoke to Reverend Michaels this morning at the farmer's market, and he said he knows a minister of a good congregation in Providence you should check out. The church is young and hip," Hanna's mother said and poured milk into her coffee.

They were sitting at the breakfast table. Her father was diligently eating his cornflakes in silence, as he always did. His brown hair had greyed in places and thinned considerably. Even though it had only been a month since graduation, she couldn't help but continue to notice the way her parents seemed to have aged since she last saw them over the winter holidays. That was the thing no one told you: while you are growing up and getting older, everyone around you is, too. She had been shocked to see the silver strands in her mother's brown hair. Her fringe bangs were peppered with grey and white, and there was a layer of what Hanna could only describe as "age" on her pale skin.

"Thanks Mom, we shall see if church is for me when I get there."

"Well, there's a band and everything, and they make their own music too, very rock and roll," her mother pushed, as

Hanna knew she would. "It might be good for you to meet some new people your age, especially since you won't really know anyone—" she paused, then added, "besides your roommates. Have you figured out who they are going to be yet?"

Hanna hadn't told her parents anything, only that she'd gotten a job in Providence and would be taking a gap year before deciding if she wanted to fully go into medical school or do research. She had the grades for Brown's medical school too, should she decide that's where she wanted to apply. In the meantime, she would be working at Planned Parenthood's Southern New England office as a research and policy clinician. This had also been a bit of a test, revealing where she was working to her parents. Her dad hadn't really said much, which was expected, and she could tell that while her mother perhaps didn't *love* the idea, she had latched onto the thought of Hanna continuing on to medical school.

"I have some ideas, talking with some people to see if we click..." Hanna hated lying, but she told herself it wouldn't be for that much longer. The summer would end, and her mom *would* find out.

"Okay well, let us know, we want you to be safe. We know you're an adult now, but you're still our baby," her mom cooed a bit on the last word.

"Of course, I have explicitly explained that I am NOT okay with living with a serial killer or killers," Hanna said, and her mom scoffed and waved Hanna away playfully with one hand.

In another universe, Hanna was blurting out, "Just kidding! I am moving in with my *two* girlfriends, because surprise, I'm bi and apparently like my lovers in twos." But of course she didn't say that. Instead she went up to her room determined to pack but instead climbed on her bed and escaped into a swoony sapphic romance — *these have really turned into my thing.*

"UH FUCK, yes, right there, Jesus, don't stop—" Some of Hanna's hair was plastered over her forehead and she could feel the rest of it sticking to her neck and back.

"Mmmm I don't know about Jesus, you better know who you're in bed with, church girl," Lily whispered, her fingers expertly moving in Hanna, her thumb rubbing just enough of her clit.

"Lily!"

"Mmmm better babe, don't worry, I know where you need me, right here." She pressed down further into Hanna, stretching her in a way that made her ankles flex.

"Fuck I'm going to come," Hanna said, her orgasm building.

"No you won't, not like this Banana," Maya said from where she was, naked, behind her. She had a leg on either side of Hanna and when Hanna looked back she could see that Maya was slowly stroking herself, looking down at her with heavy-lidded eyes.

"No I won't, not yet," Hanna repeated and fuck yes she loved it when Maya told her what to do.

"Not until you've tasted me," Maya said, and Hanna let out a moan because Lily hadn't stopped fucking her, and that coupled with watching Maya touch herself was going to send her over the edge.

"Hurry, I need it, need you now," Hanna said, as Maya got up on her knees and lowered herself onto Hanna's face. She loved having Maya like this, completely surrounded by the smell of her, the taste of her, the heat of her. And Hanna showed it in the way she tongued her, her tongue sliding over Maya's slickness to greet her clit.

"Like that, good girl," she heard Maya moan.

Ever since they'd discovered Hanna had a praise kink, they

had to use it sparingly because that's all it took to light her up. Hanna came, moaning into Maya. She felt Maya twitch on top of her, and then slide off and roll over on the bed.

Hanna loved it when this happened; she was still tingly all over and cooling down but turned her head in time to watch a naked Lily climb on top of Maya and fit her body to hers.

"God I love fucking you two, my girls so good for me," Lily said as she began riding Maya to her own orgasm, which didn't take long. The sight was unbelievably hot, her two women naked together. It was like live porn or her own personal sex dungeon.

"I swear I have never had success with scissoring like I have with you," Maya said, panting as Lily rolled off of her and they lay on the bed breathing heavily, Lily and Maya side by side and Hanna at their feet.

Nights in the treehouse were everything this summer. They were *the* reason Hanna had been so excited to come home for the summer instead of working back in Boston. She supposed she, Maya, and Lily could have all found work in the city or stayed in Maya's apartment, but being with Maya and Lily, occasionally working on the orchard — she knew Diana would put that in heavy quotes— and sleeping where it all began felt right. Plus it was a great way to see if moving in together was happening too fast. Lily always joked that she never thought she'd fit the U-Haul stereotype, and here she was doing it times two.

"Holy shit," Lily breathed, "it just never gets old."

"If anything, it keeps getting better and better," Maya said.

Hanna moved up the bed and squeezed herself between the two women. Their bodies were slick with sweat and without AC, the summer humidity clung to them. Hanna didn't care, she leaned into them. She felt like every time she was sinking deeper and deeper in a dream, one where she felt so damn free.

"I love you both," she said quietly, and as if they'd rehearsed, Lily and Maya both sat up on their arms and turned to face her. "I love you Lilith, and I love you Maya," Hanna said again, louder this time with what she hoped was a certainty that left no room for doubt. Because she had never been so certain of anything in her life.

# 34

## MAYA

Maya was in love. She was deeply *in love*. In love with both Hanna and Lily. She wasn't sure it was something she had fully admitted to herself, considering she had seen how fleeting the feeling could be as she watched her parents' marriage implode, but last week when Hanna had said it, it was like the last knot inside of her slackened. Hanna loved her and Lily, and yes, Maya loved them too.

"*Me?*" Lily was the first to utter a word after Hanna's declaration, and she sounded so shocked and vulnerable that whatever wall Maya was scrambling to build crumbled.

"Both of you," Hanna had said.

"I know, it's just that—"

Before Lily could finish Maya said, "I love you too. Both of you. Hanna and Lil–Lilith." Maya kept the tradition of using Lily's full name when being especially playful or serious. "I love you, and it scares me because I just saw a love die that I never thought would, but also I know my mom has no regrets, and I don't want them either. I love you both and I am so fucking excited for Providence."

Lily had swallowed but Maya noticed her eyes were glassy. "I love you both too," she'd said, "Maya and our Banana, Hanna, I love you both so fucking much," and she'd leaned down, and pulled Maya down with her so that their three foreheads touched. And then they kissed, in that three-way playful move they took a little more seriously these days. It was what they did to symbolize having worked out something *together*.

"I HOPE it's me or Lily or both putting that goofy grin on your face, lady." Hanna's voice brought her back down to earth, or more specifically, back to her room where she and Hanna currently were sitting and trying to think of what to do for their girlfriend's upcoming birthday. They hadn't talked about these scenarios in detail, but they hoped because they were meeting to plan *for* Lily, this wasn't a moment when they were leaving her out.

Hanna was sitting on Maya's bed, and Maya was sitting cross-legged on the floor, laptop in her lap open to a page of their brainstormed ideas. Hanna had worried, but Maya reminded her that one, having a friend over isn't weird, especially since they'd been working at the orchard together, and two, her mother wouldn't be home anyway. She was off doing whatever mysterious thing was keeping her occupied and happy these days.

"Of course," Maya smiled back at her. She went to kiss her but knew it would make Hanna even more nervous, so she winked instead. Maya thought love *did* make her a little *goofy*, but she was into it. "What were you saying?"

"I was just saying, I don't think Lily has ever had a proper birthday party before."

"No? Not even when you were in high school?"

"I honestly thought I just wasn't cool enough to get invited maybe, but when I asked Diana for some ideas last week, she just said she liked to let Lily do her own thing."

Maya's stomach sank at that, thinking back to how amazed Lily had been at the fort and their sleepovers. It all continued to make sense, the more she got to know Lily at home. "Okay, but she has friends, right? That Eve girl she talks about sometimes?"

"Yeah, I think Eve is her *only* real friend though? She was the only person I saw in her grad photos." Hanna paused and sighed. "I really shouldn't have stopped us from going, it would have been so cool for us to have shown up for her. It was selfish, I'm selfish."

"What's done is done, Banana. Besides, I don't think Lily needed us there; like you said, she had Eve. In any case, she has us *here* and that's what matters. One day versus the many we'll have together, remember that." Maya smiled at Hanna. "So what should we do? Should we hire a clown? A stripper? The latter feels more like Lily's speed."

Hanna laughed. "Oh my god, can you imagine?" She grabbed a pillow from the head of Maya's bed. "You can, can't you? You're thinking about it right now, aren't you?" Hanna threw the pillow at Maya.

"Is that so wrong? We're young! We can look, fantasize," Maya said, grinning. "Besides, it's only hot to me because you both would be there."

Hanna crossed her arms in feigned indignation. "I can't believe I am dating you two!"

"What would Lily do?"

"Oh you know she'd agree with you, you both would be sitting there thinking about it!" Hanna was laughing now, and it made Maya's chest warm.

"You love it, Banana," Maya said, and Hanna's face flushed, because she knew she did. Their little brat.

"I do not."

"You do, you're thinking about it right now, some hot brunette's running her hands through Lily's hair, touching what's yours. You're thinking about how you'll throw a fit and get what you want by the end of the night, aren't you?" Maya hadn't meant to go that far, but she was there now.

Hanna's eyes went dark and soft. "Don't do this to me in your mother's house."

"What would you like me to do in my mother's house?"

"Maya!"

Maya laughed but let the matter go. She wouldn't torture Hanna any further.

"Can we focus?" Hanna said in the tone of voice Maya associated with deflection.

"Yeah okay–we could do something fun and kinda retro? Is there a roller rink around here?"

"Oh, I really like that, and then we could do pizza and beer after?"

Maya nodded. It was very tenth-birthday-meets-adulthood. It satiated Maya's need to give Lily everything she missed. Just when she was about to start looking up the roller rink, Hanna's phone lit up with a call. Hanna grabbed it.

"You're on speaker," Hanna warned.

"Let me in!" Lily's voice answered back.

"Where are you?" Hanna said, looking slightly panicked, as if Lily could see into Maya's room where they were conspiring. Maya found it endearing.

"Uh, where our super hot Papaya lives–hurry, it's hot out here!"

"Wait why—"

"Hanna let me in, or I am going to feel left out here!"

Maya knew Lily wasn't serious, but an impatient Lily was not to be questioned. Hanna sat up, giving Maya a pointed look, and left the room to retrieve Lily.

TWO MINUTES LATER, both Lily and Hanna were laying on Maya's bed. When Hanna had tried to move away, Lily had latched onto her, exclaiming, "Maggie isn't even home!"

"So this is a pleasant surprise, how'd you know we were at my place?"

"Spies," Lily deadpanned.

"Seriously," Hanna tried to wriggle from her arms but gave up.

"Why do you two need some time alone without me? Hmmm?" Lily pretended to look upset. Since their conversations after spring break, they all had agreed that it was fine for there to be time spent with just two of them at a time; it was unrealistic to think they could do every little thing together, and sometimes they might not want to. While they were lovers, they were all also friends.

"You're ridiculous," Maya laughed, looking up at the two women on her bed. God she was in love with them.

"A little birdie may or may not have told me you guys are trying to plan something for my birthday." When Hanna went to speak Lily continued, "Don't deny it, we don't lie to each other."

"Okay, so what if we are?" Maya asked.

"Don't, please, I have everything I want with you two here."

"Okay but, Lilith come on, we missed your graduation and —" Hanna started again.

"And I had a blast partying with Eve. Who, by the way, insists we video call one of these days, considering she's in Zurich for the summer."

"Uh okay, sure, but—" Maya started.

"But nothing, seriously, every day with you two feels like a gift." There was a very pregnant silence as even Lily seemed taken aback by what she'd said. "And anyway, my mom wants to have a barbecue at the house."

"Oh?" Hanna said. "She didn't mention it when I–I mean–"

Lily laughed. "We just decided last night. I told her I didn't want anything big when she asked on both of your behalfs, not too subtly by the way, and apparently she has something she wants to talk to me and Maya about."

"What?" Maya asked.

"No idea," Lily shrugged, "but figured let's just invite your parents, Banana, and get it over with? I mean if you feel comfortable with that? It might help to do so in a place where there is an escape à la the treehouse and available booze."

After a long moment Hanna said, "It's actually kinda perfect. All of our parents will be there, and we won't be in public. I love it, actually."

"You sure?" Maya asked.

"Yeah. I mean, it has to happen and it's your birthday Lily, I can give you this," Hanna said and smiled.

"You can't do this for me, Banana. I told you I already have everything I need."

"I know. I mean that I can give us this, give *me* this."

Lily kissed her, and Maya leaned in to plant a quick kiss on each of them.

# 35

## LILY

Lily walked into the kitchen to find her mother leaning over her laptop. Her shoulder-length light blonde hair was askew, like she had been running her fingers through it — which meant she was stressed.

"What is it?" Lily asked, as her mother looked up at her.

"We've got a fire blight problem," she said, almost hissing. Lily knew it pained her to see the trees suffer. That upset her more than how it might impact the business.

"I thought you got it under control?" Lily said, leaning over the counter. Her mother had seemed a bit distracted lately, more so than usual.

"I thought so too. I think I'm going to need to get some outside help this time." Diana Blake sighed. "Anyway, nothing is going to change today. You ready for your dinner in a few hours?"

"Yeah I think so. What is it that you wanted to talk to me about? And why would Maya need to be there?"

"I didn't say Maya had to be there, it just might be nice. I know you two have gotten close."

Lily's anxiety sparked. Why would her mother need her to have someone she was close with when they talked? Was it sad news?

"Mom?" Lily asked.

"It isn't anything to worry about!" her mother said, rubbing her shoulder against Lily's. She was the same height as Lily, and they were built relatively the same. Lily liked that she looked like her mother, though her mom had thinner lips and always joked that she didn't know where Lily had inherited her boobs from. "I just thought it would also be nice because it's your birthday."

Lily was unconvinced, but her mother was unmovable. Diana didn't say or do anything she didn't want to. "Fine, but you're being weird," Lily said, adding, "Oh– I invited Hanna and her parents too."

She felt her mother slightly stiffen. "You did?"

"Is that alright? It's not like there won't be enough food. I saw what you bought, we have enough for a football team."

"Oh, well, yes, I just wished you'd have told me." Her mother, who was rarely unnerved, looked a bit pale.

"Yeah sorry? I hang out with Hanna as much as I do Maya, and since you and Maggie are going to be there, I told her she could bring her parents." Lily's anxiety started to snowball, but she kept her voice calm, not wanting to betray that the girls were coming out tonight over dinner. What was going on with her mom? She made a mental note to bring something stronger up to the treehouse later, just in case.

"Makes sense," her mother said, sounding flustered and strange. "I uh—I'll just go check on some things." She quickly moved from the room, leaving Lily in a flurry of uncertainty and unease.

～

LATE AFTERNOON CAME MORE QUICKLY than Lily had prepared for. Ever since the run in with her mother earlier that day, she'd been tangled in her thoughts, trying to figure out what was possibly going on. She'd been distracted and sent a silent thank you to Maya for putting in the extra effort to reassure Hanna in their group chat.

Lily was dressed casually, in a cotton tank top and jean shorts, but because she thought this moment festive, Lily threw on a purple lipstick she wore like twice a year, which also was about how often she wore lipstick.

Once outside in the back of the house, she made her way down to where her mother was grilling.

"There she is! Ah and purple, nice, looks so great with your hair," Diana said, smiling. All of the discomfort from earlier had apparently evaporated.

"This looks amazing Mom, thank you," Lily smiled.

"Sure thing! You know, you never had any parties here, this is fun. I wish I could have done this more for you when you were little."

"Mom, you never asked if I wanted to do anything," Lily countered, though she wasn't truly surprised by her mom.

"Well honey, my approach was to let you lead," her mother said genuinely.

"I was a kid," Lily started, but then thought better of it. "Doesn't matter, thank you for this today." She leaned over and kissed her mother on the cheek, then felt her phone buzz.

PAPAYA MAYA

Let's get this thing started. I am here.

HANNA BANANA

We here!

LILITH

Guys I want a fruit nickname

PAPAYA MAYA

You get what you're given

HANNA BANANA

Lilith is BADASS. Now come get us!

LILY SLID her phone in her pocket. "Looks like everyone's here," she said over her shoulder as she made her way back into the house.

"I dig the purple," Maya said as she, Lily, and Hanna moved towards the backyard, their parents in tow.

"Thanks, I wanted to be festive. You two look amazing," Lily said, and it was true. Maya looked gorgeous and chic as always in a pair of flow pants and a cropped v-neck, revealing her golden brown skin in patches Lily wanted to lick. Her curls and coils were loose and she'd done her makeup. Hanna was stunning with her long black hair in a high ponytail and simple makeup, save for a shimmery layer of gold eyeshadow that worked well with the rosiness the summer had put into her pale skin. She wore a purple maxi dress that Lily noticed accentuated her bust in the best way.

"When was the last time you were here?" Lily heard Mary McAvoy ask Maggie.

"Oh, uh, well I—we've—been back in town for some time and Maya has been helping here over the summer," Maggie responded, and Lily exchanged a knowing look with Maya.

"Interesting, because the last time I remember you being here—" Mary started.

"I always liked it here," Evan McAvoy chimed in. Lily's ears perked up because she rarely heard him speak.

They made it to the grilling area. Diana had been sure to clean the outdoor furniture and set up couches and chairs, so they wouldn't have to sit at the table the whole time while she was grilling.

"Dinner will be ready in about fifteen minutes! Feel free to grab some drinks and get comfortable, of course there's plenty of cider," Diana said from the grill.

"You ready to do this?" Lily said, once they were alone and the parents of the group, save for Diana, had walked over to the cooler for drinks. Lily could hear them making small talk.

"I mean, no? But I think we have to do it. It's the end of July. We leave in two weeks, so even if there's a fallout, it won't be for long."

"We can all run away together to the treehouse," Lily said. She watched Maggie take an extra bottle of cider from the cooler and head towards Diana.

"Like I said earlier, we got you," Maya said reassuringly. Lily wanted to pull Hanna into her arms but didn't dare do so. It was clear she was nervous.

"Maybe a drink to take the edge off?" Hanna breathed out.

"Don't have to ask me twice," Maya said.

Lily agreed and was going to say something when she was distracted once again by Maggie and her mother. This time they seemed to be having a very fiery, whispered conversation.

*What the fuck?*

When her mother caught her staring, she turned to Maggie and said loudly, "Dinner is ready if y'all will take your seats." She said it sweetly, but Lily knew her mother and heard the dismissal in her voice.

"Let's do this," Maya said, and Lily tabled the questions that were starting to bloom in her mind. She would get to those after.

## 36

## HANNA

Hanna let out a shaky breath. Dinner had started and there was the expected small talk, Diana and her mother, Mary, doing most of the talking, though it did sound *forced*, and for whatever reason Maggie seemed subdued—*all joking aside, maybe Maya and Lily were on to something?*— and it was no surprise that her father wasn't doing much talking. Hanna really thought he'd married her mother partially so he wouldn't have to. Hanna thought Lily and Maya were quiet in solidarity.

Around the table, she and her parents were on one side, with Maggie, Maya, and Lily on the other and Diana at the head. Lily sat closest to her mother. There was no way to even reach out and touch one of her girls under the table for fear of accidentally reaching her foot out and touching Maggie. *How mortifying that'd be.* Then again, Hanna wasn't sure she'd notice, as Maggie was staring down at her plate of untouched food. Hanna decided she wasn't missing much. Diana was a vegetarian *and* a bad cook — a lethal combination in the kitchen. Hanna shoved a piece of what looked like charred eggplant into her mouth and began to chew. Her mouth felt dry from nerves, and that only made the food move around like sand paper. When she went to swallow she choked, and to quell her coughing fit she took a sip of her Blake Cider. The sip helped, but before she put the bottle down she thought, *fuck it,* and downed the rest of the relatively full bottle in a gulp.

The motion momentarily slowed her mother down from whatever she was going on with Diana about. "Hanna?" came her mother's voice, and she could hear that she was taken aback a bit.

"Mom, Dad, I'm bi," Hanna blurted out. From the corner of her eye, she saw Maggie's face jerk up and felt her gaze. The table went silent.

"I'm sorry?" her mother finally said.

Diana said, "Good for you, kid."

"I'm bisexual. I like—men and women, and more?" Hanna didn't know why she was asking a question.

The table was once again quiet.

Hanna looked up at her girlfriends without a clue what to do. She knew her face was crimson and air didn't seem to quite make it to her lungs, even though she was taking deep and rapid breaths.

"Um, I'm pan, pansexual," Maya announced to the table.

"All of the above, right on! I myself have been dabbling in my fluidity again recently," Diana said to the whole table.

Lily turned to look at her mother, and then shook her head and looked back at Hanna.

Hanna couldn't look away from Maya and Lily.

"I'm *very* gay," Lily announced proudly, picking up her bottle and holding it up in a cheers. Diana clinked her glass and then so did Maya, who turned to meet Hanna's eyes and burst into laughter.

Lily began to laugh, and so did Diana.

It was contagious, and Hanna found herself laughing too,

not even from relief at finally saying it out loud but from the sheer ridiculousness of the situation, and the love and gratitude she felt towards her girlfriends who were being *there* for her in the best way.

"Well then, congratulations ladies, but I already knew about you, kiddo," Diana said, taking Lily's hand and giving it a squeeze. "Came out to me and my sister back in—what was it, seventh? Eighth grade? We took her out to celebrate," she continued, like it was the most normal thing in the world.

Suddenly, Hanna remembered she'd only gotten half of it out. "Um and Lily, I'm dating Lily, and Maya. I'm dating both Lily and Maya. We are together. The three of us."

Silence returned back to the table, until Diana said nonchalantly, "Triads are poly on hard mode, but y'all are young."

"Hanna?"

She turned to her mother this time and forced herself to meet her gaze. "Yeah Mom?"

"So, you're–so you're interested in girls? But Jeff—"

"Boys, girls, and well, I'm bisexual."

"Okay, and so, what, the three of you are–together?"

Hanna turned to look at Lily and Maya, who looked at her as they nodded.

Mary let out a little laugh. "Is this real?"

"Yes, Mom, I'm moving with them to Providence, they're who I am moving in with."

"I knew based on your chart you'd be a U-Hauler," Diana said to Lily.

"You can't, I mean, come on, is this why you are holding off on med school? To play out some fantasy?"

Her mother's words sent ice down her spine, and she could feel her eyes sting with the threat of tears. "It's not a fantasy, Mom," Hanna said quietly.

"Well then what is it? I thought you had a plan, and now

your plan is—" her mother couldn't seem to complete sentences. "Is that why you brought us here? To tell us all together?" She looked around the table.

Hanna fixed her eyes on her hands in her lap. Finally she heard her dad say, "Mary, I think it'd be best to—"

"I'm just trying to understand. My daughter got into Tufts, she volunteered at our church, she got great grades, graduated summa cum laude for crying out loud, was going to be pre-med, and all of the sudden, she starts hanging out here at the Do Whatever You Want and Live However You Want to Live Orchard and telling me she's bisexual — okay, but this?" From her peripheral vision, Hanna could see her mom was gesturing towards Lily and Maya, "Going to forgo med school to live in, what? A brothel—"

"Mary!" Her father's voice was a volume she'd never heard before. It was enough to make her look up again, eyes full of tears that began to spill over.

"Listen Mary McAvoy, I do not care what you say about me and how I run things, but you will not talk about my daughter and who she decides to love this way." Diana's voice was low and cool, something Hanna had not heard before either.

"Hanna." Hanna looked up at the sound of her name and found Lily's eyes. "Come here," Lily said, getting to her feet.

"Hanna," her mother warned.

Hanna pushed back from the table and walked over to Lily, who pulled her into her arms.

"We love your daughter," she heard Maya saying. "We are in love." Hanna heard Maya stand and then felt her warm hand on her back. That's when she broke. She turned her face into Lily and began to cry.

"Hanna," she heard her mother almost hiss.

Hanna was able to pull together her composure just enough to say, "It's true Mom, I love them, they're my future too. I'll still go to medical school if it still feels right, but loving them isn't throwing my life away, it's making it better."

"Are you not going to say anything?" Mary turned to Maggie, who hadn't said a thing.

"I love my daughter," she said weakly and shrugged, "but sure, this is super surprising."

Mary scoffed and then looked at Diana. "Well I don't expect *you* of all people to do anything, probably your whole lifestyle dragged these girls into this —"

"Be very careful what you say next." Diana's voice was even lower and left no room for games.

Mary swallowed. "Well, I —"

"I think we best get home, have a sleep, and talk about this when we have had a chance to process." Hanna's father grabbed his wife's arm as he stood from the table. "Hanna, we will see you when you're ready?" He let go of his wife and walked around the table.

Hanna felt Lily's arms grow tighter around her, but when her father got to her, she turned slightly away from Lily to face him. He gave her a small smile and then put his hands on either side of her face and kissed her forehead. "I'll talk to Mom. You're our baby girl," he whispered and then turned to join his waiting wife.

"You really have no issue with this?" Mary said, glaring at Diana.

"In this economy? A three-income household sounds like a good idea," she said, not looking at Mary and instead giving Hanna a wink.

Mary sputtered, "Of course you haven't changed since high school." She walked off, her father following silently, something sad in the way he moved.

Hanna felt Maya hug her from behind, and she allowed herself to be squeezed by her lovers.

After a moment Diana spoke again, "Listen here kiddo, Hanna, what you just did was very, *very* brave. It takes guts to do what you did. You are welcome to stay here for as long as you need, even if you need to stay till moving day, okay?"

Hanna nodded. She was beyond being able to talk, the tears fighting their way out of her.

Diana must have gotten up from the table because the next time she spoke she was closer but just as loud. "Look, there is never a right time. For whatever reason, big or small, some people go their whole lives not being true to themselves, and it eats away at them. You get to choose love, you get to choose freedom. It may feel like shit now, but I promise, that choice is a gift."

And with that, Hanna let go and wept.

## 37

## MAYA

Maya wanted to cry too. She wanted to hold on to Hanna and fix all the pain inside of her, having watched everything Hanna had feared come true. Well, almost. It was clear that it wasn't so much the bisexuality that unnerved her mother as much as the fact that she had two girlfriends.

They were still in the Blake's yard. Lily had taken Hanna to the treehouse, and Diana had disappeared somewhere inside the main house. Now it was just Maya, standing in the evening light watching her mother, who sat at the table as if she were afraid to move.

"Mom?" When there wasn't an answer, Maya started to worry. This whole time they had been so focused on supporting Hanna, and Maya never considered that this was the first time her mother was hearing about her relationship. Having so readily accepted her pansexuality, she'd never even considered her mother wouldn't accept her polyamory.

She cautiously pulled out the chair next to her mother and sat down, angling her body towards her mom, who almost imperceptibly turned towards her. "Mom?"

"Hey bug." Her mother hadn't used that nickname in years. Not even when she had told Maya about the divorce.

"Mom?" Maya tried again. "So, are we, is this ok?" She wasn't really asking permission, but she didn't really know what to ask because she was unsure as to what the issue was.

"I uh, didn't know, didn't realize," Maggie began.

"Didn't know what? That I also date women? I told you I am pan," Maya said. She hadn't been shy about her crushes on celebrities of many genders. Her mother had never said anything; her dad every now and then agreed or disagreed with her, but no one had ever told her that her sexual or romantic interests weren't okay.

"I guess, well, there were just boys in high school," her mom said.

"Well I am pan, so I am attracted to people." Maya spoke slowly at first, trying to reiterate some definition of pansexuality in case her mother had been unclear. "That includes all genders, though admittedly there are challenges with cis men," she joked to try and break through the tension.

"Is that it? You can't find a good guy to date?" her mother asked.

Disbelief slammed into Maya. "What?" she said dumbly.

"The reason...never mind," her mother cut herself off with a sigh.

"Mom, I am not into women because I can't find a good man. I am not even into Lily and Hanna because they're women. Like I said, I am into them because they are *them*."

"I see," her mother said plainly, and then she finally looked up into Maya's eyes. Maya saw desperation there and maybe something like shame. "Is this, did I do this to you?"

"Mom what are you talking about, what are you trying to say? You don't like that I'm not dating a guy? Or is it that I am dating *women*?"

"Well, this is certainly layered. There were only boys in high school so I just assumed– I mean, your generation has all these trendy names." Her voice fell again and she dropped the sentence.

Maya couldn't believe what she was hearing. Her mother, who had moved away from this small town and married a Black man, even though she knew what that would mean. "Pan isn't a *trend* or something fleeting—"

"I didn't mean—" her mom began, but Maya kept going.

"There are some things that have *always* existed, but we didn't have the vocabulary for them. Just because language has finally caught up and there are words to describe things doesn't mean they've been forced into existence suddenly. Rocks don't exist because man suddenly came up with a word for them." Maya felt impatience slip into her tone. She couldn't believe she was having to have this conversation now, with her mom, while Hanna was falling apart. She took a moment to be briefly thankful that they did have Lily, that they had the three of them, so someone would always be there for each of them.

"Hanna," her mom began slowly, "I'm sorry, that isn't what I meant. Look, I'm not upset; I'm just processing. Okay, so two women at once? Are you lonely? I know the divorce was a lot." Maggie swallowed, "I was a lot."

Her mother looked down then and Maya reached to gently grip one of her forearms. Her mom looked up with tears in her eyes.

"Mom, please listen to me carefully. I fell in love, okay?" Maya said clearly and calmly.

"When?" Maggie's voice came out as a whisper.

"After last fall, we all kept in touch and hung out over winter break and spring break and, well, it just sort of happened. Okay? This didn't come from something ugly, I am in love, it's really beautiful. I need you to understand that."

Her mom nodded and smiled weakly. "I just don't want life to be any harder for you than it has to be. People won't understand...I don't even know if I understand."

"Mom, I am a Black, queer woman in a country that loves to remind me it doesn't care. Shouldn't I be holding onto all of the love and positivity I can? Life is too short not to." Maya gripped her mother's forearm a little tighter. "I am in love, and I am loved, really loved, how is that something to be worried about?"

"I just want you to be ok," her mother breathed, turning fully towards Maya and squeezing Maya's hand.

"I will be, okay? I trust them, and I have you and Dad, right?"

"Yeah bug, of course you got us, we love you, I love you. I just need to process and adjust, okay?"

Maya smiled weakly and leaned in to hug her mother.

"How did you get to be so brave?" her mother said over her shoulder.

"I don't know, how about you? Leaving this town, marrying Dad?"

Her mom weakly chuckled. "Well, look at how that worked out, trust me, I am not as brave as you. I wanna be you when I grow up." They both laughed, even though Maya could see they both were crying.

# 38

## LILY

"It's going to be okay, no matter what, I promise." Lily was not in the business of handing out promises she couldn't keep, so it was a word she rarely used. But as she held Hanna close to her on the bed in the treehouse, she meant it. She knew she and Maya had her, that they all had each other.

Lily didn't think Hanna was fully aware of all she had given Lily—Lily suspected Maya absolutely knew, but it was unreal how attuned she was to people's feelings—and she wanted to give back to Hanna in this moment. "We got you," she cooed as Hanna lay on her chest. She wasn't sobbing, just crying and sniffling — still, it felt like progress to Lily.

After a moment Hanna said, "It's strange, because I am relieved, is that weird?"

"No, everything you're feeling right now is true and makes sense," Lily said quietly, threading her fingers through Hanna's hair.

"It honestly wasn't as bad as I thought. Looks like the way to have a very traditional parent not care about your sexuality is to also reveal you're dating two people," Hanna quipped and Lily snorted. "Do you think everything is okay with Maya?" Hanna added.

"I don't know, I mean, it is taking her a while." Lily fought the urge to text Maya. Hanna needed them, but she was starting to suspect that Maya was going to need them too. Maggie had behaved so oddly at dinner, first the hushed argument with her mom, and then her silence and detachment towards the end. When Hanna had come out and then they all revealed that they were dating each other, she hadn't really reacted in any way that made sense to Lily. It's like whatever was revealed *added* to whatever conflict was brewing inside of her. Her mom also never shared what she'd wanted to talk to her about. Another tense wave of emotion rolled through Lily. Here she was at the next chapter of something new and beautiful, and she was wracked by trepidation of what was old. In any case, she still had two weeks to put some of it to bed. Right now, Hanna needed her, and if Maya also did when she got back, she would be there for both of them.

Finally, Maya appeared at the door and slipped inside the treehouse. "Hey sorry, I uh, had a really rad conversation with my mom," she said, her voice dripping with sarcasm.

Lily and Hanna were sitting up on the bed, each holding a cider. Lily had one arm around Hanna, and she motioned with her free hand for Maya to come join them.

"Going to need one of those first," Maya said, taking off her shoes and heading over to the cooler. Lily watched her grab a cider and make her way into the room. She removed her pants and got in the bed with her bottle.

Lily handed her the bottlecap opener she had on the bed, and Maya thanked her. Searching her face, Lily could see a soft flush across Maya's brown skin. Something had happened. Before she could ask though, Maya leaned over her and planted a kiss on Hanna's forehead. "You okay? Well, all things considered."

Hanna gave a watery chuckle. She'd long since stopped crying, but her face was still blotchy and red in areas. "Yeah, actually, I think I am," she said. Maya let out a breath and Lily felt her body relax a bit.

"Are you okay?" Lily asked, looking over at Maya, who was settling into her side.

"Yeah Papaya, you took a minute, I didn't even think. Well, how did Maggie take it?" Hanna added.

"Not what I was expecting," Maya sighed, "I had to re-explain pansexuality to her, and she made it sound as if all of this was her fault somehow." She shook her head, her curls brushing against Lily's shoulder.

"Ooof, I am so sorry," Hanna said.

Lily was surprised, considering Maya said she'd been out since high school, but maybe the whole two girlfriends thing was a hard pill to swallow. She was grateful her mother didn't seem to care, not that that was surprising. By her own admission, Diana's approach was to let Lily figure it out herself. It had been something that Lily had resented, but in this moment, she was grateful; she thought it meant her mother had a great deal of trust in her.

"Anyway, we talked and it's fine, I think? She just said she needs some time to adjust." Maya took another sip of her cider and sighed.

"Something is going on with our moms I think," Lily said. "I saw them arguing, and your mom was being so strange at dinner."

"Yeah totally, I just don't know what it is, and truthfully I'm not sure I can take it on after the divorce," Maya replied.

"That's fair, but yeah, even I noticed in my craze of anxiety that your mom was very quiet at dinner," Hanna said. "But hey– these next two weeks don't have to be heavy. Maybe we even go up a little earlier? You said the place is ready, right Lil?"

"Yep, you guys are going to love it."

"It's not a sex dungeon or a frat house, is it? I realize perhaps we shouldn't have left the digs up to you — hey!" Maya let out a laugh and Lily pinched her.

"No, you both are going to love it, have a little faith," Lily said with feigned indignation.

"I can see it now, a tap in the kitchen and a heart-shaped be—"

Lily cut Hanna off with a pinch right over the ticklish spot on her side. Hanna erupted immediately in laughter and seeing a smile finally back on her face warmed Lily.

"You both suck," Lily said, laughing.

"But seriously, thank you for taking care of that, I just was so bogged down with school stuff," Maya said, and Lily could see her smiling at the fact that Hanna was smiling too.

"Yeah thank you," Hanna said as she came down from her fit of giggles. "I had a bunch of certifications and stuff to prep for before work."

"No problem, I told y'all I'm your sugar momma," Lily joked. And it really was a joke to her. She had money for doing nothing but simply being born into her family, and if she could lean on that and the free time it gave her to take care of her girlfriends, she would do it.

"Stop, we are going to pay our way," Hanna said, and Maya agreed.

"We'll see, you both are just getting started, let's not deal with money right now. Everyone just does what they can when they can."

Lily knew they weren't done with the conversation, but she

wanted to be done with it for now considering the evening they'd just had. Her girlfriends seemed to agree because they dropped it.

"God I'm exhausted, and it isn't even late," Maya said, taking another sip.

"Snuggle party?" Hanna asked.

"Fuck, yes," Lily said, something she never imagined she would be enthusiastically agreeing to.

A comfortable silence fell between them as they each undressed. No one asked, but they all got completely naked, like the thin layer of clothes would be too much space between them right now. After Lily turned off the lights, save a tiny portable lamp that was really just a lantern full of solar-powered fairy lights, they climbed back into the bed, Hanna on one side of Lily and Maya on the other. The subtle glow allowed Lily to see her two girls, her lovers. She couldn't help smiling at the romantic intimacy between all of them. A love that was theirs. Lily held them and kissed the top of Hanna's head and then Maya's temple. They were a tangle of limbs as they touched, soothing each other with occasional kisses.

"I love you," Hanna said.

"I love you too," Maya said.

"I love you three," Lily said and they all laughed at her bad joke. "There has to be a way to just say it. We all know we mean all of us, right?" Lily asked.

"Yes, yes," Maya said, and they each said, "I love you."

And while the summer was coming to a close, Lily thought the love they had declared during it was endless.

## 39

## HANNA

This was it. Hanna stared up at her kitchen ceiling as she waited for the moment her parents would come home. Nerves wracked her, and while she knew her girls would be there for her no matter what, she had insisted that she needed to talk to them alone. Maya and Lily would be there for her after, no matter the outcome of the conversation.

She didn't expect for everything to be fixed, not really, but Hanna had realized just *how much* she and her family didn't talk about. The unspoken walls between them. This had just been the thing that, when she'd pulled it out into the open, had destabilized everything else and brought it all crashing down. It would take a long time for them to sort through the mess. But at the end of the day, these were Hanna's parents, and she wanted to at least give them the *option* to make it right before she went off to Providence.

She'd texted them the night before to say she'd be waiting for them after church. She and her father had texted back and forth; namely he'd wanted to make sure she was somewhere safe. She hadn't heard from her mother, but she assumed her father was acting as their go-between.

Hanna had avoided her parents over the last couple of weeks by essentially living at the Blake's. She hadn't seen her parents since Lily's birthday dinner. Instead, along with Lily and Maya, she'd gone by the house one Sunday when she knew her parents would be at church and grabbed the things she needed. Since the treehouse really wasn't suitable for full-time living, she, along with Maya, piled into Lily's room.

Maya wasn't really in the same boat. She and her mom spent dinners together talking and sharing, and then Maya would come back to the Blake's and climb in between Hanna and Lily —just the way they liked it. Diana didn't seem to mind; if anything, it was like she understood.

As if to distract them, Lily had been presenting Hanna and Maya with various potential apartments, asking them to pick their top three. She was adamant that the final choice would be a surprise.

"You both have a lot going on, let me take care of the home, as your soft masc housewife," Lily had said, making Maya and Hanna laugh.

Hanna's heart startled and a pit bloomed in her stomach as she heard the sound of a slamming car door. She looked from the ceiling to the microwave on the counter: 12:43pm. Right on time. She waited in anticipatory silence. It wasn't far from the car to the front door; Hanna suspected her father and mother were prepping on the doorstep before coming in.

She hoped her father was talking some sense into her mother. He was often a quiet but strong presence in the house. If her mother was the captain of their ship, her father was the wind in the sails. She'd never seen him angry or even raise his voice before Lily's birthday dinner. It seemed though, with people who were of few words, when they did speak, you listened, for they made them count.

Hopefully they would today.

Hanna heard the jingle of the bells her parents kept around the handle of the front door, the telltale sign they'd entered the space.

"Hanna?"

Hanna was surprised to hear that it was her mother calling out for her. "In the kitchen," she called back.

There was a pause, some rustling as they took off their shoes, her father dropping his keys into the dish as he had for as long as Hanna could remember, her mother putting her purse next to that very dish. Same every time.

It wasn't long before she was staring at both of her parents as they entered the kitchen. Her mother wore her signature low bun and a multicolored coral dress that fell modestly to her knees. Her father was in his usual slacks and button-down, even in the August heat.

"Do you–do you want lunch," her mother started, her voice shaky with what Hanna knew were nerves. This was uncharted territory for them, they'd never had to have a tough conversation with *each other* before. "We ate at church, but I can—"

"It's okay Mom, I grabbed something earlier with Maya and Lily," she said the names of her two girlfriends defiantly. She watched her mother swallow and her father set a hand on her shoulder as he walked them both over to the kitchen table.

The table was a rectangle, and so her parents sat opposite Hanna. Hanna had never felt that the table was particularly big, but now it seemed obscenely small. She removed her hands from the top and dipped them in her lap to create some space.

"So, thanks for letting me come say goodbye," Hanna started. She had tried to rehearse what she was going to say with Maya and Lily, but in the end, decided to go off vibes. The situation was too unpredictable.

"Hanna, this isn't goodbye," her mother's voice was at the high pitch she used when she was momentarily shocked.

"Well I mean, before I leave for Providence," Hanna offered.

"So you're going then?" her mother asked.

Hanna stared back at her.

"Mary," her father's deep voice seemed to float out of him and attempt to fill the space between them.

"Mom, of course I'm going, I got a job I'm excited about and I get to be with two people I love."

At the last part her mother scoffed. "You're young, you —"

"You and Dad were married at twenty-five," Hanna countered, already feeling anger prickle down her spine.

"Yes well, I mean," her mother took in a deep, shuddering breath. "Hanna, when did all of this happen? I just don't understand."

At the sound of her mother's voice breaking, she knew her mother meant it. It was a bit of a plea. The sound of it quieted Hanna's building anger.

*They just want you to be okay.*

"So, you also like girls or–" Hanna's eyes flicked over to her father, who had gone red in the face but seemed determined to marshal on. "Because we don't care about that. We've known about Lily for years, and Mary and Diana were even friends back in high school."

Hanna's chest swelled at her father's peace offering. She was so grateful for his declaration of acceptance that she didn't even try to work out the part about Lily being the poster child for homosexuality in Maplewood, nor what he meant by bringing Diana into the mix.

"You don't?" and Hanna heard the need in her voice, more need than she had wanted to admit to herself. She looked at her mother, who she saw had started to cry.

"Hanna, what makes you think we'd care about that? If that's what is making you– experiment," her mother replied, rekindling the anger Hanna had quieted.

"Experiment? I'm not experimenting!" Hanna gritted her teeth.

"Perhaps, Mary, we can hear from Hanna?" her dad tried.

"Yes, well, okay, so you like girls and boys, I mean men and women or–? Because you had Jeff in—"

"Mary," Evan McAvoy cut his wife off, another rarity. Hanna couldn't help but let the gratitude for her father in that moment wash over her. They were never particularly close, in that they didn't spend a lot of one-on-one time together, but she had always felt *loved* by him. And in this moment, that's what mattered.

"I am bisexual, like I said, so for me, yes, I am attracted to both those who identify as men *and* women. That's what I know for sure now, though, I could see that evolving over time. I don't think I'm pan like Maya, I definitely seek out body—-well," Hanna took a deep breath, "I am bisexual, at the very least."

"At the very least," her mother repeated, not as a question, but as a statement she was trying to digest.

"And," Hanna continued, "it appears I am also polyamorous, because yes, I have fallen in *love* with both Lily and Maya."

"Love," Mary McAvoy said the word like it was dirty.

"Yes Mom, *love.* I love them."

"Hanna, if you want to experiment, you can keep it behind closed doors, keep it in the bedroom. I mean you can't honestly think there is any longevity to this 'relationship,'" her mother spat out the last word.

"Mary we—"

"I mean okay, so you all live together, but come on, you can't all get married? Kids? How would that even work? And you're throwing away your future to play house in that—"

"Mary!"

At the harshness in her father's voice, Mary McAvoy took a

breath, but still pushed forward. "I knew I shouldn't have let you hang out at the Blake's house so much. And that Maya girl—"

"Let me? Mom. I am over twenty years old, I go where I go. And just so we are clear, it's not like I caught Lily's gay or whatever." Hanna was fuming.

*Seething.*

She thought she might be able to take whatever her mother had to say about her, but she saw red at the mention of Lily and Maya.

"Oh I know that! I am not this uptight ignorant woman you'd like to think I am! I'm just practical, we have sacrificed so much for you, given you *everything*, and now you're, you're—"

"Mary, don't you dare, we—"

"It's okay, Dad. I don't know what the future brings, all I know is how I feel right now. *Right now* I am in love with both Lily and Maya. Right now, I am in a relationship with them. A real relationship, not an experimentation that is purely for 'the bedroom,' but something that is ours, something we plan on carrying with us as we move through the world." Hanna was breathing quickly now, trying to keep her voice cool and controlled. She felt her eyes sting with tears. This was one of the hardest conversations she'd ever had, mainly because it wasn't like she and her family had any practice at this. And now she was sitting here having to fight for validation from her *mother.* If her own mother wouldn't believe her, believe them, then who would?

Hanna took another breath and let her tears fall. She was coming to the conclusion that it *did*, in fact, *matter* to her what her parents thought when her father spoke.

"Look Hanna, we love you, okay?" He reached across the table and turned his hand over. Hanna took it.

"Yeah you love me because you have to," Hanna spit out, and she was crying now, chest heaving with the fear she'd buried long ago. She could feel the questions that were going to fight their way out.

"Oh my girl, yes, because you're our daughter." Her father paused as if waiting for her mother, but Hanna couldn't see their exchange. She was focused on her hand in her father's on the kitchen table. She held on to it as if she'd blow away if she dared let go.

"Hanna, of course I love you, I just—this is your life, and you're not thinking—"

"Mary." Her father's voice was a warning.

"Do you both regret it?" Hanna said softly, her mouth thick with saliva.

"What do you mean?" Evan McAvoy asked, squeezing her hand.

"I mean," Hanna took a breath and looked up through her tears at her parents, "are you upset that I am your daughter now? Do you think–" She took a moment to work through another wave of tears and sniffled. "Do you feel like you picked the wrong kid?" With her last fear bared, she put her head down on the table and sobbed.

Never letting go of her hand, her father suddenly crouched down beside her, pleading "Hanna, Hanna, look at me," but she couldn't. She thought if she saw the slightest bit of confirmation in his face, she really would shatter and blow away, never to be seen again.

"Okay, okay," her father said as he enveloped her. "You are my daughter, and I know, there is a lot going on right now, but that will never change, will it Mary." Her father raised his voice on that last bit.

There was a long pause as he stroked Hanna's shoulder and rested his head next to hers.

"You are our daughter," she heard her mother quietly say, as if resigned. It hurt like hell to hear it the way her mother had said it, but she had said it.

They sat like that for a while, Hanna crying and her dad rubbing her shoulder. Eventually, she felt her father pull away from her and then his steady hands in her hair, guiding her to lift her head from the table. When she did, she saw that her mother was no longer in the kitchen with them. She turned to face her father, tears still making their way down her cheeks, but she had stopped sobbing. At the sight of her mom's absence, she thought she'd start again.

"She just needs some time, okay? This is new for us, and we are processing. Your mother just has a different way of doing so. I hate to ask this of you, but please just give her some time?"

Hanna let out a shuddering breath and nodded.

Her father pulled her in for a hug. "Listen to me Hanna, you are our daughter, that will never change okay? Give it some time honey, just give it some time."

# 40

## MAYA

LILITH

Where are you Papaya?

HANNA BANANA

I told her to wait but...you know what that's like

PAPAYA MAYA

Just finishing up and about to head out now, my mom is already outside

LILITH

MOVE THAT SWEET ASS THEN

Better yet....

HANNA BANANA

Don't...

PAPAYA MAYA

Hanna just take her phone away?

LILITH

SEND NUDES

Specifically that SWEET ASS

PAPAYA MAYA HAS LEFT THE "MY GIRLS"
GROUP CHAT
HANNA BANANA ADDED PAPAYA MAYA TO THE "MY
GIRLS" GROUP CHAT
HANNA BANANA

Nuh uh

LILITH

What were you going to do? Leave and then...
what would you say when you got here?

HANNA BANANA CHANGED THE NAME OF THE CHAT
TO "A FRUIT BASKET FOR LILITH"

HANNA BANANA

Happy?

LILITH

Niiiizzzeee

It's time to hit the road, I have a sexy apartment
to woo you both with!

PAPAYA MAYA

...I was already wooed, but now that you've
mentioned the digs...

**M**aya smiled to herself and slid her phone into her back pocket. This was it. Her mom was going to drop her off at Lily's, and the three of them were going to make their way to Providence. To the "grand reveal," as Lily put it.

"You ready?" Maggie's voice came from the front doorway. Maya thought her mother looked more at ease, and she was grateful to her over the past couple of weeks. Especially after seeing how Hanna's mother had reacted. It broke Maya that Hanna had seemingly had all of her worst fears confirmed, especially how the conversation had gone yesterday during her 'goodbye' talk. Maya had held her for the rest of the night before coming home in the morning to have one last breakfast with her mom.

Over the last couple of weeks, Maya had thankfully had great conversations with her mom, helping her see the validity of her relationship. Maggie had initially worried that Maya was experimenting or latching onto the other two women as a means to soothe the pain of her own family being pulled apart by the divorce.

"I don't think we are pulled apart Mom, I think we've just changed," Maya had told her mother, who looked immensely relieved and grateful for that shift in perspective. "And even if it seems like I have acquired two lovers instead of one for the sake of a found family, would that be so bad? I love them and I am loved. They make me happy, they make me feel safe, they make me feel seen." Maya had said these words in a serious tone, but her cheeks burned with how hard the truth in the words made her smile.

"It's just, it was so hard for you in Boston, being different, being Black." Her mom had looked into Maya's eyes with such sadness, but there was also an understanding she and Maya had never confirmed out loud before. "You're my baby girl, and I love you more than anything, and I never want anything to hurt you, you know that? I felt like okay, so your life would be a bit more challenging for something as dumb as the color of your skin, but now–I just want you—"

"You just want me to be ok." Maggie had made this clear to Maya, unlike Hanna's parents. Maggie smiled in confirmation. "I am okay, Mom," Maya assured her. "Being different is ok. Sure it has been hard, but I love my brown skin, I love me, just who I am. You and Dad always made sure of that. I'm okay. More than that–I'm happy."

And then they'd hugged, and her mother had cried, and

whispered "thank you" into Maya's ear. That felt heavy, but there were no more words needed, all they had needed in that moment was each other, the feeling of *home*.

"Maya? Where are you right now? Let's go!" Maggie said, moving back into the house and gently nudging Maya's shoulder, bringing her back to the present.

"I was just thinking how funny it is that I'm kinda going to miss this house that I basically haven't lived in. But more funny to me is that I have that feeling like I am going to miss home, like when I first moved out for school," Maya said.

"Well, it's not like this is your last time here, you can come back whenever you want. Maplewood will be your home too."

Maya looked into her mom's topaz blue eyes, beaming.

"Playlist?" Lily said from the driver's seat of her brand-new electric SUV. She'd insisted they needed something for the "whole family" that was good in the snow, and she flat out refused to 'fulfill the Subaru stereotype' since they were already U-Hauling.

"Got it," Hanna said from the front seat.

They were all in, packed to the brim and sitting in Lily's driveway. Diana and Maggie stood in front of the car, having just hugged each of them. Hanna had been watching Diana and Maggie sadly, but then, in a very unexpected turn of events, her father had arrived to say goodbye to everyone. He had since left, but Maya could tell the gesture had meant everything to Hanna, and so it meant everything to her and Lily.

"Can we at least get an hour into the drive before you turn on your investigative podcasts about what goes bump in the night?" Maya said from the back seat. Lily laughed and Hanna feigned offense.

"I'll have you know that I only listen to ethical true crime."

"Whatever that means," Lily said. "Alright girls look alive, they're waving."

Maya shifted to look around the front seat where she could see the two moms waving through the windshield. She smiled and waved back, as did Hanna and Lily.

"Alright ladies, wait till you see the final place I got for us," Lily said, starting the car and sliding the gear into reverse.

"Ah, we're on the lease too, right?" Hanna asked.

"No, I took all that personal information from you and had you sign that paperwork so that I could steal your identity and run for mayor," Lily said, turning to back out of the driveway. Even though the car came with a backup camera, Maya noticed Lily still liked to check.

"Mayor, huh?" Maya said, shaking her head.

"Yes, to answer your question, you are both on...the deed."

Maya felt the floor give away from her. "The—what?"

Lily reached the end of the private driveway and swung the car onto the path that would lead them to the main road. She beeped the horn and everyone gave one last wave to Maggie and Diana at the end of the driveway. As they pulled away, Maya saw them hug. It was sweet that Diana was going to be there to comfort her mother. She knew Maggie was going to have a tough time with her gone.

"Lily, the what?" Hanna repeated, bringing Maya back into the shock she'd previously felt.

"Yeah well, one way my mom has continued to grow her wealth? Real estate, baby. And look, if we are going to share a home, I want it to be something we actually share, something that benefits all of us."

"Lily, but—" Hanna began, her voice revealing the same nerves that Maya felt.

"We already agreed on the rent. That will just go towards the mortgage."

Maya rolled her eyes, "But we didn't help with the down payment! We can't buy you out if something—"

Lily cut her off. "Stop! I'm trapped. We're U-hauling. You both are stuck with me. I don't expect any of the down payment money, but this way we all build equity for ourselves."

"Lily—"

"I don't know, look, reparations? Am I allowed to make that joke?"

"Holy shit," Maya said, and she found that couldn't find anything to say beyond that.

"Okay so no, not a great joke, but let me do this okay? I love you both, and I'm invested in us, okay? This hasn't done anything to hurt me in any way, so win-win, it's done."

There was silence in the car.

"U-hauling huh? So you're admitting to it?" Hanna said.

Maya and Hanna had been so distracted with their own personal affairs, Maya kicked herself for not looking at the paperwork more closely.

"Fine, fine, but know that I don't expect to be a kept woman," Maya said.

"Mhmm speak for yourself," Hanna joked.

"Listen, this place will be ours, and I wouldn't have done it if I wasn't sure that I want you both with me. And this way, if something does happen, neither of you feel like you have to stay because of finances. This way we're all financially equal when it comes to our home."

Maya took a beat to digest, and then she felt immense gratitude to Lily, not simply because she had quite literally bought them an apartment, but because of the thought process behind it.

"Okay," Hanna said.

"Yeah, okay," Maya said, smiling. It truly felt like she was leaving one home to find another. Thinking back to a conversation she'd had with her mother long ago in the car, she closed her eyes. *Your home is where you are loved, completely, totally, deeply.*

Maya sighed and sat back in her seat and said, "Yeah, let's go home."

# PART V

# EPILOGUE

FOUR MONTHS LATER

# 41

## HANNA

**LILITH**

MAYAAAAAA

HANNNAAAAAA

**HANNA BANANA**

Oh wow she's using our given names...

**PAPAYA MAYA**

Must be bad...

**LILITH**

It isn't good

Well it isn't bad it is just....

Are you two on your way home?

**PAPAYA MAYA**

Yeah, leaving the library now, but I need to call my mom back on the way home, so was going to pick up some food. Thai good with everyone?

**LILITH**

FOOD AND WINE

HANNA BANANA

Lily, what the hell? Also we have plenty of your family's cider in the fridge

LILITH

FOOD AND WINE

I NEED an ABV of at least 10%

PAPAYA MAYA

Okay so now I'm worried

HANNA BANANA

I'm leaving the office now, should be home in 25…should I call you first?

LILITH

No I need both of you here, Maya you will too

With that last ominous text, Hanna began shifting gears on what she *had* been planning for that Friday night. She *had* been planning on going home and seducing her two beautiful girlfriends, considering they all had a weekend that aligned: Maya didn't have a paper and Lily wasn't working towards a client's deadline. It sounded like those plans would have to take a back seat.

Hanna stuffed her phone into her new leather shoulder tote, a congratulatory present from her parents, aka her mother. While they still weren't talking, nothing really beyond proof of life conversations, Hanna felt that perhaps this was her mother's way of trying to take a step in the right direction. With one last adjustment of her shoulder strap, she continued down the hall of Planned Parenthood New England.

"Sorry, Ms. McAvoy, one last question?" A soft voice came

from behind her as she made her way through the waiting room towards the exit.

Hanna turned to see the curly-haired student she had met about twenty minutes before. "Hey Serena, was there more you wanted to ask?"

The young woman's light brown cheeks colored, but she nodded her head.

"Do you want to step back in one of our—"

"Will I still like my boyfriend after?"

Hanna shut her mouth and took a pause. They were alone in the waiting area, since it was the end of the day and Hanna was closing the place down, so she wasn't surprised that Serena was okay with having the conversation there; she was surprised because she knew Serena had just been in with one of their medical providers to discuss changing her hormonal birth control. Hanna had stepped in to shadow the consultation, acting as a liaison between the patient and the medical professional. This location found that adding a Patient Advocate–her official title–helped build trust and understanding and therefore improved outcomes for their patients.

Hanna loved her job and was floored by the amount of misinformation when it came to certain bodies out there. She was used to being surprised by questions like, "Can I douche with Mountain Dew after sex to keep from getting pregnant?" or "My partner says because it's anal we don't need a condom," but this question was unexpected.

"I'm sorry, your boyfriend? Will you like him after..." She trailed off, waving her hands slightly to encourage the young woman to fill in her blanks.

"I saw on TikTok that birth control tricks your body into thinking you're pregnant so you crave a certain kind of partner, like one that protects you, like a friend? But then when you get off of it you want another kind of partner, one who is more–sexy, I guess." She laughed at the last part sheepishly. "So I was thinking that if I change the type of birth control I'm on, and Dr. Lutz explained I might have new side effects–and I was thinking, what if a side effect is that I like a different kind of guy?" She shook her head, her face turning almost scarlet. "You know what, you're trying to leave for the day, never—"

"Whoa, whoa, whoa," Hanna said, while her mind raced to catch up and sort through the logic and misinformation to find a way to soothe the woman's very real fears. "Let's slow down for a second. Come here, let's sit."

She guided the young woman to a pair of seats that couldn't be seen through the windows. While no one was in the building besides the cleaning staff, Hanna was all too familiar with the protestors outside and how much they liked to try to catch a glimpse of the people in the waiting area, even though they tried to shield it as much as possible.

The protestors assumed every single woman walking into the building was getting an abortion when that was less than 1% of the work they did at the location, like many locations. Mainly they just spent their days providing medical care and information that the community they served otherwise wouldn't have.

"First, call me Hanna. I'm not that much older than you, you know," Hanna said as they sat. It was true; she was 22 to the young woman's 17. "Second, I totally get that navigating hormonal birth control can be a crappy process until you figure out what works well with your body."

Serena nodded. "Yeah, and I'm not even taking it for birth control."

"A lot of people aren't," Hanna replied.

"Why do they even call it that then?" Serena inquired, finally making eye contact with Hanna.

"Because that's what it was originally developed for and

that's how it's remembered. But I know lots of girls who take it for the same reasons as you: they have really painful periods and basically see the whole pregnancy prevention piece as a bonus."

Serena laughed at that. "It's basically our backup. Even though my boyfriend isn't crazy about condoms, I don't want to risk it."

"It's your body that he gets to be invited to, so you get to make the rules on how it's entered."

Serena's cheeks reddened with discomfort. Like so many teens Hanna saw, she wasn't experienced at talking openly about sex, and Hanna mentally commended her on working through it.

"Now," Hanna continued, "you're afraid that birth control will alter who you are attracted to?"

Serena nodded. "It's been coming up on my TikTok."

"Ah," Hanna started, internally shaking her head at the nonsense on social media. "Okay, so first off, in terms of *how* the pill works, it's a little bit more layered and nuanced than your body believing it's pregnant, especially if you're not taking a mono phase pill. I'll leave that up to your conversations with Dr. Lutz, but in the meantime I'll also send you home with one of our pamphlets, I know—" Hanna acknowledged the slight eye roll the girl tried to fight off, "but you deserve to know what's happening with your body. Second, attraction and desire are impacted by hormones, sure. There are times of the month you may feel *more* interested in sex than others, but *who* you're attracted to is *who* you're attracted to."

Serena nodded, eager to be convinced but not seeing the logic.

"Imagine if what you saw on TikTok were true," Hanna continued, "do you know what the divorce rate would be? And what about women like me? I have two girlfriends, and while I am not on the pill, what if I were? According to the logic you found on TikTok, if my body thinks I'm pregnant I should suddenly want to be with a man for the sake of protection? There's just too many instances where if this were true there would be some very obvious societal reactions and problems."

Serena let out a breath. "True, true, and that would mean that people who get pregnant in relationships would suddenly change their minds about their partners," she said slowly.

"Exactly," Hanna said. "So no, one of the side effects will not be that you lose interest in your boyfriend. If that happens, it's one hundred percent not the pill."

"Okay, okay," Serena said, laughing. Her brow furrowed as if she was just realizing something. "Wait–you have two girl-friends?"

Hanna had to be careful about this information because she knew poly relationships weren't always understood, but she had promised herself that she'd always be open with the patients. "Yes, I'm bisexual and fell in love with two of the best women," Hanna said proudly.

Serena's face turned serious as she pondered the informa-tion, and then she grinned. "Yikes, the spend on tampons monthly," she said, and then more seriously added, "Sounds fun though, getting to go home with two women."

"It is great, no one ever falls into the toilet," Hanna joked, because there was so much more to it than that.

Serena smile widened and she said, "Well, thank you so much, sorry that I held you—"

"Never be sorry! I love my job, and this is what I'm here for." And it was true, Hanna knew she had made the right choice in holding off on going to medical school and working as a Patient Advocate. It was helping her figure out the best path for *how* to serve these communities.

She said goodbye to Serena and then locked up, navigating to her car through the "you're going to hell" rants of the "pro-life" protestors. She went to plug in her phone when she saw that Maya and Lily had been texting. The last two messages showed a preview.

> Papaya Maya: HANNA BRING WINE.

> Papaya Maya: HANNA OUR MOMS ARE BANGING.

## 42

## LILY

HANNA BANANA

Sorry I got pulled into another crisis, heading to grab wine and then home to you both. See you in 30!

Okay sorry are we drinking red or white? I know its fall and everything but…???

Nothing like texting with myself to spike my anxiety….

Well shit.

You know what? I'm getting both.

L ily heard the front door unlock as Hanna made her way inside. She heard it because the apartment was open-concept– a lofty, warehouse-style that Lily thought resembled some of her acquaintances' places in

Brooklyn more than Providence—and even if it hadn't been, it was otherwise silent.

Maya and Lily sat on the couch in the living room, just past the small front foyer. They'd been sitting there, stunned. Maya had gotten home about twenty minutes before Hanna. Lily had been in the third bedroom she had turned into a studio of sorts, working on some freelance graphic work, but she went immediately to meet Maya in the living room.

Since moving into their apartment, they had worked to make the space fit for each of them, to make it a safe space, to make it a home. There were three bedrooms, though they only used one as such, making the other two workspaces for Maya's school-work and writing, Lily's art, and Hanna's work. While the space was fairly raw and open, they'd warmed it up with plenty of color: teals, mauves (namely a large mauve couch Maya *had to have*), and yellows, and some ceramic pieces of Lily's. Some were purely for aesthetic, but some functional, like the custom mugs she made for each of them to have their morning coffee together. While Lily would likely never be a morning person, it was the time of day they dedicated to just *them*, before the day spun off into school and work.

Lily had known what Maya had discovered on her latest phone call with her mother. It was the same thing she'd discovered perhaps a half hour earlier than Maya: Diana and Maggie were *dating*. Not just dating; her mother had told her it was serious, that there was some convoluted back story they could discuss next week when they went to the orchard for Thanksgiving—where Diana and Maggie would be hosting. *Together.*

Maggie hadn't officially moved in, but she might as well have, according to her mom, who then swore her to secrecy. In the midst of Lily's shutting down to process, she had told her mother that would be impossible. She, Maya, and Hanna were completely open with each other and something like this would've killed Lily to sit on. So Diana must have told Maggie and Maggie called Maya. Afterwards, Maya had found Lily and shouted in disbelief, the two of them then laughed hysterically till they melted into a silence that was equal parts shock and needing Hanna.

"I got wine, both red and white!" Lily heard Hanna shout, followed by rustling as she removed her shoes and coat. Hanna walked towards them and dropped a cloth shopping bag in between them.

"I am going to assume you meant Diana and Maggie, and not Diana, Maggie, and Mary," Hanna said, looking down at them.

"Hanna," was all Lily could get out.

"Somehow, though, I am not sure if that's better or worse," Maya said.

Hanna bent down and kissed the top of Lily's forehead and then pulled back and said, "I will be back for both of you, I am going to get glasses."

"Just bring jars," Lily said. They were about to get sloppy, and she had no desire to have to clean up glass. Their everyday glasses were surplus canning jars from the Blakes, and now they made a much safer choice.

Hanna returned with three jars and plopped down on the comfy couch between Lily and Maya, who seemed just as eager as Lily to get close to Hanna.

"So catch me up, tell me what happened," Hanna said, twisting the caps off both bottles of wine and pouring a glass of red for Maya, and a glass of white for her, and Lily felt her heart warm at how well Hanna knew them. Having her back at the apartment centered her, as she knew it did for Maya.

Hanna poured herself a little red and then scooted back on the couch so that Maya and Lily could lean on her from either side. Maya slouched down and laid her head on Hanna's chest and Lily curled into Hanna's side, leaning her head into the crook of Hanna's neck, soaking in her warmth and scent. With each breath, she felt her shock dissipate and turn into something nameless but far more manageable.

"Okay so, where to even begin, I *knew* my mom was seeing someone? But—" Maya started, and Lily took a long pull of her wine, the bright citrus notes dancing on her tongue. And while they had a lot to get through that night, she knew they would, and it would all be okay.

## 43

### MAYA

Even after three bottles of wine, and two rounds of lovemaking where Hanna *delivered* on a promise to take their minds off of things, Maya couldn't quiet her mind. She lay naked in bed between Lily and Hanna—the way they often did—and tonight she needed it more than anything.

Discovering that her mother was in a relationship with Diana was shocking for a whole host of reasons. Namely, Maya hadn't even known her mother liked women. She'd never said anything—not when Maya came out as pan, not when she'd her first girlfriend, nothing. The second reason was harder to face: shame.

The fact that her mother felt ashamed for liking women was a heartbreaking revelation for Maya. It left her with so many questions—questions she knew she couldn't have asked over the phone—but it made her mother's parting words before she moved to Providence feel all the heavier, and Maya's heart broke for her. To think she had felt she needed to hide all this time.

She'd told her mom they would talk more, promising she wasn't mad—just surprised, and that she needed time to process. Her mother had said she hadn't wanted to tell her over the phone, but Diana had told Lily. Maya said it was okay; at least it gave them a couple of weeks to process before Thanksgiving.

And process she would need to do. On the one hand, she was relieved that her own struggle with sexuality had helped her understand why her mother needed time to process Maya's relationship. It hadn't been a hate response, she realized, but a fear response–Maggie projecting onto her. Maya didn't think her mom was prejudiced, and she wasn't sure her heart could take it if she ever found out otherwise.

The fact that she was dating her girlfriend's mother was...not ideal.

"So, if you both get married, Lily and I..." Maya hadn't even been able to finish the sentence; it had inexplicably, shamefully slipped out — she hadn't tried to make her mother's news about her. She had a fleeting, bizarre thought about karma and how often she'd turned up her nose at step-sibling romances.

"Whoa, look, there's so much we need to discuss, you and I, and then the four of us—of course Hanna is welcome to join, too," her mother had said, and the inclusion of Hanna had quieted something in Maya. Warmed her. Her mom was *trying*. Of course Hanna would join.

"Okay so, terror aside, hear me out," a red-faced Hanna had said, pouring more wine,"*if* they get married—"

"Hanna! Be on our side!" Lily had interrupted incredulously.

"I am! Just listen to me," Hanna said, placing a finger on Lily's lips. "If they do get married, then yes, you'll be step-sisters—"

"Hanna, EWWW," Maya had said, only to get shushed by Hanna.

"If that happens, then you both will be *family*, and then that means if two of us get married, *we* are all family. Does it make things much easier when we think about that and...and—"

Hanna actually hiccuped, which Maya found adorable, "property and children and stuff," Hanna speed-mumbled through that last bit.

"Children?!" Lily said, smiling wide.

"Are you trying to lock us down, Banana?" Maya had teased, but she couldn't help but grin too—so wide it hurt her face.

"I'm just saying," Hanna began, turning even redder, "I'm not saying now, just saying—"

"Oh my god the trap tightens its grip," Lily had said in mock lament. "Trapped by two lipsticks."

"Shut up! You're like a chapstick at most." Maya had taken a teal throw pillow and thrown it at Lily, who dodged while laughing.

"Yeah, yeah." Lily was absolutely cracking up.

"Okay Banana, lock us down," Maya had teased as Hanna took a long pull of her wine, switching to white to keep Lily company. Maya thought they'd all reached a point in the night where it didn't matter.

"Honestly, you both are the worst. I was trying to put on a positive spin, but whatever, laugh it up," Hanna had said without any real bite.

Lying awake now, Maya thought about how Hanna coming home had centered both her own and Lily's energy, how she had held them, made them laugh, and listened. Maya turned over and wrapped an arm around Hanna. She felt Lily shift in her sleep behind her, Lily's naked body finding hers and one of Lily's arms sliding around her waist. They'd be crazy hot in the morning, but as always, Maya decided it was worth it.

# PART VI

# FINAL EPILOGUE

## FALLING FOREVER

## 44

HANNA BANANA

Lil, where did you go?

PAPAYA MAYA

If you ran away without us, you suck.

LILITH

Well you own part of the apartment so....

HANNA BANANA

!!!

LILITH

Chill brat, I decided that this morning needed some well earned grease and better food than we had in the fridge. Getting breakfast.

PAPAYA MAYA

And coffee?

HANNA BANANA

We have coffee here....

PAPAYA MAYA

But not coffee already made in a fancy machine

Like if you're already out....

HANNA BANANA

LILITH

Yes, yes, I am getting coffee too

HANNA BANANA

Don't encourage her

PAPAYA MAYA

ENCOURAGE ME

LILITH

Are you guys up?

HANNA BANANA

Just got up and didn't know where you were

PAPAYA MAYA

Still in bed

Actually...

*Sent an image*

LILITH

!!!

I will be home stat! DO NOT put clothes on.

I have been waiting too long for this moment!!!

L ily bounced on the balls of her feet as she waited for the last of the order to be ready. She knew if she showed up empty-handed that would be enough for both Hanna and Maya to riot, and she had plans for them. She couldn't wait to get back to their little corner, to be enveloped in her girls. She smiled to herself at the thought of them waiting for her...

HANNA ROLLED onto her stomach and stretched.

"Holy shit," she said.

Maya laughed. "I know, had I known that was what would happen if we sent nudes..." She buttoned her silk pajama top.

Hanna smiled. She loved the way that Maya couldn't help wearing her pajamas when in bed, even though Lily had just fucked their brains out. Hanna wasn't sure she was ready to break the moment with clothing and besides, she loved the way Lily looked at her body.

"Lily, how can you be on your feet so soon?" Hanna teased over her shoulder, as Lily's blonde head disappeared from view.

"Food is getting cold," she heard Lily shout from the kitchen.

Hanna rolled onto her back and then sat up. Maya leaned over and planted a soft kiss on her cheek.

"You're not going to freak out if we eat in bed, are you?" Hanna asked her.

"She better not, I didn't get my snuggles in this morning," Lily answered, coming back into the room wearing a pair of boxers and, to Hanna's delight, nothing else. She set a bag on the bed and carefully placed a cup holder with three coffees on the nightstand.

"You would have been able to snuggle if you hadn't run off," Maya said, smiling as Hanna opened the bag and began to hand out their foil-wrapped food.

"I had to provide for my babes," Lily said, shrugging as she handed a coffee to Maya. Hanna watched Maya kiss Lily's hand before taking the cup. Her stomach swooped as Maya took a sip and moaned in pleasure.

"That good?" Hanna said.

"Of course it is, it came from me," Lily said.

Maya rolled her eyes. "I will make an exception for food in bed, because there's a special occasion we haven't called out."

Hanna turned her face to Lily and saw her own confusion mirrored back at her.

"It's fall—just past the time of year I first met all of you," Maya said, smiling and taking another sip.

"Oh my god," Lily said, kneeling onto the bed and handing Hanna a warm cup. "It totally is, and we missed it!"

"I can't believe we missed it!" Hanna said. "But in our defense, it has been a crazy fall with the move, new job, new school schedule. I guess we've really just kinda fallen into routine, fallen into things."

"Well what's important is that we are addressing it now with bed food," Maya said, leaning around Hanna to set her coffee down and then grabbing a bagel sandwich.

"'Bed Food,'" Hanna and Lily both air quoted.

"It's how you get ants!" Maya said.

"In November? In New England?" Lily settled in next to Maya and wrapped an arm around her, grabbing her own sandwich with her free hand. "Can't believe we blew it, we should at least get gifts or something."

"You got a gift, you got nudes this morning," Maya said.

"The gift that will keep on giving," Lily smiled.

"And we def got something in return," Hanna said, leaning over to kiss first Maya, then Lily, on the cheek.

"Mmm, we sure did," Maya said as Hanna leaned back into her spot and grabbed the last sandwich. "Besides, I don't think we need to do something big," she continued around a small bite of bagel and egg. "Not after the year we've had—I'm actually so proud of us." She took a moment to chew, and the pause seemed to spread through the room and settle around them.

They had gone from hooking up, to falling in love, to moving in together. Sure, cue the U-Hauling jokes, but it had taken them a whole year. There were still things to navigate with their parents, school, work, but Maya was starting to understand that was probably a constant of life.

Maya thought about how *good* they all were, even if she was going to have to de-crumb their bed. How one night of stumbling into a steamy encounter had planted something between them, and Maya couldn't wait to keep watching it grow.

They finished their food in the same old easy silence, then cleaned up before climbing right back into bed. As they settled in to pick a movie, Maya could almost recall something her mother had said at the start of her journey to this point—something about home, and about people. In the haze of a wine hangover and a greasy-food Band-Aid, she could only smile at the thought that she finally understood.

Like the noise of life, the day was grey outside the apartment, but their bed was a refuge. Maya knew she wasn't alone as she snuggled between her two girls, sturdy and warm — there was no place she'd rather be than in the soft light of this room, their hands sliding into hers.

# ACKNOWLEDGMENTS
## (AND WHAT'S NEXT!)

If you are still reading (thank you!), I hope it is because you liked what you read, or at least you're willing to give me some benefit of a doubt as to why you didn't like what you read (thank you!).

*Let Them Fall* has been a journey, like any work of art or writing. It also happens to be the first full length work I have attempted since a little project I flirted with over a decade ago, so this did not come without its fair share of learnings.

So first off, I need thank some folks! Thank you to my wonderful mother and father who instilled in me the value of reading and storytelling. Thank you both for always encouraging me to follow my heart and invest in my dreams.

Thank you to my mother, who I watched be a single mom and career woman all while continuing to challenge herself and grow. I will never forget all those early 4am mornings where I'd peek into your study and see you at your desk working on your dissertation. You taught me what it *takes,* and what it means to have something that is truly *yours.*

Thank you to every teacher that ever took the time to SEE me and encourage me. To name a few standouts, Mrs. Davidson from second grade, Ms. Debbie from third and fourth, and Ms. Dunnel all through high school. I simply wouldn't be who I am today without these individuals approaching the little Black girl in their classes with love and acceptance.

Thank you to my supportive husband. You are a true partner and don't confine our partnership to gender roles, so I was able to come back to myself postpartum via writing. Thank you for always believing in my work and listening to every iteration of my ideas!

Thank you to my daughter, who will always be my very best creation, the single most important aspect of my life (sorry any future kiddos but you don't exist at this time of writing). I have spent my whole life wanting to write books, and I don't think it is a coincidence that I found the inspiration and drive to do so after you came into my world. I will always be grateful for that and I love you more than anything and that will never change. Thank you for inspiring me to strive to be my best and true self, the mother you deserve.

Thank you to all the friends, family, writing group and care-takers who have supported me, this also wouldn't be here without you.

A huge "thank you" to my amazing editor, Megan Kruse, who isn't afraid to push me and willingly reads my insane first drafts. I deeply value our working relationship and feel so lucky that I get to work with such a kind and inspirational person who isn't afraid to also tell me like it is.

Lastly, thank you to all the amazing artists who helped me bring aspects of this work to life!

In a quest to always explore identities other than my own, I do think I was able to also explore what it means to be a racial minority in a predominantly white space, even if that space is still one shrouded in love. But, I also hope that I was able to highlight that white people who love us can also be confronted with these worries and challenges without devolving into guilt or hostility. Lily has her girls, and they know that and appreciate her willingness to listen and acknowledge them.

I will say I may not have gotten all the voices right, but I hope readers feel seen and acknowledged — or enjoyed reading a book with some diversity. Lastly, it was pretty cool to also create an entire book without men. No shade meant, just as a US resident and all the decisions that are being made about women by men, it felt oddly gratifying.

So what's next? Well I have been thinking about the moms since I first wrote the first short story, and can't wait to share theirs. While both MCs are white, common in the FF space and something that just had to happen based on the above, I promise the next book will also explore multiple identities and give voices to other marginalized people as well. I also want to know more about Aunt Julia, and hear the conversation between Felicity and Sruti at some point. There are so many ideas bouncing around in my head. Hopefully, these will get better as I write, and I hope you'll follow along with me!

Cheers,
    Simone Holiday

# STAY IN TOUCH!

You can (please lovingly and kindly) follow along with me on Instagram (@authorsimoneholiday) or if you'd like, you can sign up for my newsletter for exclusive content, reading recs, thoughts, and more.

I do not have a TikTok or other socials and don't plan on doing so anytime soon. I can barely keep up — and I'd rather stick to platforms I can be thoughtful about and put the time and care in. For now you can find me on Instagram only.

—Simone Holiday

# ABOUT THE AUTHOR

Simone Holiday is a queer Black author who loves exploring all of the elements that make us human and how they can lead to a HEA. She writes mostly contemporary romance, and the Fall Series is her debut. When not writing and contemplating all the things, you can usually find her hanging with family or curled up with a book and a cat.

# ADDITIONAL WORKS

If you enjoyed her work and want more of a paranormal romance vibe - you can find her alter ego, Billie Simone Baldwin via Instagram @BillieSimoneBaldwin.

For more information about purchasing and permissions, please reach out to Simone Holiday at authorsimoneholiday@gmail.com.

www.simoneholiday.com